# THE
# NIECE

# BOOKS BY GEORGINA CROSS

*The Stepdaughter*
*The Missing Woman*

# THE
# NIECE

## GEORGINA CROSS

*bookouture*

Published by Bookouture in 2022

An imprint of Storyfire Ltd.
Carmelite House
50 Victoria Embankment
London EC4Y 0DZ

www.bookouture.com

ISBN: 978-1-80019-903-3
eBook ISBN: 978-1-80019-902-6

*To the Decatur Crew. Thank you.*

# PROLOGUE

## BETH

Friday

The smoke chokes my lungs. I reach out, clutching nothing but air until my hands land on a wall, then a doorframe. But the landing above the stairs is dark, the smoke pluming black, and it's difficult to see where the railing ends and the top of the stairs begins.

My hand covers my mouth, the heat stifling, the fumes toxic as I let out a rattled pant. Below, the crackle of flames gets louder, closer. The fire is tearing through the house, the flames alive while wanting to kill everything in its path.

I call out for my daughter, and there's no answer. I'm hoping she's escaped. She's flung open a door and is running far from here. She'll find someone to help, and we can both be saved.

*Run, Hannah, run. Be brave.*

But what if someone has gotten to her? What if whoever set the fire hasn't left the property and they're chasing her down? They're dragging her back to this place.

I try to scream but not much comes out. A frightened whisper, a relentless cough, then a terrible barking sound that takes over my body. I bend at the waist. I'm not sure if I can take this much longer.

Orange flames lick the top of the staircase. It's too hot; the air is stifling and sweat pools at my chest. Backing away, I find my daughter's room and fall into a corner. Tucking my knees beneath my chin, I know it won't be much longer before the flames will find me in here too.

How long will this take? Will it hurt? Or will I suffocate from the smoke first? *Please let me be gone before the flames hit.*

Outside, the sound of someone shouting, their high-pitched laughter—and a burst of fear shoots down my spine. They're thrilled at what they're seeing: my house burning, me along with it. I know exactly who it is.

*Run, Hannah. Be brave.*

# ONE

The first phone call is heart-wrenching. My sister is dead from a house fire. Her teenage daughter is the only survivor.

The second call is a punch to my core. Someone purposely set the blaze and the police don't know who it is. Someone has killed her.

With trembling hands, I reach for the window and rip open the blinds. My backyard is empty, and on the other side of the fence is my neighbor's roof. Everything remains quiet. It remains quiet for now.

*They're coming after me next. First Beth, then me.*

The detective says, "Why? Why would you think that?" And I startle, not realizing I've spoken the words out loud.

"I-I don't know. I'm sorry. This is just a lot to take in."

Detective Gillespie is calling from Louisville, Kentucky, the site of our family farm, and what used to be our family farmhouse. I grimace, imagining what's left behind: the burned-out shell and caved-in walls, the stained-glass window that my mother loved so much. They found my sister's body reduced to bones in the rubble.

*The fire burned quickly,* the detective said. *Your niece is lucky to have gotten out alive.*

But I can't help thinking: *She was trapped.*

"When was the last time you spoke to your sister?"

"It's been years," I answer.

He doesn't ask me to elaborate. Either he doesn't know much about our family, or he's keeping silent for now. He's biding his time, and that's fine because I have no desire to explain anything to him, not the reasons why I left Louisville thirteen years ago and started a new life in Alabama. The reasons why I haven't spoken to my sister, Beth, and why she refused to speak to me.

Something tells me the detective will learn this soon enough.

I press my forehead against the window. "Beth," I sob.

Someone calls for Detective Gillespie and he tells me he needs to go. "Again, Ms. Jenkins. I am very sorry for your loss. We'll keep in touch."

The next day, I'm still reeling. My twelve-year-old daughter, Cassie, is in her room listening to music, oblivious as to what is happening. She doesn't know about her Aunt Beth as they never met. She doesn't know that she has a cousin either. The next call takes me by surprise.

The attorney talks to me, slowly, remorsefully, and it's so unlike the crisp, efficient tone of the detective. But there it is: the familiar drawn-out sigh in his voice and the gentle twang of a Kentucky accent, and the homesickness washes all over me again.

But the hair on the back of my neck rises too—something is up. Carl Fredericks only gets involved when there is something difficult to share or formalities that need to be discussed. The last time we spoke, our parents died and he was executing their will.

The time before that... well, that's another story.

He pushes the receiver against his mouth, muffling his words. How old is Mr. Fredericks these days? Mid-seventies? He must love his work.

"How are you, Ms. Jenkins? Tara," he adds, returning to our shared familiarity.

I swallow the lump in my throat. "Not well, to be honest."

"I'm so sorry," he says, releasing another sigh. "It's horrendous, this tragedy. Everything that's happened to your family. What they've been through."

*What they've been through.* He doesn't include me.

He still suspects me of doing the unthinkable, does he? And the shame rises to my cheeks.

"What is it, Mr. Fredericks?" I ask. "What's going on?"

Beth and I are estranged—he knows this. He was there when it happened. After our parents died, everything went to my sister: the property, our parents' life savings, the house that as of Friday night has gone up in flames. There is nothing left to settle as everything will be passed to her daughter, Hannah.

"Your niece," Mr. Fredericks tells me. "She's coming to live with you."

I don't respond at first.

"She's only sixteen," he says.

The air releases from my mouth.

"Tara?" he prompts. "Did you hear what I said? Hannah. Beth's daughter?"

Of course I know who Hannah is. How could I forget my own niece? I'm not speaking because I'm in shock, that's all. Only yesterday, I found out my sister was killed... my only sibling... and now this?

Hannah is the niece I'd forgotten.

But I haven't forgotten about anything else. The good times and the bad from growing up with my sister, Beth, the rift I caused with our parents, how everything went to hell. The words that were exchanged, the cover-up—every part of that is seared into my memory, branded into my brain. Even when I hoped moving to Alabama would give me a fresh start. I could escape the memories.

I got pregnant with Cassie a year after I moved, her father taking off before she was born. That wasn't a surprise either. But we were fine, and it's been just the two of us. We've never needed anyone else. That's what I tell myself.

And now there will be someone else in our home.

Hannah, my niece. Why would Beth purposely leave her only daughter with me?

The last time I saw Hannah she was three years old, a toddler with shiny black hair that is so similar to my daughter Cassie's. Hair that slid past her cheeks, and Beth was constantly trying to hold it back with a clip. Hannah couldn't say her *R*s and pronounced my name *Auntie Tawa*, which I thought was the most adorable thing in the world. As the first grandchild, she was the highlight of our world and we doted on her, my parents especially. The last time I saw Beth, I didn't realize that would be the last time I saw Hannah too.

My niece sat on the front porch playing with her doll. By then, my sister had moved back into our parents' house, which left me homeless, penniless, and very confused. *This is our parents' decision. Not mine*, is what Beth told me. She didn't do anything to help.

I should have told Hannah goodbye. I should have wrapped my arms around my niece's small frame and kissed the top of her head. But my sister didn't give me the chance; she practically rushed me out of the house and down the front steps, screaming that she never wanted to see me again. I told her the same.

Hannah was silent as she watched me go. Did she cry later?

I wondered. Did she call for me or did she simply go back to playing with her doll?

But my niece was only three years old at the time and won't remember much except for what her mother must have told her over the years—Beth's own version of things. But does she know what role her mom played in everything too? Could she ever guess?

*I kept my end of the bargain, sister. Did you do the same for me?*

The line goes silent. Mr. Fredericks must be giving me a moment to let this all sink in so I can process what he's said. But it feels impossible. My brain spins while it also feels as if time has come to a standstill.

Beth is gone, and now there is Hannah.

The attorney coughs a dry hacking wheeze, the result of years of smoking cigars, if I had to guess. Even back then, he peered over his desk to read our parents' will and the cigar rested in the ashtray. The lingering smell made me sick.

Mr. Fredericks coughs into the phone. There's the clink of a glass, a slurp of water as I haul a deep breath.

"Hannah?" I ask. "She's coming to live with me? But how?"

"Your sister made a few updates last year."

Beth *did* authorize this. Even after all this time and us not speaking to one another, she purposely included my name. She officially designated me as Hannah's legal guardian. What changed her mind?

The act seems absurd, a last resort. But with Hannah's father dead also—a bus accident while he was on tour with his band, and not a very good band I admit—and with our parents deceased, Beth had no other options. I'm the only remaining relative, along with my daughter. Our home is Hannah's last stop before foster care.

"There's no way she could have foreseen this," Mr. Fredericks explains. "But your sister was quite adamant that it was the responsible thing to do, that if anything were to happen to her, an illness or an accident, she needed to know that Hannah would be cared for. She turns eighteen in two years so we're not talking about a long amount of time here. Your sister probably thought this was something that would never transpire. A formality. Something that would never come to pass."

*Something that would never come to pass.*

But it did—it happened. Beth died and I'm the one appointed to care for her daughter.

What would my sister say if she knew this was actually happening?

"I don't know..." The words don't come easy.

I wait for Mr. Fredericks to tell me he's discovered a long-lost relative, someone on Hannah's father's side, and he'll tell me he's calling them next. He'll let me off the hook.

But that's not possible. Family members on her dad's side are long gone too.

"You'll be okay," Mr. Fredericks says, and with the pause in his breath, I wonder if he still considers me as that sad, lost twenty-five-year-old who sat before him all those years ago, my sister not able to meet my eyes as he relayed our parents' decision. The attorney tried to be diplomatic, even when it was obvious how shocking my parents' last wishes would be.

By the way Beth hung her shoulders, I imagined she'd already seen an advance copy. She had known this was coming.

The paperwork dropped from my hands; I remember that clearly. My parents listed their reason for cutting me out, their will letting me know what they thought of me.

*You shamed us*, Mom said. I should have known Beth was the favored one.

"Tara." Mr. Fredericks says. "This is a good thing, what's happening. It's a way to make amends. You're still family and Beth trusted you. She came around."

When I speak, my voice is a whisper. I know the truth. "It's because there's no one else."

He doesn't say anything at first. He knows the truth too. "But there's money," he adds. "Money that will be passed down to Hannah when she turns eighteen, plus funds that will be provided to you in caring for your niece. It's enough to cover her expenses and college tuition if she chooses to attend."

A tiny bubble of hope ripples through my chest. The knowledge that there's money to raise Hannah with, and it's money I might be able to use for my daughter too.

Does Mr. Fredericks know I've been raising Cassie by myself since she was born? Was Beth aware of my circumstances? She was a single mom too.

I step away from the window, tears burning hot on my cheeks. "How does this work? Do I come and get her?" The thought of returning to Louisville makes my stomach flip.

"No, she's flying to you."

"When?"

"Tomorrow."

Tomorrow, and a bolt of lightning strikes my lungs. That's soon.

"I met with her. She's a good kid. Quiet, and understandably grieving with losing her mom, but she's lovely. She doesn't get into trouble and is quite good with school. I've been keeping tabs on her over the years, your sister too. I owed your parents that much after they died."

"Did you keep tabs on me also?" I ask. Immediately, I regret my question.

"Your family has always meant a great deal to me," he says. It's not a direct answer.

"Hannah already knows she's coming? You've already told her?"

"Yes. This must all happen quickly. She's a minor without a home. She stayed with your sister's neighbors last night, the older couple, the ones she ran to for help. But that's not a long-term solution. We must get her placed with you as soon as possible and I've been working with Child Services to execute everything as fast as we can."

"But what about Beth's funeral? Won't she need to stay for that?" *Shouldn't I be there too?*

"She didn't want a ceremony."

I push the phone against my ear, not sure if I heard the attorney correctly. Not wanting a funeral? That doesn't sound like Beth. I have no idea who her friends were anymore—I don't think she ever remarried—but there are family friends and former classmates who will want to pay their respects, clients who bought her artwork over the years and will want to send flowers. The Beth I knew would have wanted something small, wouldn't she?

"Beth became a bit of a recluse over the years," Mr. Fredericks explains. "She wasn't painting as much either. She might have sold a few pieces here and there, but she wasn't pressed to have any big shows. Hannah is shy too, and from what I understand, she prefers to be homeschooled. But that will have to change now as she'll be in public school when she comes to live with you. They lived a quiet life, the two of them. They had enough funds to get by."

They had enough funds while I—

I pinch the space between my eyebrows. "This is all happening so fast."

"I understand. But I'm taking care of all the details, don't worry. I've got the paperwork."

I glance down the hall where my daughter Cassie remains in her room. What will I tell her? How will Cassie respond?

*I'm sorry, but there are reasons I never told you about your aunt and cousin before.*

"Hannah is hurting and lost her mother in a very tragic way," Mr. Fredericks continues. "She escaped tragedy herself too, running from the fire like that, and it must be traumatizing. It's important she's with family, don't you agree? It will bring her some comfort. You can do that for her, can't you, Tara?"

I close my eyes. Of course I can. Of course I will.

This is not what I ever expected to happen, but I could never push my niece away, not when I know she's out there somewhere and needs help. Because my sister would never forgive me. I would never forgive myself.

I survey my house, the small, brick ranch that I'm proud to call my home. We don't have much, but there is a spare bedroom that we've been using as storage. We can clear it out. We can turn that room into a space for Hannah.

My head spins. There are so many things we need to do. We'll need to help Hannah cope—that will be critical. She needs to be able to grieve for her mother. I'll explain why I haven't been around for thirteen years, why I never sent her a birthday card.

Will she forgive me? Will she understand? Hannah may never fully comprehend what happened between her mom and me, and many of those details will need to remain hidden, but we can give this a shot, can't we? After all, that's what the attorney is asking.

I will take on raising a teenager. I will do this for my niece.

Hannah's voice rings in my head... *Auntie Tawa*... and I'm picturing her at her birthday party, how we spent the morning hanging pink streamers and balloons. She was so happy with her present, a cocker spaniel puppy just for her. We had no idea everything would fall apart that afternoon.

"What time does she arrive?" I ask.

Mr. Fredericks relays the Delta flight information as I fumble for a pen and write it all down. I check the calendar app on my phone, knowing I'll have to block out the rest of my afternoon at the office in order to meet Hannah. It's only a twenty-minute drive to the airport and then a return trip to Decatur over the Tennessee River.

Hannah and I will sit down and talk. I might have to take off the rest of the week as there will be so many things to do to get Hannah settled, Cassie also. I should notify my boss. I'll call my best friend Cynthia at work. But not yet. I've got to get things settled in my mind first.

Tomorrow. Hannah arrives *tomorrow*.

Fear takes over and I once again peer through the blinds, staring at my backyard. Is it safe for Hannah to live with us? She only just escaped death herself.

Someone purposely set a fire and burned down my sister's house. Hannah would have died if she hadn't escaped.

Fire. Their use of flames, and it's too similar. This isn't some random case of arson. This is revenge. Someone wants to take revenge on me too.

Whoever did this to Beth will try to find us next, and it will be easy to do. A quick Google search and they can track us down. They'll know where I work, Cassie's school. I have a Facebook account and I hardly post there, but my location can be easily discovered.

Hannah could lead a path straight to us.

"Who else knows she's coming?" I ask.

Mr. Fredericks coughs. "What do you mean?"

"Who else knows that Hannah is coming to Alabama?"

"My legal team, of course. And Child Services in both states. But no one else."

"The neighbors she stayed with last night. Do they know?"

"Yes. But don't worry, Tara. I've already explained to the Chandlers not to share details. An airline rep will also ensure that Hannah is cared for during the flight." The clacking of keyboard keys sounds in the background. "I'm sending you documents to review. Please go over them as soon as you can. I'll need you to sign them."

But I'm not thinking about paperwork. My throat constricts at the thought of seeing Hannah after such a long time.

"How will I recognize her?" I ask. "How will I know it's her?"

"She has long black hair like your sister," he says. "Like you too, Tara." He pauses. "You won't be able to miss her."

# TWO

## Sunday

I must tell my daughter what's happening.

Cassie's bedroom door opens, and with it comes the tell-tale zip of her soccer bag. She has afternoon practice and I almost forgot, the coach asking to squeeze in extra drills the day before a game.

She finds me in the kitchen, her bag is hoisted over her shoulder. "Ready to go?" She's already chomping on a piece of gum, something she says helps keep her focused during practice. Her hair is pulled into a ponytail.

I grab my purse and avoid her gaze. My hands tremble. "Yup. I'm ready."

We don't talk much on our way to the field, and if Cassie notices anything wrong, she doesn't say. She turns up the radio, one of her favorite songs, even though I can't focus on the beat, can't focus on anything except not to drive like a maniac. I grip the steering wheel and do my best to keep my breaths steady, not wanting to give it away to Cassie just yet that our world is about to change. I can't drop a bomb on her right before practice as there won't be enough time to explain. We'll need to talk immediately after.

My stomach churns.

Tomorrow... Hannah arrives *tomorrow*.

At the practice field, Cassie jumps from the car and sprints toward her teammates. She's confident, my daughter, and far more capable than I ever was at her age. We're like a team, the two of us. She can make her own dinner if I'm working late. She knows to throw the towels in the dryer and bring in the mail if I run out of time. If Cassie had been in my shoes, I bet she would have made better decisions than me.

I don't go home, and I don't run errands. Instead, I drive around aimlessly, my brain in a fog, until I find myself heading south on U.S. Highway 31, passing restaurants and drycleaners, fast-food places and churches. Several miles later I pull over when I reach the greens of the Decatur Country Club.

The homes are larger in this part of town and the course is beautifully maintained. With mild winters in Alabama, golfers can play throughout the year. It's late February but not too cold as several golfers cruise by in their carts. I watch them disappear at the next turn.

But I'm not here to golf—I don't even play. I just need somewhere to think. I need to come up with a plan.

Cracking open the window, I kill the engine, my mind mulling over everything that needs to be done, the ripple effects that Hannah living with us will bring.

We should prepare her bedroom as soon as possible—we'll do this tonight. She has to have somewhere to sleep, and I'll be damned if her first night is spent on the couch. I'll swap places and give her my own room before it comes down to that. But where will I find an extra bed? Where will I find spare furniture?

Do we have enough spare sheets, clean towels? When was the last time we went to the grocery store?

Hannah won't be carrying a bag, that's what Mr. Fredericks told me. Everything she owned burned in the fire, which means she'll need new clothes. A whole wardrobe and every basic essential. She'll be starting from zero.

I stare at the time on my dashboard. Within the hour I'll be sharing the news with Cassie about a cousin she never knew about. I'll explain how we're about to go from a family of two to having one more person at the dinner table. There will be someone new sitting with us in the living room.

Will my daughter understand? Will she forgive me for keeping this part of our family away from her? Will she be saddened that Aunt Beth never reached out to her either?

I hang my head, the tears pricking my eyes. *It was pathetic, Beth, staying apart like this. What were we trying to prove?*

I unlock my phone and find an email from Carl Fredericks with several attachments—it's the documents he promised to send me. The PDF opens slowly and when it does, my eyes swim at the endless blocks of information and complicated legalese. It's too much to take in, and I'm not sure where to sign or which paragraphs to focus on first. I close out my email, knowing this is something I will deal with later.

But for now, questions swirl in my brain about the things I don't know, the information about what I truly need to care for Hannah. What should I prepare for? Has she developed any allergies over the years? Are there certain items I need to pick up at the store?

But Hannah is sixteen, I remind myself. She'll be able to tell me these things herself. We can navigate what she needs together.

But what about other issues? Details about her life that she's finding difficult to express right now, especially after the trauma of losing her mom. Everything she owns is burned and gone, and now she's moving two states away to live with people she doesn't know.

How much does she understand about the police investigation? Does she know her mother's killer is still out there and is frightened they could come back for her?

The poor girl will need therapy and I'll sign her up with someone as soon as possible, perhaps as early as this week. And what about school? Mr. Fredericks told me she was home-schooled but with me working full-time and lacking the patience to help Cassie with her own schoolwork, that's out of the question. Hannah will need to be enrolled in our local district just like her cousin. She can attend Austin High.

I start up the car, knowing I've sat here long enough. It's time to pick up Cassie.

The girls are still running drills when I arrive, and I impatiently tap my fingers against the steering wheel. Practice should be ending soon. Why is this taking so long? I'm anxious to get this over with. I'm nauseous about where to start.

I practice what to say instead: *So, Cassie, I have a sister— had a sister. She died and her daughter is coming to live with us. You have a cousin.*

Knowing my daughter, she'll fall silent the same way I did. She'll try taking everything in while waiting to see if she's misheard something. She might think this is a joke.

*No, sweetheart. This is real.*

The coach calls the girls into a huddle, and they circle around, stacking their hands together for their end-of-practice cheer. Someone shouts, arms go up, and my daughter breaks free from the pack. She scoops up her bag and jogs toward me, her cheeks splotchy red.

My stomach tightens. The innocence of her. Her dimple and the pink headband. The dirt and grass that cling to her socks as she grows closer.

Somewhere in the parking lot a car door slams, and my heart jolts. A man walks onto the field. He squares his shoulders and walks directly toward Cassie—he has her in his sights. My hackles rise. He's someone I don't recognize.

My hand flies to the door handle and I push to break free. Cassie is still running, unaware that anyone is approaching her, unaware that she is in danger. Her eyes remain glued on mine.

The man closes in. He's less than ten feet away.

My heart flies to my throat. *They found us.* They got rid of Beth Friday night and drove to Alabama. They will attack my daughter first and force me to watch. They will come for me next.

*What goes around comes around,* I hear the voice repeat.

"*Cassie!*" I scream and wave my arms. She halts, a puzzled look crossing her face before she resumes her jog.

The man—dark hair and black windbreaker—continues to walk too. But just when they're about to intersect, just as he's close enough to strike her, he sails right past my daughter to someone else, another soccer player, and he greets her with a hug. When he pulls back, he whips off his sunglasses and my heart could burst with relief. It's Zach Hillier, Fiona's dad, and she tells him something that makes him laugh.

Cassie eyes me warily as she approaches the car. "Are you okay?"

I force myself to get back inside. "I'm fine." I sit down and busy myself with the seatbelt. "It's nothing."

Cassie drops in beside me, and at once, the smell of my daughter's sweat and the spearmint gum she's chewing rushes into the car and skims past my cheeks. Her ponytail whips across my arm as she tosses her bag into the backseat.

Cassie says, "Emma had better step up and play defensively. Tomorrow is a big game and Coach made us run extra laps." I know this is important to Cassie. They have a championship title to defend and my daughter aims to be named team captain next year.

I reverse out of the parking space but my heart is still

pounding, my fingers knuckle-white against the steering wheel. I make another sweep of the parking lot, looking for—what exactly? An unmarked van? A car with tinted windows? Someone standing in the middle of the road with a lighter in their hand?

*They used fire...* and I blink away my thoughts.

Cassie tugs her ponytail free from her neck. She removes each cleat and pulls off her socks and shin guards as bits of dirt and grass float to the floor. But I don't say anything. We practically live in here, eating fast food between tournaments with a daughter who plays year-round sports. I'm almost positive that if I look between the seats, I'll find rock-hard French fries and balled-up napkins from several months ago.

"It's so annoying when Stacie and Anna won't shut up," Cassie says. "Everyone got into trouble, including me. More laps." With a yank, she pulls at her practice shirt so it's no longer tucked in her shorts. She stretches her long legs and points her toes while I increase the air conditioning. It's not just to cool Cassie down, but me too. It's hard to relax and my mouth runs dry, my tongue weighing like a brick.

I should tell her... but where should I start? How do I do this?

"Cassie," I begin.

She reaches for her drink bottle. "The team we're playing tomorrow is supposed to be tough. Rolling Hills is undefeated."

"Cassie—"

"But Coach thinks we have a chance. When we get home, she says we need to stretch."

"We're not going home yet."

This gets her attention. "Are we stopping for food first?"

"Yes. No." I turn on my blinker and merge to the next lane. "I mean, we can get food later. We need to go to the store first."

"But we just got groceries last week."

The contents of our kitchen pantry cross my mind. Is it enough? Is there anything in there that Hannah will like?

"Maybe a few more groceries," I tell her.

She shifts her eyes to me. "You're acting weird." She waits for me to say something. "What's going on?"

I say it in one long exhale. "You have a cousin. A teenage cousin. And she's coming to live with us. We're picking her up from the airport tomorrow."

She breaks into a smile. "Okay, Mom." She laughs.

"I'm serious."

She stares right back. "What cousin?"

I grip the wheel as my eyes turn to the road. "Remember me telling you about Grandma and Grandpa and how they died before you were born? I never went back to Louisville?" She nods, but it's slow, cautious. "Well, I have a sister—had a sister. But she died too. And in her will she asked that her daughter come live with us."

Cassie takes a sip from her water bottle. "Wow…" she says, and she's silent for a long time.

"What's her name?" she asks.

I blink, realizing I left out this part. "Hannah."

"How old is she?"

"Sixteen. But when she turns eighteen, she can leave and decide what she wants to do." I'm not sure why I add this part except to give my daughter a timeframe, as if knowing it's only for two years will make it sound more manageable, more palatable. More doable.

Cassie fiddles with her bottle cap. Her eyes flit back and forth. I can only imagine the thoughts streaming through her mind.

"You *had* a sister?" she asks. "What happened?"

"A house fire," I tell her, and swallow.

"Oh my God. Why didn't you tell me about her? Before?"

"We had a fight years ago, before you were born. It was... complicated."

That's one way of putting it.

"Where do they live?" she asks.

"In Kentucky. The same house where I grew up."

Cassie lets out a sigh and it's painful. She's frustrated, and she has every right to be. When she was little, I would describe the family farm, the apple orchard we loved so much, the creek where we'd fish. She'd beg to visit, but I always told her no, that Grandma and Grandpa didn't live there anymore and we no longer owned the property. But now she knows that was a lie. She knows I have been lying to her for years.

The guilt overwhelms me, it consumes me, and I bite down on my lip.

Cassie says, "I'm sorry, Mom. I'm so sorry about what happened to your sister."

"I'm sorry I never told you."

"And now Hannah is coming to live with us?"

"Yes," I repeat. "She arrives tomorrow."

"Don't worry, Mom. We'll make it work." She offers a shrug. "It's kind of cool knowing we have more family."

The relief floods through me, my heart blooming inside my chest.

"We'll figure it out," she says.

And if I wasn't driving, I'd reach right over and kiss her. It's an overwhelming relief, the words I so desperately need to hear, and they're coming from my daughter.

But the doubt creeps inside my head, the moment clouding over. How will she react if the rest of the truth comes out?

# THREE

We spend more than an hour at the Target store picking out things for Hannah. Cassie repeats a dozen times that she wants everything to be perfect as we search the shelves. I want the same.

But it's hard to know what to buy Hannah when we know so little about her. For her bedding, will she prefer pinks or lime greens, or should we stick to neutral colors? *She's sixteen*, Cassie reminds me. She'll probably want something grown-up.

We settle on a navy blue comforter and white sheets, matching blue towels, and a bedside lamp. We guess at the kind of conditioner she'll like and if she'll want a soft bristled tooth-brush or something harder. Will she want any makeup?

For groceries, I throw in extra snacks, bananas, bags of oranges, plus animal crackers and Oreos that are dairy-free. Cassie is lactose-intolerant and that's something I'll need to give Hannah a heads-up about. I don't remember Hannah having a problem when she was a toddler, so we include boxes of cereal, yogurt, and milk.

But in the clothing section, we're stumped. There's so much to choose from and too many unknown factors. What's

Hannah's size? Her style? Based on our family's genes, I'm guessing she's not curvy, as neither am I. Height-wise, I'm average, about five foot five inches, and my sister was about the same. But Hannah's dad? He was more than six feet, and I grit my teeth, trying not to think about him.

We decide that clothes are something Hannah should select for herself, and instead, we pick out some underwear in basic black and white, and a set of pajamas to get her started. I decide not to order a bed since not only is this something that's not in my budget and I'm not certain when those funds Mr. Fredericks mentioned will show up in my account, but the bed won't arrive in time. I need to come up with another plan.

We're pushing the cart toward the front of the store when Cassie says, "This is fun." She smiles at the selections. "Shopping for Hannah."

I smile too, but it's strained. Does Cassie fully comprehend the situation? This isn't a sleepover or a week's vacation where Hannah will be gone by Sunday morning. A week from today, our house won't go back to normal where it's just the two of us with phone calls here and there to Hannah to stay in touch. This situation is with us for at least two years.

On the drive home, I remember one of my work colleagues mentioning that he's looking to part with some of his son's stuff. His son graduated last term and has recently moved into an all-furnished apartment.

I call Kevin and he says yes, absolutely, and that he'll meet us with his truck when we arrive home. Not only does Kevin carry in the pieces of the bed, he assembles the frame, drags in the full-sized mattress, and throws in a matching side table. "I'm ready to turn my kid's room into a Man Cave," he laughs as he pushes aside his toolbox. "Let me know if you need anything else."

But there isn't space for much more in the shoebox-sized room, maybe a rug or a small dresser that we can add later, and that's after Cassie and I cleared every box and stack of Christmas decorations we never got around to sorting. Everything is now dragged to the garage, boxes stacked against the wall.

In typical Kevin fashion, he doesn't ask much about what's going on, the fact we're preparing a bedroom for someone else. He's never been big on small talk even though we've worked at the same advertising agency for the past five years. I've put in a lot of long hours to move up from sales assistant to running several of my own accounts while Kevin stays busy in accounts payable. Knowing him, he won't think it's his business to ask and is likely relieved to be getting rid of his son's stuff.

Within the hour, Hannah's room is set up. I've washed her sheets and made her bed, and Cassie has placed her new toiletries in the bathroom. She smiles when she realizes she and her cousin will be sharing a toothbrush holder.

We stand at the doorway and admire the space. The room is decorated minimally but it's cozy enough. It's a start and Hannah can eventually make it her own.

Cassie sets a decorative pillow at the head of the bed and steps back. "I can't wait to meet her," she says.

I nod, but don't say anything. I don't want her to know how badly my chest is squeezing, how my stomach is riddled with nerves. How I'm not sure how my niece will react when she sees me.


Fire. It's the terrifying sight of flames—the flames that are outside my window.

I jump from my bed. It's too close. The distinct smell of smoke fills my airways, and I'm choking. There's not enough air and I could pass out. The police will find me on the floor the same way they found my sister.

I stare, wide-eyed out my bedroom window. Orange sparks

flicker against the night sky. Smoke rises. If someone doesn't do something about that fire soon, it will consume my house next. The flames will leap over that fence. My daughter is in danger.

I should save her, but my feet remain glued to the floor. I'm paralyzed—the shock of seeing flames so close, and it renders me helpless. This can't be happening. Not again.

The smoke rises into the air in dangerous, black wisps. Fire is what killed Beth. It's what my sister and I used to cover up our crime too.

I should move. I should run down the hall and wake up my daughter. But, instead, I clutch my pajama top and yank the material until it's beneath my chin.

The laughter from someone cuts through the air and every hair on my neck stands on end. But it's a low chuckle with someone else laughing next.

On the other side of the fence, I spot the red flannel of my neighbor's shirt, her blue jeans as she moves behind the wooden slats. The tan color of a hunting jacket can be seen next, a camo wool cap pulled tight over the man's head. I let out my breath. It's my neighbors, Dawn and Peter, and they have a fire going in their fire pit, something they do sometimes in the evenings, sitting in their backyard with a few beers.

I release my pajama top and the material crumples against my chest. My breaths slow, the air returning to my lungs. It's only a fire pit, and it's in my neighbor's yard. There's nothing to worry about. I can't let my paranoia get the best of me, not so easily. I'll never make it with Hannah if I do.

In the morning, Mr. Fredericks sends another email to let me know the funds from my sister will be deposited into my account next week. The rest of the assets, the property, including her life insurance policy, will be made available to Hannah when she turns eighteen.

The attorney asks if I have any questions about the documents. I don't, but I hurry through my shower and gulp a large cup of coffee, the biggest mug I can find, to help me get through this task. With the appropriate documents signed, I notify Mr. Fredericks when it's done.

Dressing for work, I stare at my reflection in the mirror. My eyes are puffy, the lack of sleep evident in the paleness of my cheeks, the sallowness of my skin. I fear that I will make a horrible impression on Hannah.

Down the hall, Cassie's alarm clock sounds. To my relief, Cassie looks as if she slept peacefully while I barely managed a few minutes. It was hard to relax when I was still on edge about my neighbors' fire pit, plus the additional details Detective Gillespie shared when he called last night.

He said the fire started in the living room where several of my sister's canvases went up in flames first. My niece stumbled downstairs and called for her mom, but when she didn't answer, she panicked and broke through a kitchen window. She ran looking for help. When the firefighters arrived, they had no choice but to let the fire burn out, the house a total loss. They found my sister dead and trapped inside her daughter's room.

My niece ran a half mile away to their neighbors' house. She refused to go inside even when the Chandlers covered her with a blanket and begged her not to look. But she kept her eyes to the horizon, the smoke that billowed into the air, and kept saying that she didn't run fast enough. She wasn't able to help her mom.

The detective told me that Beth likely died of smoke inhalation, but I'm not sure if that's the case. I think he wants to spare me the horror, and I tremble at the flames that may have reached her arms and legs first. Her hair, alight. Her face twisted in pain.

Did my sister know who was doing this to her? Did she look into their eyes before she hid upstairs?

When the detective questioned Hannah, she told him she didn't hear anything or see anyone. But she did provide one interesting lead, and the idea is enough to raise my pulse.

"We need to confirm a few things first," Detective Gillespie said, "but there is someone we will be questioning."

He doesn't tell me who, but I already have my suspicions. I don't say anything to him either because I need to keep my promise. *That will undo everything, Beth. I know it will.* It will uncover what we fought to keep hidden.

# FOUR

Monday

Hours later, we're standing at the Arrivals gate at Huntsville International Airport. I've checked Cassie out early from school and told my boss that she has an early game. It's not a total lie, and I plan on explaining as much as I can to her later.

It was a busy morning of meetings, but I did find time to pull my friend Cynthia aside and tell her about Beth. She was astonished at first, and sad for me too. She didn't know I had a sister.

"I'm so sorry." Cynthia wrapped her arms around me for a hug. When she pulled back, she studied me. "Seriously, T. Are you okay?"

She wanted to ask more, but we didn't have time, not with another meeting reminder pinging our phones. She promised to check in with me later and gave me another squeeze before she disappeared down the hall. But just like with my boss, I didn't tell Cynthia about Hannah. I'm not ready with that part, not yet at least. I need to see my niece first.

The airport is modest with its black tile floors and white

walls, and it's small with its single terminal, one café, and a modest gift shop that sells everything from sweatshirts to keychains touting the Rocket City—what Huntsville is known for, from its 1960s space age advancements to its current expertise in the aerospace and defense industry.

I'm too nervous to sit, so we stand. Cassie must be nervous too because she won't stop fidgeting. Someone plays on a nearby piano, but they're by no means a professional and are simply passing the time while they wait on someone. But the plunking of the keys grates my nerves, and my palms are slick with sweat. Each minute that passes is excruciating.

Passengers walk past us with their carry-ons. They stare down at phones while others are greeted by loved ones. One of the new arrivals scoops his kids in for a hug, while the rest of the crowd heads for the baggage carousel.

But there is no sign of Hannah.

The Arrivals screen shows her flight landed twenty minutes ago but she hasn't emerged, at least we don't think she has. We've kept our eyes locked on every man, woman, and child exiting the terminal and there hasn't been a sixteen-year-old girl with black hair. No one rushing toward us for a hug either.

Cassie steps from one foot to the next watching who comes down the escalator. She squeezes the plastic wrapping around the small bouquet of pink carnations—something we picked up on the way here, and the plastic crushes on one side. But I don't tell her to stop. My own hand clutches the strap of my purse as I crane my neck.

Other flights have now landed from Atlanta and D.C., which means it's no longer the passengers from Hannah's flight, which will complicate things, confuse things. There are more people to review, and more chances of losing Hannah in the shuffle.

I curse. Where is the airline rep who should be escorting her? Did they leave her at the gate and tell her to take it from there? She's sixteen and maybe they hope she can follow instructions.

The knots in my stomach tighten. But what if she didn't get on the plane? What if she doesn't want to be here and ran away? She fled to somewhere else.

Someone with long hair walks toward us—and my heart lifts—but the young woman cuts to her left and hugs someone who I assume is her boyfriend. An elderly couple passes us next; they have no additional luggage and proceed directly to the elevators.

A young girl arrives—is that her? Cassie grabs my arm and rises to her tiptoes.

But, no, this girl has blond hair and she's older, possibly in college, dressed in yoga pants and an oversized sweatshirt. Her parents, it seems, jump from their chairs and hug her. Her backpack is embroidered with a college logo.

My feet lower. Will we hug? I wonder. Will Hannah want to be held or will she shrink away from us as soon as she sees me? We're strangers... we don't know each other.

Beside me, Cassie looks ready to spin a hole in the ground.

And then I see her.

I see Beth—*my sister*. She's walking toward me.

And I can't believe it. My sister is here. Beth isn't dead. It was a horrible misunderstanding and she took a flight to Alabama. We can fix everything.

But the woman standing before us is younger and smaller. She's thin, her arms hanging limp by her sides. Her eyes dart back and forth, and it's not Beth, but someone who looks exactly like my sister. Her mirror image.

*Long black hair*, Mr. Fredericks said. *Like you too.*

My eyes prick with tears. It's a bittersweet feeling: my sister is gone but standing less than ten feet away is her daughter, Hannah. My niece. The girl I'd forgotten.

The three of us stand and stare at each other. No one moves, no one knows what to say, and the passengers clear a space around us. I'm trying to recover from that first sight of her, that split second when I thought she was Beth and I nearly bowled over.

Cassie is the first to speak. "Hannah?" she says, and her voice is pitched sky-high.

Hannah's eyes flicker to me first, then Cassie. She looks so much like my sister and the emotions storm through me. The same almond-shaped eyes, just like my daughter and me.

My niece is beautiful. She wears no makeup except for the tiniest amount of lip gloss, and her hair runs past her shoulders, but it's not in a ponytail like Cassie wears hers. Hannah's clothes are new too. I can tell by the crispness in the shirt and the straight lines in her jeans these are items that have never been washed. Someone may have bought her outfit as recently as this morning.

Did Hannah pick out the clothes by herself? Did she go to the store and select that top? I know very little about her except that, when she was a toddler, she liked *Clifford the Big Red Dog* and her doll with the blue gingham dress. She would run outside in her overalls.

But by the way Hannah stands stiffly, her hand scratching her shoulder, she's uncomfortable. Her face pales and her eyes shift. I fear she's about to turn and run.

Cassie thrusts the flowers into her hands. "I'm Cassie," she says. "Your cousin." And my daughter says this so earnestly and with such kindness that I smile, my heart warming at how much she wants Hannah to feel welcome.

But Hannah stares at the bouquet and doesn't blink. It's as if the sight of flowers is foreign to her, but that's ridiculous. She grew up on a farm. They would have maintained our parents' vegetable garden. If Beth kept things going after our parents died, the roses would have been spectacular each spring.

But Hannah is nervous, and the discomfort etches across

her face. She doesn't know what to do or where to look, except at the bouquet.

Cassie holds out her arms for a hug, and timidly, cautiously, as if cornering a wounded animal, she draws in closer to her cousin. But Hannah doesn't hold out her arms. To be fair, she's clutching a bouquet and the plastic crinkles loudly between them.

Cassie hugs her gently, then drops back with a look at me to take over.

"Hi, Hannah," I say, and reach out my hand. It's an awkward moment—everything is so awkward and new and tense—but something tells me that Hannah is not ready for another hug, at least not from me. We'll need to take things slow.

She gazes at my hand, my extended fingers, before her eyes travel the length of my arm to my face. Our eyes meet, and when they do, she flinches. Butterflies erupt in my stomach and the pain cleaves at my chest. What is she thinking right now? What does she know? More importantly, how much did Beth tell her?

She clasps her hand inside my own and lowers her eyes. She's cold to the touch, her fingers bone-thin, and the handshake must last long enough because she pulls her hand in one swift motion.

"I'm Aunt Tara," I tell her, and wince at the crack in my voice. "We're so glad you're here. We're so sorry for everything that's happened, but we're happy to have you living with us."

Hannah responds with the quietest of peeps. "Hi," she says.

I offer her a smile. But Hannah doesn't smile back.


We don't have as much time as I hoped before the start of Cassie's game. I wanted to bring Hannah home and avoid her enduring an hour at the soccer field—she could settle in at the house first. But with the delay in finding Hannah, we'll have to rush if we want to make it before kick-off.

Cassie climbs into the back of the car, already giving up front seat privileges, I notice. But she doesn't seem fazed. An unspoken understanding is taking place that her older cousin will get first dibs. I start up the car as Cassie explains why she has her soccer bag.

"I'm sorry about this," I tell Hannah. "I thought I'd have more time to drop you off first."

"It's okay," she says, but keeps her eyes to the window. "We can watch the game."

I spot my daughter's smile. She's thrilled that she'll be able to play in front of her cousin, and she continues to talk telling Hannah about her position as sweeper and how their team won the championship last year. "We have a lot of the same starters, so I think we have a good chance."

Hannah doesn't respond. I can't tell if she's paying attention, and she might not even care. She keeps her gaze out the window as we take the ramp to Interstate-565. We head west past acres of fields and red earth, the clay commonly seen in this part of north Alabama. To our east is the base of the Appalachian Mountains and the rolling hills. We pass exits leading to brand new subdivisions and schools, and when we pass signs for the historic town of Mooresville, Hannah turns her head with curiosity. She keeps her arms folded.

She's so quiet, and I don't blame her. Everything must look so different from Louisville. Up until a day ago, she never had a reason to think much about Alabama—or about us, for that matter.

Minutes later, we're on the bridge crossing the Tennessee River and we drop into the quaint town of Decatur. Cassie's school and its adjoining soccer field are only a few miles away.

At a red light, I steal a glance at the teenager buckled in beside me. She bites her lip, and with her arms strapped at her waist, her fingers dig into her sides. The tips of her fingers whiten, and she twists her mouth as if to keep her emotions in check. She's trying not to cry.

Everything inside of me wants to crumble. This poor girl and what she's been through—what she's still going through. She survived something horrific only a few days ago, and she's traumatized.

Cassie speaks up. She's asking Hannah a question, something about whether or not she likes soccer, but Hannah doesn't answer, and the silence lands heavily inside the car. My daughter closes her mouth, her cheeks reddening when I meet her gaze in the rearview mirror. She's been rambling too much.

But I'm not sure if Hannah registered the question. She appears lost in her own thoughts and stares out the window at every strip mall and gas station. Is she comparing this to her home? Is she missing her mother? Is she crying inside about how nothing in her life will ever be the same?

My shoulders lighten when Cassie's school comes into view, and it's the moment that Hannah sits up. We enter the parking lot and her eyes are glued to the red brick building: its large front portico and the flag poles that stand in the middle of the U-shaped driveway.

She looks up, her chin lifted, her wide eyes with a curious stare. And for the briefest of moments, I recognize a flash of my niece, the toddler I once knew, the way she would marvel at things when she was a little girl.

But this girl has grown up, and the sixteen-year-old Hannah beside me now runs her hand through her hair. It's a beautiful shade, jet black and like ink, it's so shiny. I remember when Beth would clip barrettes at her bangs only for them to slide out minutes later. Hannah would take off running, her nose crinkling when she laughed. She was so happy that day for her birthday party.

Hannah studies the school while my thoughts turn to the

additional information Mr. Fredericks sent me from Child Services.

Hannah Margaret Higgins, aged sixteen, is up to date with her immunizations and has no known allergies or health conditions. She's been homeschooled since the third grade and was enrolled, until recently, with the Louisville Homeschool Association under the supervision of her mother, Beth Higgins. With ACT and college-entry exams already taken, as well as honors classes fulfilled with a handful of college-prep credits under her belt, she's a bright kid, a studious kid, which means my sister was an excellent teacher.

But there is one detail that surprised me: Hannah has yet to get her driver's license. She turned sixteen in October but has not applied for the test. I would have thought a teenager these days would be gunning to get behind the wheel. But with Hannah being homeschooled and staying mostly with her mom, she must not have been in a rush to drive. My sister took her wherever she needed to go, or her friends picked her up.

But what about now? I'll be bringing her to school in the mornings, but she'll need to ride the bus in the afternoons, same as Cassie. In a few months' time, maybe I can arrange for her to take driving lessons and she can get her license. With the funds Mr. Fredericks mentioned, maybe we can purchase a second-hand car.

I remember when I turned sixteen and how eager I was to drive. I couldn't wait to climb behind the wheel of my parents' Toyota Corolla and would take off any chance I got for the mall or a sleepover. It was a half mile to our neighbors' house and then another five miles before we reached the highway that leads into town. My driver's license was my ticket to freedom—parties, mostly, as it turned out, which explains why my grades could never compare to Hannah's. For this, she takes after her mom.

The report also states that Hannah plans on studying

science in college—biology specifically since veterinary school is listed among her educational aspirations. I consider my own daughter and how her grades are okay but have never been stellar. Maybe having an A-plus student in the house will be a wonderful influence on my daughter.

We find a parking spot at the back of the building closer to the locker room. Cassie rushes from the car and shouts, "Wish me luck!", before she disappears inside the school to change into her uniform.

Now it's only Hannah and me.

She chews on a nail, and I do the same. She drops her hand, and I pull mine away too. We share the same nervous tendencies, I see.

Hannah turns in her seat, and it's the first time she's looked at me since we've been in the car. It's longer than she dared at the airport. "There's something I need to tell you," she says, and her lips tremble. I try to be ready, but the nausea ripples its way through my stomach.

# FIVE

"I miss her," she says. "And I wish I'd known you better. That you and my mom hadn't drifted apart, that we'd been around each other." I listen to her, but my chest wants to fold in on itself, the guilt and dread sweeping through me. "I wish I'd known Cassie too," she adds. "We could have grown up together. We could have been friends."

"I'm so sorry, Hannah. Your mom and me—"

"She missed you," she says, and her eyes drop. "She was lonely."

I struggle to blink back my tears. An ache forms at my temples.

Hannah says, "But there's nothing we can do about it anymore, can we? We can try to make up for lost time, Cassie and me. I'm here, and this is what we're dealing with, so we'll try to make it work. I'll live with you, and we'll do our best." She nods as if she's convincing herself. "It's the only way to make things right."

I rub at the space between my collarbones. "I'm so sorry," I whisper.

"I understand that a lot happened... between you. I know there was a lot of blame going around."

I wipe my eyes, and nod. How grown-up she sounds. How much she wants to understand why we did what we did, why we chose to split up our family. And she will try her best. She wants me to also. There is a chance we can mend old wounds because, like my daughter, Hannah has hope. She wants this to work. And I marvel at how Beth and I have raised such smart and emotionally sound girls.

I want to hug my niece. I want to stretch between our seats and thank her for her words. But I don't. Instead, I tell her, "Thank you for saying that, Hannah. I believe the same thing, that everything is going to be okay."

She looks away again, but her shoulders shrink back. I realize it's taken every bit of her resolve to say these words and now she doesn't know what to do next.

"I mean it," I repeat. "We're so glad you're here. We're happy you'll be living with us. I know you're hurting. I can't even imagine..."

She is about to speak when several girls burst from the locker room doors, several of the soccer players spotting me in the car and waving in my direction. "Hi, Ms. Jenkins!" they shout before they catch up with their coach.

Hannah lifts her head. In her eyes, I sense her longing. The girls look happy and carefree as they race to the field.

"We can go now," Hannah says, and she reaches for the door handle.

I glance again to the locker room door, knowing that Cassie will be coming out soon. She'll be lacing up her cleats and running out at any second.

Did she tell any of her teammates, I wonder? Is that why some of them turned and waved because they wanted to catch a peek of Hannah? In her excitement, Cassie told them about her cousin, our new housemate.

I step onto the sidewalk and Hannah does the same. She looks around, and so do I. The shouts from the bleachers pull my attention as one of the refs blows a whistle.

I hear Hannah say, "Aunt Tara?"

And a warmth spreads through my cheeks. It warms my heart to hear her calling me that after such a long time, and I smile at her. "Yes, sweetheart?"

"Don't think you're off the hook."

"What's that, honey?"

She stands taller. She's no longer curling in on herself like she did in the car, and she faces me, no longer timid.

"What happened between you and my mom," she says. "What you did to Grandma and Grandpa." She takes a rattled breath. "I don't know if I can forgive you for any of that."

I raise my hands to my chest. "Oh, Hannah."

"My mom never forgave you, did you know that? She was so angry. And yet, here I am. She left me with you, and I can't believe it."

But it was something her mom never thought would come to pass. *A formality*, Mr. Fredericks told me.

With a hitched cry, Hannah says, "Aunt Tara, what did you do?"


Several of the parents assemble on the bleachers while others unfold their lawn chairs and set coolers beside their feet. But all I want to do is run and hide inside my car.

I need to explain myself to Hannah, I know I do, but the sound of Cassie running past us startles us both. "It's almost game time," she says.

"Hannah," I try, but she nudges with her chin.

"The game," Hannah says, and she walks ahead.

It hurts to swallow, the panic icy cold in my lungs. What exactly did my sister tell her? She must have put all the blame on me. It's the same story she told herself after our parents died, and that's even when the police never found me at fault. Our parents' deaths were ruled an accident. But that didn't stop Beth from blaming me, did it?

*It's your fault,* Beth screamed at me. And I clenched my hands. *But I didn't kill anyone, Beth. You did.*

She begged me not to look back. *Don't, Tara. Please.* We turned away, the secret forged between us, the flames erasing everything behind us.

Numb, I follow Hannah to the bleachers, my insides scrambling. There is guilt, and anger too that my sister filled her daughter's head with lies, but then named me as her legal guardian. Why would she do that? No wonder Hannah doesn't want to be with me. She thinks I'm at fault. She's only heard one side of the story.

*This could have been handled so much better, sis. You have only made this much, much worse.*

Hannah and I don't sit in the bleachers but stand to one side. I slide my sunglasses over my face and nod to a few of the parents I know and am relieved when the game starts and there's no time to introduce Hannah.

The game moves quickly and it's difficult for me to pay attention. At one point, I recognize the long, defensive kick of my daughter as she hurtles the ball across the field. Someone chest-traps it. The team scores. The crowd cheers while several people shout, "Go Bears!" and I spot Fiona's dad whistling from the bleachers. I duck my head, cringing that I thought he was someone else.

Those squared-off shoulders, and dark hair. The way he walked so assuredly toward my daughter.

*He has to pay for what he's done,* Beth told me.

Cassie celebrates another goal, and she throws a glance in our direction. I clap, but the bones in my fingers ache, my body untethered.

My niece on the other hand is enraptured with the game. She moves her head up and down the field, taking everything in as Cassie drops back defensively and kicks the ball away from the goal. Cassie passes us another look and Hannah claps loudly.

The Bears win 3-1 and the girls jump up and down. My daughter sprints toward us, beaming with the satisfaction of playing an excellent game in front of her cousin.

But when she draws close, Cassie slows her steps. She must spot the stiffness in our bodies, our unsmiling faces, her gaze bouncing between us. "What's up?"

I'm about to tell her that everything is fine when Hannah says, "That was amazing. You're a fantastic player." She raises her arm for a high-five and Cassie's expression breaks instantly. She bursts into a grin and smacks her cousin's hand.

"Great job," Hannah says. "Seriously. Your team is really good. You especially."

I can't help from being stunned, but also relieved, by the sudden change in Hannah's demeanor. Maybe she's relieved now that she's told me how she feels, and she got it out of her system. Or maybe watching Cassie's game lifted her spirits.

"If you guys play this well now," Hannah says, "you're going to have a heck of a team next year."

"Thanks," Cassie says, her smile not leaving her cousin's. "Do you play?"

"I did, but it was a long time ago."

"What made you stop?"

"I got tired of it. But I miss it sometimes." She tents her hand over her eyes and scans the field. The refs bend down to pick up the cones while the coaches discuss something on the sidelines. "It was fun watching you out there," Hannah tells her. "It brought back so many memories."

"Awesome. Thanks." Cassie runs her hand through her ponytail, her fingers pulling at a tangle.

Hannah smiles at me, and there is a knowing look, the subtle rise of her eyebrows that says she may not have forgiven me yet, but she will not show her resentment in front of Cassie. She will not upset her young cousin when what she wants to do most is make things better. Like she said, *We can make up for lost time, Cassie and me.*

My body stiffens. *Cassie and me.* She failed to include me in that sentiment.

# SIX

"You guys hungry?" I'm positive Cassie's answer will be yes after playing a tough game, but I'm also hoping this is something Hannah will like. Our first dinner together, the three of us.

We pull up to Tommy's Burgers and there's Tommy, the owner, shouting instructions from the counter as he punches orders into the register. He holds out his arms in greeting as soon as we enter.

Over the years, Tommy has seen us come and go, often with Cassie running in to grab our to-go orders of burgers and fries, the grease seeping through the paper bags before she's reached the car. Other times, and especially after a win, we'll sit down for dinner. Tonight is definitely one of those occasions.

"This is my niece," I tell Tommy, gesturing to Hannah. "She's going to be living with us so you should be seeing a lot more of her."

Tommy claps his hands together. "Wonderful." His blue eyes shine from his deep tan resulting from the amount of time he spends on the golf course. But his mouth twitches, and it's as if he wants to ask a question. He's trying to determine if Hannah living with us is a good thing or a bad thing since he doesn't know the circumstances behind this child, or how she ended up in my care. Usually, kids not living with their parents is often preceded by something tragic or complicated, and we are both of those things.

But instead, he says, "It's nice to meet you, Hannah. Welcome to Tommy's." And he smiles in my direction before he turns to Cassie. "Another win?"

"Of course," she answers.

"Fantastic. The Bears all the way, right?"

"Absolutely."

Tommy nods at her to prompt our order. Cassie and I don't look at the menu as we already know what we want: junior-sized burgers with lettuce and tomato, and no cheese since Cassie can't have dairy. Hannah studies the menu posted on the board above Tommy's head, and it suddenly occurs to me that I didn't ask if she likes burgers, if she even eats red meat. Is she a vegetarian? Would she have preferred we go somewhere else?

I'm wondering if I should apologize when Hannah says, "What do you guys usually get?" And Cassie tells Tommy our order. She's efficient in that way, letting Hannah know what we want while letting Tommy simultaneously punch in our request.

"No cheese," she reminds him.

Hannah nods. "I'll have the same."

"Are you sure?" I ask, and Hannah shoots me a funny look. "You can order whatever you want. There are chicken sandwiches too."

"No, I'm good. I like burgers."

I add three drinks and an order of fries and pull out my wallet to pay. The girls grab a booth in the corner and I join them a moment later.

Cassie is once again talking about the game. She has a habit of doing this, providing a run-down while discussing good plays or skills that need improvement. By the way Hannah angles her body toward her to listen, Cassie is eager to discuss something they have in common. The silence in the car ride from before, magically erased.

"Emma did great," Cassie says. "She really stepped up. Which means Nikki needs to heal fast and get back on her A-game or she could lose her starting position."

Hannah asks, "Nikki got hurt? How did that happen?"

"A sprained ankle. But Emma played so good that Coach should think about starting her next time. If I were Nikki, I'd be worried."

"Is Emma one of the forwards?"

"Yeah, she scored that first goal." Cassie taps her fingers excitedly on the table, the adrenaline coursing through her. "What position did you play?"

"Center mid," Hannah answers. "It was with my school team."

"Was that your homeschool?" I ask, finding my way into the conversation.

Her eyes flicker to me, then away again. "Yes," she answers.

"Cool," Cassie says. "I didn't know homeschools have teams."

"Some of them do as a rec group. It's fun."

My daughter scrunches her nose. She doesn't mean to, but I know what she's thinking. "Do you like homeschool? I mean, I know some kids who do it, but it seems quiet. I don't know much about it besides that."

"It's good. I liked it." Hannah tucks her hair behind her ear, and it's the first time I notice she's wearing nail polish, the last remnants of a metallic-blue color chipping away. "But I know I won't be homeschooled anymore, and that's okay." She slides her eyes in my direction. "I get it."

I don't respond but am grateful this is something Child Services has already explained to her.

"So, with homeschool, how does it work?" Cassie asks. "You

guys do your assignments at home and then you meet up for practice?"

"Yes. Well, that's how I used to do it."

"Was your team any good?"

"My middle school team was. We won district and had a pep rally and everything."

Cassie looks equal parts excited and jealous. Her team qualified for the championships last year and there wasn't a pep rally or any type of send-off. Most of those events are reserved for the football team. "A pep rally for homeschool kids?" Cassie says. "Like in a gym or something?"

"Well, not really," Hannah says. "It was more like a bunch of kids and parents jumping around in a parking lot."

Cassie laughs, and a scene enters my mind of my sister doing just that: jumping up and down and waving a poster for Hannah. I bet it was the best poster in the parking lot.

"Mom, we should try something like that," Cassie says. "Even if it's just the families and stuff."

"Good idea." But I'm also studying Hannah because this is great information to know, a small peek into her life with my sister.

It's also interesting because up until a few years ago they weren't as reclusive as Mr. Fredericks described. They were attending soccer games and meeting up with families. So, what happened? In the last few years, what made Beth cut herself off to stay at home?

Did she keep in touch with any of these parents? Hannah hasn't played since middle school but maybe Beth kept in touch with some of them over the years. I should ask Detective Gillespie about this and see if he can find out anything. Maybe someone knows what was going on with Beth the days or weeks before her death. Maybe she told someone she was worried about something.

"Order fifty-seven!"

Cassie leaps from her seat and scrambles for the counter. "I'll get it."

Hannah passes me a small smile, and I smile back. Conversations from other families grow louder around us, but the noise doesn't bother me. Inch by inch, I feel my shoulders start to relax. With my niece smiling, some of her edges are softening, her anger toward me lessening.

Cassie returns with our food. She hands out foil-wrapped burgers and unfolds the bag of fries for us to share. "Ketchup?" she asks.

"Sure," Hannah says, and Cassie squeezes enough for a family of ten.

"Oops." She caps the lid.

I watch the girls eat, my daughter chewing a handful of fries before she bites into her burger. Hannah does the same. Cassie takes a sip of her drink, and so does Hannah. My niece is copying her in everything, and it's both sweet and surreal, the two of them stealing glances at one another while also giggling. They must see the resemblances with their straight black hair and olive skin, the realization they now have a sister.

I take it all in. Watching them is like stepping back in time, and it reminds me of when Beth and I would hang out on the front porch as our mom made ice cream. She'd hum while she mixed in the cream and sugar and stirred it together in a large bowl, the flavors changing with the season, with our family favorite remaining, vanilla with blackberry swirl. We'd eat pints of it every summer while we talked on the front porch.

Did Beth take Mom's bowls in the kitchen and teach Hannah how to make homemade ice cream? Did she carry on with our family tradition?

When I was a kid, Beth would let me stir the cream sometimes. She'd join in on Mom's humming, maybe a church song or a Christmas jingle, which would make us laugh especially if it was the middle of summer. I would take the spoon and sneak a lick, and Beth would catch me, but she never told. We used to keep our secrets to each other back then.

"How do you like your burger?" I ask Hannah.

"It's really good."

"We made up your room," Cassie says, excitedly. "We bought a few things we hope you'll like. A new comforter and lamp and everything."

"Thanks. That's really nice of you."

"PJs too." My daughter beams. "Mom is taking you clothes shopping tomorrow, isn't that right, Mom? You can get what you want. The mall has a whole bunch of great stores. I wish I could go too, but I have school."

"I wish you could go too," Hannah tells her. Her eyes drop at the shirt and jeans she's wearing. "It will be good to have something else." She scrunches her face.

Cassie shrugs. "I think it looks good on you." And she takes another bite of her food. Cassie has never cared much about clothes, but I wonder if that will change now that Hannah is living with us. Already, I see her eyeing her cousin's nail polish.

"Don't worry, Hannah," I tell her. "We'll pick out things you want. It'll be fun."

"Fun," she repeats, but she looks down, her voice sounding hollow.


Cassie is so eager to show Hannah her new bedroom that she grabs her cousin's wrist as soon as we enter the house. She pulls her down the hall.

Cassie insists on pointing out everything even though it's self-explanatory: the new comforter and side table, plus the items we picked out at the store. She sits on Hannah's bed and bounces a couple of times, the mattress springs squeaking beneath her. Hannah does the same and they laugh.

"This is really nice," Hannah says, and she smooths her

hand along the bedspread. She admires her new lamp before she says to me, "I hope it wasn't too much trouble."

"No trouble at all," I answer.

"Blue is my favorite color. That's cool that you guessed that." Little by little, the knots in my neck loosen. It's possible that Hannah is slowly coming out of her shell.

"You can pick out anything else you want later," Cassie says. "Picture frames or decorations or whatever."

I stand in the doorway and consider how remarkable it is that just last night Cassie and I stood in this exact spot and tried to imagine what Hannah would be like, what she would look like. And now here she is, sitting on the bed and checking out her room. Until yesterday, I didn't think this was possible. I didn't think my sister would die either.

Cassie is talking again. She's describing her middle school and how Austin High is not that far away from campus. "Your school is on the other side of the Beltway. That's a highway." She looks at me. "We'll show you around, maybe tomorrow, right, Mom? After school and you guys go shopping, we can take Hannah around for a drive?" She doesn't wait for a response. "We'll show you everything. I think you're going to like it here. You'll like your school too. It's big, but I heard the cafeteria is awesome. I can't wait for high school in two years." She tucks her knees beneath her chin and clasps her hands together.

"You'll have lockers and classes upstairs, downstairs," Cassie continues. "And tons of clubs to choose from, not just sports, but other activities, so maybe you can find something you'll like. Maybe student council or theater. I heard the principal is strict but cool."

Hannah nods. It's a lot of information to take in at once and I fear that Cassie might be going overboard. But to my relief, Hannah asks Cassie some questions too.

"Do you have friends in the neighborhood? People you hang out with?"

"There's Emma, the girl that scored that first goal. And Katie lives one street over."

"Can you walk to their houses?"

"Yeah, it's not far."

Hannah smiles. "I'd love to meet them."

And Cassie smiles. "I'd love you to meet them too. They're really fun. But there is this one girl, Marissa, who's a pain. She gets on my nerves." Cassie rolls her eyes and Hannah does the same.

"We'll stay away from her," Hannah says.

I back away. My presence isn't necessary. I'm intruding on their moment and they don't need me to hover. These are two young teens—well, one pre-teen and one sixteen-year-old—who are laughing and talking about school and friends. I smile at how Cassie's dreams of endless sleepovers have already begun.

Neither of the girls notice me leave, and I head for the kitchen where I grab a glass of water. I'll check my phone and see if there are any new messages from the detective. I hear Cassie say, "So what do you think? Are you excited about everything?"

And it's Hannah's pause that catches my attention. "Everything... well, it's new. But I'll get used to it."

"I hope you like Decatur. It's small, and not like Louisville —I mean, I don't know anything about Louisville."

"I know. You guys never came."

And my daughter falls silent. I wince that she doesn't know what to say, but she'll try to come up with an explanation. *I didn't know about you until yesterday. I wish we would have, but my mom...* But those explanations should come from me and not my daughter.

But Hannah says, "It's okay. It's not your fault." And she

changes the subject to something about music, a new band, and my daughter happily switches topics.

I'm in the living room when the door to Hannah's bedroom closes. One of them has gotten up to close it, and I'm not sure if it was Cassie or Hannah, but they want their privacy. They're forming their own little club, and I'm the boring adult who's not invited. But that's okay, and I'm glad they have each other. Cassie will be our glue.

I hear a shriek—it's coming from Hannah's bedroom.

Something heavy thuds on the floor, and my first thought is that one of them has fallen off the bed. Next, the mad scramble of feet.

Cassie wails, "*Mom!*"

And I swing open the door. Every muscle in my body is wound tight. I'm ready to launch forward, I'm ready to take on what's happening. I must protect my girls.

# SEVEN

"What's wrong?"

The girls are no longer on the bed but are standing at the window. They're not hurt, which is a relief, but they're also not moving. Their backs are to me as they peer outside.

We didn't put up curtains and the same plastic blinds that are in every room of this house hang in Hannah's window also. The blinds are open, providing a full view of the driveway and what's taking place to scare the girls. The distinct flicker of flames.

I don't believe what I'm seeing. For the second night in a row, there is a fire burning outside our house, but this time it's out front.

I rush to the window. This is not my neighbors' fire pit but something else. The fire is near the sidewalk, the flames rising higher.

Orange flames crackle and smoke billows from what appears to be a trash can. The black rubber melts as the can droops from the heat. On the ground next to it is a large, dense mass, but I can't tell what it is. It will catch on fire next, the whole thing going up in flames as the blaze spreads to my house.

My pulse hammers in my throat. Hannah led a path straight to us. Whoever this person is, they will destroy the rest of our family.

Hannah backs away from the window, her hands trembling. "It's a fire," she whispers, the orange flames reflected in her eyes. "*A fire!*" she screams.

I pull at the girls' arms and drag them behind me. "We need to leave right now." We run from Hannah's room and burst through the front door as I instruct them to stay in the street. Cassie holds onto Hannah, and Hannah does the same.

The trauma of Hannah witnessing this is not lost on me. I should do something soon. I step closer to my yard and tell myself I should alert the neighbors. I will call 9-1-1.

I pat my hands at my pockets, but I don't have my phone. Dammit, I left it inside the house. The wail of a firetruck sounds in the distance, the siren getting closer, as the truck hurtles through our neighborhood. Someone has already called 9-1-1.

It must be our neighbor, Bobby, because he comes running from next door, his hair wet, his shirt damp as if he's just gotten out of the shower. He waves his arms as he runs.

"Everyone stand back!" he shouts.

The trash can is on the sidewalk and not on the grass, but I sidestep quickly to the concrete. The can is full of twigs and grass clippings with snarled branches sticking out. The wood burns hot and crumbles to black, the green leaves disintegrating into ash. On the ground are stacked-up pieces of a tree trunk that have been sawed into rings.

Bobby pants when he reaches the sidewalk. He's dragging a garden hose but drops it when the firetruck careens around the corner.

"I'm so sorry," Bobby says. "My brother-in-law is an idiot."

"What?"

"He was smoking a cigarette. He must not have put it out all the way and tossed it in. Those leaves, and those branches, everything is so dry, it caught fire." He rakes his hand through his hair and winces at the firefighters climbing out of the truck. "This is so embarrassing."

Two of the firefighters approach as I swing my attention back to the girls. They're safe, they haven't come any closer, but their eyes are as wide, especially Hannah who looks like she could leap out of her skin.

I could kill Bobby's brother-in-law for doing this.

"I'm so sorry," he repeats. He explains to the firefighters, "We had a tree that needed to come down and my brother-in-law came over to help. He was careless. It was a lit cigarette."

They put out the blaze with a steady shot of the hose, but the blast knocks the can to the ground and it spills over. What remains is the putrid smell of melted rubber and a wet, soggy mess scattered across the asphalt.

"It goes without saying how dangerous this is," one of the firefighters says. "With a strong gust of wind, if the flames had caught on to any other debris, it could have spread to the houses."

"I know. I'm so sorry." Bobby peers at his front door like he's minutes away from strangling his brother-in-law. I could help with that, I think.

I stare at the blackened heap before us.

"Are you okay?" Bobby asks.

I don't say anything. I don't want to lose my cool, especially in front of the girls. I also don't want them to see how this experience has rattled me—another fire, two nights in a row.

It was an accident, I tell myself. It has to be.

"We'll clean up the mess," Bobby says. "Don't worry. We shouldn't have left it so close to your yard." And he hooks a thumb to what I assume is his brother-in-law's truck which takes up part of the street.

The firefighters ask Bobby if they can go inside and speak to his brother-in-law.

"Absolutely," Bobby says. "And while you're at it, can you tell him to knock off the smoking too?"

I instruct the girls to stay in the living room. There's no need for them to watch from Hannah's window. Someone is outside shoveling the burned mess. Even with the door closed, we can hear the sickening scrape, the smoke finding its way into the house and seeping into our clothes.

I check on Hannah. It wasn't long ago that ash and smoke clung to her face too.

She remains still on the sofa. Cassie says something about watching TV and Hannah nods, but her eyes don't focus on anything and she's shocked. Finally, she curls up beside my daughter and tucks her hand beneath her chin. It's sweet, the two of them together, looking like sisters.

I find my phone and head for my room, shutting the door so I can call Detective Gillespie. He owes me an update.

He answers on the third ring. "Yes, Ms. Jenkins?"

"Have you learned anything?"

Something double-clicks in my ear, his pen. Another phone shrills in the background. It's approaching eight o'clock and he must still be at the police station, which is good. *Keep working*, I implore. Keep investigating. We need to get to the bottom of this, and soon.

"What do you know?" I ask.

"Ms. Jenkins, I can't share any of the specific details right now, but please know that we are following up with everything. We're talking to the individual in question first thing tomorrow."

"Who is it?"

"I'm afraid I can't tell you that."

"What makes them a lead?"

He skirts the question. "We're going through your sister's

phone records. Her computer burned so we lost the hard drive but there are several files backed up to the cloud. We're going through those files too."

"And?"

"Your sister received several messages. That's all I can say for now. That, and combined with what your niece told us, we feel confident about bringing this person in."

"My niece is living with us now, did you know that? Beth's daughter."

He pauses. "Yes, I'm aware."

I want to tell him that my niece is in danger, and so is my daughter. But instead, I ask, "The person who sent my sister the message, was it a man or a woman?"

"I can't tell you that right now."

"What did the message say?"

"Ms. Jenkins," he says slowly.

"Can you let me know tomorrow?"

He clicks his pen again. "I'll tell you as soon as I find out anything concrete. Don't worry, Ms. Jenkins. You need to trust us. We're doing everything we can to find out who did this."

I lower the phone and hang up. *We're doing everything we can.*

Isn't that what they always say? But he has no idea what he's searching for, and for that part, I am certainly to blame.


Tuesday

In the morning, Hannah asks if we can buy flowers. "White roses for my mom," she says after we drop off Cassie at school. "I thought it would be something nice to do for her. Seeing as my mom didn't want a funeral or anything." Her eyes redden.

"Of course," I tell her.

I pull onto the street when Hannah asks, "Is there a park we can go to? Or somewhere near water? Mom always liked the water."

I nod and consider the park nestled against the Tennessee River.

I remember the creek where Beth and I learned to fish with Dad. We had matching fishing poles and we'd roll our jeans above our knees and stand on the creek bank for hours. Beth was always more patient than me.

Before we left home this morning, I emailed my boss and let her know that I would be taking personal leave following my sister's death. Since I have a few days accrued, it would be no problem and I spent time last night rescheduling my meetings and pushing them to next week. My boss, the owner of Kelly Bishop Advertising, responded with exactly what I wanted to hear: *Take your time. Do what you need to do.* Kelly has always been good at recognizing when one of us needs to use sick leave or needs a personal day. I'm also lucky to have found a job where I have found something I can stick with.

I shot a quick text to Cynthia to let her know too. She came back with a rapid-fire response.

*Should I stop by after work?*
*Check on you? Bring you food?*

I told her no, but her offer brought a smile to my face. Cynthia knows how much I don't like to cook and she'll be imagining me with another bag of takeout.

*I'll be okay,* I responded. *I just need some time.*

Our plan for today is to shop for new clothes for Hannah and enroll her in school. But since we have an hour before the mall opens, we can absolutely fulfill Hannah's wishes and select flowers for her mom.

Hannah picks out a small bouquet of white roses and clutches them to her chest. She doesn't say much as we drive to the river and park at the harbor. The sun is shining, there's a cool breeze, and it's not too chilly for a walk along the riverfront. I suggest we go near the pavilion where there's a large grassy area.

Hannah walks ahead. She keeps her head down, lost in thought, and I follow. I'll go where she goes. I'll stop when she's ready.

Hannah wears the same pair of Adidas lace-ups she had on at the airport, gray with white stripes, casual but trendy. She likes them, which worked out well since we're not the same shoe size. Everything else she has on is from my closet.

It took us a few minutes this morning to find something, clothes of mine that weren't too big or "too stiff"—Cassie's words. *Mom's work clothes*, she teased as she pointed out my gray suits and black trousers. Hannah gave her a knowing glance, but she eventually settled on a pair of jeans that were, admittedly, too loose in the waist so we added a belt. She picked out one of my lightweight sweaters.

"Don't worry," I told her when she eyed herself in the mirror. "You can find something else at the mall."

Hannah moves toward a row of trees at the water's edge. She studies the water with the roses in her hands.

In the silence, I wonder if I should say something, if I should speak up with a few words about my sister, a poem, or a eulogy of some sort. Hannah is only sixteen and has most likely never had to do something like this. She was too little when her grandparents and father died. Going through this will be devastating for her.

Hannah lets out a sob. She is no longer silent, and it's as if someone has reached into my chest and wrenched at my heart. She pulls one of the petals from the bouquet and lets it drift to the ground. She picks another one, and the breeze catches it, the petal fluttering side to side before it lands on the water.

"I really miss her," she says.

"I'm so sorry, Hannah. Your mom... she was a wonderful person." My throat burns.

"Why did this have to happen?" she cries. "Who would do something like this to her? Did they want to kill me too?" At this, she shivers.

"No, Hannah," I shush her. "Please don't think that way. No one is going to hurt you." I grimace, not wanting her to see my face.

"But they almost did," she says. "What if I hadn't gotten out of the house in time? And I was trapped? I could have died. It could have happened." She chokes on another sob. "But I shouldn't have left her. I should have gone back for Mom."

I cradle her to my shoulder. "She would have wanted you to save yourself, Hannah, and you did. You did the right thing. You got out and you survived."

"I just..." She whimpers, and the tears splash from her chin to the top of the bouquet. "It's my fault."

"You needed to find help."

She cries, and I'm crying too, but soon, she quiets. She sniffles as she looks at me. "I heard you last night, you know. Talking. Was that the detective?"

I wipe my eyes, realizing she must have stood in the hallway and heard me. "Yes, it was Detective Gillespie. He's the one you met with, right?"

"What did he say? Does he know anything?"

"There's someone they're talking to. But he wouldn't say much." I eye her cautiously. I'm not sure if this is the right time to ask Hannah questions of my own right now. "It's something about that lead you told him about."

She nods.

"What did you tell the detective, Hannah? He wouldn't say. Do you know who could have done this?"

"She was going on a date. She met someone. They met

online, some kind of dating site. She was excited about seeing him at first but then..."

Another instance when my sister may not have been as much of a recluse as Mr. Fredericks thought. She had been reentering the dating scene and making plans with someone.

"What happened? This man...?" A thought strikes me. "Do you think he did something to your mom?"

She shakes her head. "No. I don't know. She never met him. She didn't show up to their date."

"Did she say what happened?"

"That she changed her mind and didn't want to go. But he sent her some messages afterwards. He was pretty angry."

"But it was a first date," I tell her. "It shouldn't have been that big a deal, right?"

"He didn't seem to think that way. He said he sat and waited at the restaurant for more than an hour and felt like an idiot. Those messages... what he said to her... he was really mean."

My voice shakes. "What did he say, Hannah?"

"That she had no right to stand him up. That she made him feel like a fool. That she would pay for wasting his time."

"Jesus," I whisper.

"I know. And that's why I had to tell the detective. Their date was supposed to be last week."

I nod at her. "You did good, Hannah, telling the detective. That was very brave."

But she's crying again. "My poor mom," she says. "Of all the guys she could have met online, would he really do something like this? Get that angry and kill her? It's insane, right? Over something like a missed date."

It is insane, and my stomach twists. It's diabolical. This person must be deranged. The police need to find him as soon as possible.

My heart hammers too. Who is this man, and what if it's the

person we've been fearing for years? He's come back from the shadows. It's exactly what I thought. He'll be furious that his plan to kill Hannah didn't work out.

I ask, "Do you know his name? The man your mom was going to meet?"

"Rick Joffrey." And I blink. The name means nothing to me. "Mom showed me his profile pic. At least that's the name he went by on the dating site."

"Did you see him?" I ask. "Did you see whoever came to the house? Who set the fire?"

"No, and that's what's so weird. I told the detective too. I was hanging out in my room, and my room filled with smoke. I ran downstairs but couldn't find Mom. The fire was spreading fast. It was in the living room and everything was so hot. I was so scared. I broke through a window."

"Did you see a car? Someone running away?"

"No, because where did he go? I never heard anyone driving up either. I didn't hear them leave. You remember that gravel driveway, right? How you can hear everyone and anyone that comes up to the house. I heard nothing."

She's right. With the farmhouse as the last property at the end of Route 30, we always knew when someone was arriving, the postal worker or Dad returning from work. In high school, it was helpful because Beth and I would know exactly how much time we had before our dates picked us up. The crunch of their tires on gravel would give us another few minutes to finish our makeup.

The tip of Hannah's nose flares pink. "Mom..." she sobs, and she tugs a rose from the bouquet.

The stem sticks at first, its thorns tangling with other thorns in the bunch, until she pulls at it and drops it in the water. We watch it float, the rosebud and green stem skimming the surface. It's a beautiful sight, a lovely gesture, and Hannah adds another flower until there are two roses floating in the water.

"The two of us," Hannah says. "It was always the two of us."

My heart breaks. That's how I think that about Cassie and me too.

*We didn't have to be so alone, Beth.*

"I love you, Mom," Hannah whispers. "I will miss you forever." She adds, "We will find out who did this. We'll make sure they're punished. We'll do whatever it takes. I promise you."

I startle at the intensity in Hannah's words, at her anger, the vitriol in her voice. But she has every right to want revenge. She needs justice. And so do I.

## EIGHT

We walk slowly to the car when I stop her and say, "Hannah, can we talk about yesterday? About what you said at the game?"

She carries what's left of the bouquet. She looks at me, a confused expression crossing her face before the memory hits her. "I'm sorry, I really am. I'm just... I'm so confused. Everything that Mom told me. It's what she told me for years, and it's all I ever heard." She ducks her head. "It's what the Chandlers told me too."

My shoulders straighten. "Charles and Regina Chandler? They told you what exactly?"

Hannah stops walking. She squirms. She's so different from yesterday with that outburst that was full of anger. Now, she's uncomfortable to talk further.

"Hannah," I say, "I didn't do anything to hurt Grandma and Grandpa. Please, you need to believe me. It was a tragic accident. A big misunderstanding." She doesn't look at me and I stop myself from raising my finger to lift her chin. "It's horrible, what happened. It's made me sad knowing all these years that your mom blamed me. It's one of the many reasons I left." I do not—and will not—include the part about her mom kicking me out. "I hate knowing the Chandlers thought this way too. But I didn't hurt them, you have to know that. I loved my parents. I miss them every day."

"But Mom said..." Her cheeks redden. "She said that if you hadn't been there..."

"She's right, Hannah. I shouldn't have been there that night, but that's not why it happened. That's not why they died. Grandpa—"

But Hannah stops me. "Aunt Tara, is it okay if we don't talk about this right now? My mom..." And she drops her gaze to the flowers. "It's just a lot for me to handle at the same time, you know?"

The flush rises to my cheeks. I feel awful. I am the most inconsiderate person in the world. I want so badly to explain myself that I'm forgetting her current state of grief. We just held a memorial service for her mother, the two of us, and while grieving, she doesn't need to be grieving for her grandparents all over again too.

We have time, I remind myself. It's important, and I will plead my case to Hannah at some point. It's crucial that she knows she's not living with a murderer.

*It's not me*, I want to tell her. *It was never me*.


The mall isn't crowded and since the doors have just opened, it's mostly senior citizens in their bright white walking shoes and exhausted-looking moms pushing their baby strollers and stopping to window shop. The babies nap peacefully while some of them kick their socked feet.

We check out the Belk department store first. That's where I'm hoping Hannah will find a few basic items.

We browse aimlessly, and I stand back, not wanting to hover as she checks out the Juniors section. She pushes several hangers to one side and inspects the clothes before she drifts to another rack. At a table display, she picks up a sweater.

But Hannah soon finds the Calvin Klein section, and she eyes a cropped hoodie with a pair of matching jogger pants. They're gray and white to match her shoes. She holds up the outfit for me to see, and I give her a thumbs-up. She nods, the tiniest smile upon her lips as she folds the clothes over her arms.

"Do you guys have an Express?" she asks.

I remember the store on the upper level. "Yes. But I haven't been there in ages."

She looks at what she has in her arms. "Is it all right if I get these first?"

With the swipe of my credit card, I remind myself the funds are coming, it's going to be okay. Mr. Fredericks assured me the deposit will be made to my account next week so we can buy clothes for Hannah. I don't need to worry.

My niece carries the shopping bag as we exit and head for the escalators. We find the store and she moves to a front table display with black tops and sequined straps. But it's a bit dressy, and she puts it down. I wander to the back where I find shelves filled with every type of jeans imaginable: stone-washed, black, skinny, jeggings, high-waisted, low-waisted. My eyes roam the shelves. What do teenagers wear these days?

Thankfully, a saleswoman glides over and flashes a smile, which earns a shy smile from my niece. The saleswoman wears a stylish black turtleneck and red suede pants. Her arms are laden with bangles, the jewelry jingling as she rummages through the clothes and pulls out outfits for us to assess.

Eventually, Hannah is shown to a dressing room where she can try on the clothes. I wait patiently, the dressing room curtain fluttering as she moves around to try things on. I resist the urge to ask her if she needs help, the way I would if it was Cassie, but the saleswoman is on standby and ready to assist, so I hang back.

Hannah steps out and shows us the first outfit, but she's shy and can scarcely look at herself in the mirror. She wears a pair of stone-washed, mid-rise jeans along with a light pink sweater.

"That looks really nice on you," the saleswoman says, and I nod my agreement. Hannah runs her hands along the sweater and peeks in the mirror.

The saleswoman mentions they're having a sale, which has me suggesting that Hannah pick out a few more items. She finds a pair of white jeans and several more long-sleeved tops, plus a couple of camisoles she can wear beneath her sweaters if she gets cold.

"What about underwear?" I ask. We've bagged her latest treasures and carry them out of the store. She'll need more than what Cassie and I picked out. She'll want another set of pajamas too.

We head to Victoria's Secret, and to my relief, she passes everything with lace edging and heads to a table with modest bikini-cut designs and T-shirt bras. She doesn't select anything that would raise my eyebrows, and I let out my breath again, feeling guilty this is something I have to worry about with a sixteen-year-old. But what about later? What if Hannah meets someone and she wants to date? She's growing up. She may want something more playful. She'll be meeting new friends, which might also lead to parties and drinking. I'll have to enforce a curfew. We'll have to establish some rules. These are issues I have yet to deal with when it comes to my own daughter, and now they're staring me in the face.

Hannah picks out a blue cotton pajama set and a pair of lounge pants. She eyes another stack of clothes before she selects a black pair of sweatpants also.

She looks to me. "Is this too much?"

"Get what you want, Hannah. You need clothes for both school and home." She looks away as if not convinced. "It's fine," I tell her, and we head to the counter to pay.

Her smile is so appreciative, so gleeful, the smile reaches her eyes this time. And my breath cuts short—I see my sister in that moment.

"Thank you, Aunt Tara," Hannah says.

We could actually be making headway.

In the check-out line, she admires a display of body spritzes and picks up a pink bottle tied with a satin ribbon. She sprays it on her wrists and I crinkle my nose. It's sticky sweet and exactly the kind of scent a teenager would wear. She also picks out some lip gloss and places everything on the counter. Once again, I hand over my credit card.

When we leave, Hannah swings the bags in her hands as I look around at the rest of the mall. Where to next?

We stop in front of a boutique called Francesca's and she asks if we can take a look. She finds a few tops she likes as well as a pair of gold ballet flats.

She studies a table covered with candles, copper jars with bright gold lids and blue containers boasting lavender scents and lemongrass sage. Hannah lifts a jar to her face and breathes in the scent.

"Do you like candles?" she asks.

"Yes." I smell one of the candles also. It's jasmine.

"My mom loved them. She would light candles at night, or during the day. Whenever, really." She sets down the jar. "It was so peaceful, just the two of us."

I can picture my sister doing this. She would do this while she painted too.

"Which scent was her favorite?"

"All kinds. But vanilla was probably the one she liked most." She reaches for one that reads Vanilla Bean and breathes in the scent. Her smile is bittersweet; memories of her mom must be flooding back to her.

"Can I buy a few?" Hannah asks. "It would be really nice. It would remind me of Mom."

"Of course."

After paying, I remind Hannah that we should leave soon. It's time to meet the registrar at the school, and she flinches slightly, the trepidation of a huge public high school possibly hitting her. She doesn't say a word as we place the bags in the car. She doesn't speak to me during the drive.

We arrive at Austin High and Hannah is visibly bracing herself in her seat. Is it too soon? Am I pushing her too hard? Maybe we should wait a few more days before we launch something like school on her. She's barely had time to grieve. But Hannah is the one who said she didn't want to fall behind in her school-work. She said it was okay this morning. She wants to keep her grades up.

Hannah stares at the brick and concrete exterior. A wall of windows rises all the way to the roof with the words Austin High prominently featured above the cornice.

As we park, Hannah checks out the student section where student cars are lined up, their car tags hanging from rearview mirrors with their bumpers covered in stickers. She lets out a strangled sound.

I reach to start the ignition. "We can try again tomorrow. We can reschedule."

"No," she says, but she doesn't move to get out of the car. She watches as a girl is dropped off at the front by a parent. She walks through the front doors, her backpack looped over her shoulders.

Hannah fidgets with her hands. She lowers her eyes. She knows absolutely no one. This will be nothing like her homeschool.

Hannah says, "I can do this, right? I'm more than ready. And who knows? Maybe I'll like it."

I wait for her to open the car door, and she does. She walks slowly.

I push the button at the top of the steps and stare into the security camera until someone buzzes us in. A loud tone blares from the speakers and an announcement is made about the next class. We stand in the lobby behind a set of glass doors, but the stampede of teenagers fills the hallway. Their laughter is loud and abrupt, along with the skidding of tennis shoes, the slamming of lockers. A girl calls for her friend to wait up.

Hannah cranes her neck to watch. Thankfully, she no longer looks nervous, and her eyes track the students as they holler down the hall.

I fill out an information sheet on a clipboard while the student aide notifies us the registrar will be with us soon.

Hannah steps in front of a display case that's filled with trophies. She grins when she spies the track team trophy for winning state last year. Will she want to try any sports while she's here? Will she join a club as Cassie suggested?

A woman bustles toward us, greeting us warmly. "I'm Mrs. Carlisle, the school registrar." She extends her hand to shake mine, then Hannah's, before she motions for us to her office. She's short with gray hair that bounces above her ears, and she wears a pair of green horn-rimmed glasses that instantly make her look friendly. A stack of folders is piled high on her desk with each folder labeled with corresponding stickers.

She moves the stack to one side and clears a space for her arms. "Please sit," she says and gestures to the matching armchairs. "You must be Hannah." She smiles at my niece.

"Yes, ma'am," Hannah answers.

"Welcome to Austin High. Welcome to Decatur, Alabama." The registrar smiles at me next. "We already have Hannah's coursework faxed from the homeschool association and everything is in tip-top shape. Hannah's credits are right on track for her junior year, if not accelerated." She gazes at my niece.

"You're a bright girl, Hannah. Remarkable, in fact. You should be proud of all you've accomplished as your homeschool group did a wonderful job. There's no doubt you are going to pass through our curriculum with flying colors."

For the first time I see Hannah is beaming, the same way Cassie did after the game. They're rubbing off on one another.

Mrs. Carlisle thumbs through papers on her desk. "We're sorting out your classes and finalizing a few things," she continues. "We want to make sure you keep up with your level of education, Hannah, and that you stay in those advanced classes." She ticks something at the top of the form. "We'll be ready for her Thursday morning. Does that sound all right to both of you?"

That's two days from now, and I check with Hannah, who checks with me. She shrugs. "Okay," she says.

Mrs. Carlisle folds her hands together. "You'll be fine, sweetheart, I promise. You're going to love it here. You'll see."

She hands me a stack of documents to complete while she types at her keyboard. I fill out our home address, then list my number as the sole emergency contact. I want to be the only one authorized to check her out of school, that's important.

I ask Hannah for her social security number, and she relays the number to me. I fill out the rest of the documents and check several more boxes before I hand the papers back to Mrs. Carlisle.

Hannah is issued a school laptop, which she clutches to her chest. Mrs. Carlisle tells us she'll send Hannah's class schedule by tomorrow. "No later," she says with a smile. "Hannah, we're looking forward to having you join us."

"Yes, ma'am," she repeats.

We're at the door when Mrs. Carlisle places her hand on Hannah's arm. "Hannah, I am very sorry to hear about your mom. We all are. So, if there's anything you need, anything at all, you come and ask. We have a guidance counselor on site and she's wonderful. You can talk to us any time." She slides her eyes to me with a compassionate look, and I nod my appreciation.

But once we're in the lobby, and Hannah is a few steps ahead, Mrs. Carlisle places her hand on me next. She lowers her voice. "We'll take good care of her, Ms. Jenkins. Don't worry. We'll notify you if anything happens." She motions to the security cameras in each corner of the lobby, their red lights flashing. She acknowledges the locked glass doors that separate visitors from the students in the hall.

My heart thuds. What information did Child Services include when they sent over Hannah's transcripts? Has Detective Gillespie been in touch?

My eyes race back to hers. Why would the school registrar feel the need to assure me about their security?

# NINE

We should stop for lunch. Hannah hasn't eaten anything since breakfast, and neither have I, but she hasn't complained. She seems intent to go with the flow and cause as little disruption as possible. She wants so much for this to work.

We find a table at a local café where I ask for a coffee. "A latte, please. Skim milk, one sugar."

To my surprise, Hannah also orders a coffee. "Black," she tells him.

When the server leaves, I ask her, "Wow, black?"

She shrugs. "I like it that way. It's something Mom and I used to do together. It's called a *fika*. Swedish for coffee break, a way to take time out and enjoy the moment with no rush. Mom loved everything about it." Her eyes light up with the memory. "We would have a *fika* together every afternoon and it was so nice." She watches one of the baristas grind the coffee beans, the cappuccino machine frothing in the background. "I'm really going to miss that."

"You still can do that," I tell her. "We can have coffee together, me and you."

She drops her eyes, but I know what she's thinking. It won't be the same. "You'll be at work," she says.

"How about when I get home? Or on the weekends?"

"Maybe." She fiddles with the menu.

I drop my eyes to the menu too.

I told Cassie this morning that since I won't be at work and will be free this afternoon, she doesn't have to ride the bus. We can pick her up straight from school.

We finish our lunch, both of us ordering club sandwiches, and it's nice. Pleasant. We take our time and sip our coffee. Hannah asks about my job, and I explain how I'm taking a few days off to be with her. She asks what I do, and I describe several of the advertising campaigns we're running, including the one for a local fitness center that is already resulting in increased memberships. "That's great," she says, seeming genuinely interested.

I also tell her about my friend Cynthia. "I hope you can meet her soon. She has two boys, but they're much younger. Maybe this weekend? She can come over?" She doesn't respond. "Or whenever you're ready. No rush." I clear my throat. "So what about you? Your friends?" She doesn't mention any specific names but says that she'll miss them. They spent years in homeschool together and they can always stay in touch through email.

"I mostly hung out with Mom," she says. "We didn't go out much and Mom didn't like to. She was kind of a homebody." She shrugs again. "We had our *fika* breaks instead."

I'm still struggling that Beth was a homebody. That's not what I would have imagined my sister being. The attorney went so far as to use the word *recluse*, and I'm still grappling with that description.

Day by day, year after year, Hannah became her mom's only friend.

*What happened, Beth? What made you pull away from everyone?*

Cassie is practically skipping toward the car when she sees us. She's so used to taking the bus, this is an absolute treat, and she's grinning from ear to ear, her happiness skyrocketing when Hannah joins her in the backseat to show her the new clothes.

They talk non-stop, and I lift my eyes to the rearview mirror more than once as their heads move closer together. Hannah shows Cassie a sweater. My daughter nods her approval. She holds up a long-sleeved top and Cassie says she likes that one too.

"There's more." Hannah points to the back.

"So cool," Cassie says. "I want you to show me everything."

"I will," Hannah tells her. "When we get home."

*Home...* and the word flutters in my chest. We're doing this. We really are going to be okay. Hannah is settling in, little by little, and it's going to be all right. We have our new little family.

Pulling into the drive, I try not to look at the black smear left behind from the trash can fire. With the next bout of rain and a few more days in the elements, I'm hoping the mess will lighten over time. I don't need it upsetting me, or Hannah.

Cassie carries several of the shopping bags while Hannah grabs the rest. They're in Hannah's room as soon as we enter the house with Hannah's new clothes spilling across the bed and the girls popping the price tags off each one. I leave them, another smile warming my face at the bond they're creating.

I set my purse on the counter and plug in Hannah's school-issued laptop to charge it. She'll want to be ready when classes start Thursday morning.

Taking out my phone, I check my email in case anything has

come through from work. But almost everyone at the office knows I'm taking time off after my sister's death and they're limiting their contact with me. It's nice to have the space, and I release my breath. There are no issues or questions from my clients either, which is a relief. No demands that need to be taken care of.

But I do find one email from Mr. Fredericks and he asks about Hannah. He lets me know that someone from Child Services will be in touch soon.

I make a note to ask Child Services about counseling. They should have recommendations for appropriate therapists in the area, especially for children in situations similar to Hannah. Grief counseling.

The girls' laughter spills from the room, and another smile crosses my face. Perhaps being with Cassie is the therapy Hannah needs right now to get through these first few days.

Another burst of laughter, and I'm tempted to cross the living room and peek my head around the corner to watch, but just as I'm about to, one of them gets up to close the bedroom door. Like the night before, it's a soft click, their secret girls' club taking place. I remember how Beth and I used to do the same thing.

I consider calling Cynthia, but she might still be at work, and if she did leave early, she'll be rushing her twin boys to another lacrosse practice. I shouldn't bother her if she's in the middle of packing their gear either. I'll want her complete attention when I tell her about Hannah. I need her to figure out something with me too.

I step out the front door and collect my mail instead. Returning to the kitchen, I toss random shopping catalogs into the recycling bin, and set aside our latest mortgage statement, when my hands wrap around a square envelope. It looks like an invitation or maybe a wedding announcement. The envelope is beige in color and it has no return address. The postmark lists Louisville, Kentucky. The date is from two days ago.

Louisville, Kentucky...

Perhaps it's a condolence card from Mr. Fredericks. He's sending his sympathy regarding my sister's death, and this sounds like something he would do. But why not include a return address?

I tear open the envelope and admire the card with its beautiful watercolor scene featuring a single dove clutching a ribbon in its beak. The words *With Sympathy* are printed across the top.

I open the card.

> *Strike the match and the flames get closer.*
> *Watch your back.*

My hands shake, and the card flutters between my fingers, my eyes zooming in and out until I'm no longer able to focus on the words. The threat.

They found me. It was only a matter of time. I knew this would happen.

The card falls to the floor. We're not safe. We haven't been safe for days.

I should pack the girls' bags and tell them we should go. We'll leave Alabama and drive... where? And what? I'll call Cynthia—she has a condo in Gulf Shores, some sort of timeshare? Or we can go to a hotel. We'll check into a new one every few days as I try to figure out what to do next. Until Detective Gillespie calls and says they've arrested someone, and we're finally safe.

But the girls... how would I explain this to them without terrifying them? How can I risk them falling apart? They're too young. They won't understand. They shouldn't *have* to understand.

I need to call Detective Gillespie.

*Strike the match.*

Beth died in a house fire, the flames consuming her. Hannah barely escaped.

Years ago, my sister and I struck a match too. The flame, ever closer.

I call the detective and he's either screening my calls or he's busy in the interrogation room because he doesn't answer. Maybe he's meeting right now with Rick Joffrey. The man has confessed and they're pressing charges.

If Rick Joffrey sent my sister threatening messages, could he have sent this letter too?

The card was mailed on Sunday, the day before Hannah boarded her flight to Huntsville. Did he already know she was coming here?

I call Detective Gillespie again a half hour later and he answers.

"I know about Rick Joffrey," I tell him. "Hannah said he's your lead, the person she was worried about. Did he admit to killing my sister?"

"Rick Joffrey claims he was out of town on Friday. We're in the process of verifying his alibi."

"Out of town?" I purse my lips. "That sounds pretty convenient, don't you think?"

"A gas station receipt places him just outside the Louisville city limits, but he could have turned back. He could have easily made the drive to your sister's property. We're not ruling anything out yet."

"Where is he now?"

He pauses.

The realization hits me. "You released him, didn't you?"

"We had to. There's nothing tying him to your sister's death right now."

"Is Rick Joffrey even his real name?"

"What?"

"Is that his real name?"

"Yes. Why would it not be?"

"That message," I tell him. "Those messages that he sent to my sister. Hannah told me what he wrote. Could that be his motive?"

"It's definitely a concern. But without someone placing him near your sister's house, and without us finding something that directly links him to the blaze, we can't hold him."

"So, he admits what he wrote to Beth?"

"Yes. And he admits that he was wrong. He lost his cool. But he said he would never kill her."

"Do you think he would come to Alabama?"

"Why would you think that?"

I ask him instead, "Did you tell the school anything about Hannah?"

"The school? No. That's out of my jurisdiction."

I frown. So why did the school registrar act that way? Or was it Mr. Fredericks who called her? With everything that's happened, he took it upon himself to alert the school.

*I kept tabs on them over the years. I owed your parents that much.*

I repeat, "Do you know if Rick Joffrey is still in Louisville?"

"He's been instructed not to leave the city limits until he's no longer in our line of questioning."

"I think he may have sent me something—or at least, someone sent me something. They mailed it two days ago." The card remains face-down on the tile.

"What was mailed to you?"

"It's meant to look like a condolence card, but it's not. And what's written inside, it's a threat. It has to be."

A door closes and it's as if the detective has stepped into another room, the background noises hushing. My heart beats double-time that he is taking this seriously.

"What does it say?"

I pick up the card, but the words swim before my eyes. I steady myself to focus on the handwriting and read the sentences to him out loud. I breathe hard into the phone.

"You have this card in your possession?"

"I'm staring at it."

"Is there anything else they've written?"

"No. There's no signature, no return address. But it's from Louisville. The postmark is from two days ago," I repeat.

"Okay, I need you to take pictures of the front and back and send them to me. You need to priority mail the card to the Louisville Police Department and post it to my attention. It needs to be to *my* attention, you got it? We'll check for fingerprints."

I swallow—but my prints are all over the card and across the envelope also. I've already dropped it on the floor and now it's spackled with whatever lint and dust is on my tile. My stomach twists. Have I already ruined the evidence?

"But my fingerprints..." I begin.

"It's okay. We'll look for anything else this person could have left behind. Saliva from the envelope. Sweat." Repulsed with the idea, I fight not to drop the card. "Once you take the pictures," he says, "ship everything to me.."

We end the call and I set the card and envelope on the counter. Taking several shots with my phone, I include the front and back along with close-ups of the message.

*Strike the match...* the words swim before me, and I shut my eyes.

Down the hall, Cassie and Hannah are talking. They've turned on some music and Cassie is singing one of the songs.

I'm thankful at how oblivious they are to what is happening. They can't ever know. I can't frighten them.

I text the pictures to the detective and search for a ziplock bag. Sliding the card and envelope inside, I make sure to squeeze out the air so the bag lays flat.

The detective told me to overnight the card which means I need to find the closest FedEx office.

With a quick knock on Hannah's door, the girls quiet down long enough for me to tell them I'm running a quick errand. "I'll be back soon."

"Sure thing, Mom," Cassie says. Hannah doesn't even look up.

With the card inside my purse, I hurry to my car.

*They know where we live.* They have our address.

As soon I get home, I'm ordering a house alarm. We can't take any chances. The danger is here. It has reached our front doorstep.

# TEN

The FedEx clerk assures me the package will arrive by noon the following day, but that doesn't stop me from demanding to see a tracking number before I take several additional photos of the FedEx envelope. I need proof that I have mailed this to Detective Gillespie.

My eyes tear to the door every time the chime sounds and someone walks in. The salesclerk keeps one eye warily on me as I pace in front of the counter.

I take deep breaths, wanting this transaction to be over with. I need to get home to my girls.

After the salesclerk runs my credit card, he places the envelope in a shipping bin, and that's my green light to run for the door.

The girls are in the kitchen—they're safe. Something is warming in the oven and Cassie says it's chicken strips she found in the freezer. "They'll be ready in twenty minutes," she says. But I'm not hungry.

The girls offer me a plate, but I tell them I have work to

catch up on and go to my room. They don't say another word as I grab my laptop and disappear down the hall.

Sitting on my bed, I open a browser. I shouldn't type his name—I shouldn't even try.

I try talking myself out of it, but the pull is too real. It's too tempting because, after today, and especially after that card, I need to know what he looks like. I need to know if he is in any way connected to a certain family. A family we've tried years to forget.

Rick Joffrey. I type his name and click search. I hold my breath—I'm seconds away from seeing the face of the man who killed my sister. At any moment, I could be looking into his eyes.

The page loads with articles citing the character Joffrey from *Game of Thrones*, the murderous prince turned sadist, but nowhere can I specifically find a *Rick Joffrey*.

I search the more formal names of Richard and Frederick and numerous results pop up. I sink against my pillow. This is going to be more difficult than I thought.

What about Facebook? I don't find much for Richard or Rick Joffrey either, and no one has Louisville set as their hometown.

*Is Rick Joffrey even his real name?* That's what I asked the detective. Clearing the search, I try again. Do I dare type in *his* name? *The* name? Am I ready to see what he's been up to after all these years?

Has he moved on and has a family of his own? Maybe he has a wife and a couple of kids. Do they know what he's been up to, his sick, twisted methods for seeking revenge?

I freeze my hands over the keyboard—I can't bear to look— and I slam my laptop closed.

Wednesday

"You're so lucky," Cassie says the next morning. She and Hannah are sitting down for a quick breakfast of waffles, a glass of juice for Cassie. "You have one more day until you have to go to school."

"Hey," Hannah says, "I thought you said I would love it there."

Cassie grins. "I did, and you will. I'm just jealous you get to hang out with Mom again." She looks at me. "What are you guys going to do today? More shopping?"

I blow across my coffee, waiting for it to cool enough before I drain the whole thing. At this point, there's not enough caffeine in the world to make up for my lack of sleep. The bags beneath my eyes are a purple-gray smudge that no amount of concealer will be able to cover. And trust me, I tried.

Hannah and Cassie, on the other hand, are well rested, as they should be. They still have no clue what's happening.

"Since Hannah's class schedule came in," I say, "we're picking up school supplies. She needs a backpack, some notebooks, pens, that sort of thing."

"Fun." Cassie frowns. "I'm missing out on all the good stuff."

"No, you aren't," Hannah says. "You have soccer practice this afternoon, right? That's fun."

Cassie pushes aside her plate. "True. I just wish I could be with you guys instead."

"We'll catch up tonight," Hannah insists. "Don't worry. Playing soccer sounds a whole lot better than picking out notebooks anyway." She flashes me a smile. "No offense."

I don't respond because I'm too busy checking my phone and refreshing the FedEx tracking app. As of thirty minutes ago, the package arrived at a warehouse outside of Louisville, Kentucky, but has yet to be assigned to a delivery truck. I squeeze my phone, wishing I could beam the package directly to Detective Gillespie's desk instead.

"Are you okay?" Cassie asks.

I soften my expression. "I'm good, sweetie." I take a sip of my coffee, but it's still hot, and I wince.

But glancing at the time, we're going to be late. I pour the coffee into a thermos and motion to Cassie to take their plates to the sink. She gives them a quick rinse while Hannah loads them in the dishwasher. The two of them working like a team.

In the car, Cassie says, "So, after buying school supplies, what else are you going to do?"

I peer at Hannah, and she peers back at me. Honestly, I haven't thought that far. I just need it to be noon when the package arrives and the detective runs it for prints.

"I'm not sure, what do you want to do?"

Hannah stares out the window. "Actually, is it okay if I get a phone? I used to have one, but it burned in the fire."

My eyes widen. Of course she would want a phone. She's sixteen. She'll want a way to stay in touch with her friends or use Instagram or Snapchat.

Hannah having a phone is a good idea too. She needs a way to call me if there's an emergency. She should be able to contact 9-1-1.

"Yes," I tell her. "You should get a phone."

"So cool," Cassie says. "You can pick out a fun case too. Maybe something with sparkles or a pink case. You think there will be a two-for-one sale, Mom, and I can get one too?"

Cassie has been begging for a phone for years—*Everyone in my school has one* is something I've heard more times than I can count. But I've been holding off for as long as I can. I don't want her getting sucked into the world of social media just yet, the allure of accruing likes as a way to either boost her self-confidence or have it come crashing down. It's my job to protect her from the creepers too, the pervs who could reach out and send her inappropriate messages also. Trust me, I'm aware of these types of men.

But what if Cassie is in danger too? She'll need a way to call me. What if someone tries to grab her when she gets off the bus?

I don't answer Cassie, but I don't tell her no either, and a hopeful smile crosses her face. Hannah winks at her.

After we drop off my daughter, we head to a local office supply store where Hannah finds a backpack and a lunch tote. We gather several notebooks and binders, highlighters and graph paper too.

"So no more taking the ACT exam?" I ask as we place the items at checkout. "You have such a great score already, you probably don't have to take the test again unless..." I slide her a look, "unless you want to. I mean, you can take it as many times as you want."

She smiles. "A twenty-eight is pretty good."

"I thought you got a thirty?"

"A thirty," she says and reaches for the binders. "I don't know, Mom made me take it so many times it's hard to keep track. But maybe I could take the test again?" She bites her lip, and I spot her competitive drive. "Maybe get a higher score?"

"At this rate, you could get a scholarship," I tell her, and she grins.

The Verizon store is around the corner and Hannah picks out the latest iPhone model with a screen so large it dwarfs the one I currently have in my hands. She also selects a case in a pretty blue paisley pattern. "What do you think?"

"It looks great."

"And what about Cassie? She seemed pretty excited about the idea. It might be..." she tilts her head, "helpful?"

For pushing the emergency SOS button, yes. For sharing her last known location so we can track her down, absolutely.

Instead, I tell her, "I know. She's been wanting one for a while."

"Cassie seems pretty mature to me. She's a responsible kid. A great kid."

I smile, appreciatively. "She is... I just worry."

She shoots me an understanding look. "It's okay. I'll help her. I'll make sure she doesn't get sucked into TikTok."

I mumble, "Great. TikTok." And I suppress a laugh. But my fears are well beyond social media at this point.

Hannah runs her fingers along a display until one of the phone screens lights up.

"Hannah..." I say casually, "when you talk with your friends back home, can you be vague about where you're staying?" She turns to me curiously, and I pause, thinking how best to phrase this. "Can you not tell them where you live?"

She stands still for a moment. A few more seconds pass before it registers. "Is it because of...?"

"We don't know," I tell her. "The police aren't sure. But let's play it safe, okay? Don't tag our location. You can talk to your friends, and that's fine—I don't want to keep that from you—but don't them exactly where you are. Not until the police can catch whoever did this to your mom."

She bites her lip, then puts on a brave face. "I understand."

"Just for now," I repeat, keeping my voice low and hating every part of this conversation. I smile at her. "Hey, chin up. This is exciting. A big day. I'm getting Cassie a phone too."

Her face brightens. "Really? She's going to be so excited. I bet she wants a sparkly case. That's what she said in the car."

She moves to the shelf to find something for Cassie, and any worries about what I just warned her about disappear. She is simply a teenager who cannot wait to show her cousin what we bought for her at the store.

# ELEVEN

It takes nearly an hour to set up both phones with Hannah deciding her own password and me coming up with one for my daughter. I want to be able to access Cassie's device at any time and see what she's doing, who she's talking to. The sales rep shows me how to set restrictions too.

"You can block phone numbers," he says. "Set time limits. Restrict content they might search for online."

"That's great."

"Do you want my password too?" Hannah asks. "It's okay, I don't mind. Mom would check my phone sometimes."

I think it over. But it's a tough one because where do I draw the line? She's sixteen and will want her privacy. I should give her some accountability. "It's okay, Hannah. I trust you."

She turns to me with a slow smile.

As soon as we're home, Hannah says she wants to sort through her school supplies and pack her backpack, but I know what she really wants to do, and that's to play with her new phone. It's already in its blue paisley case, and on the drive, she was already downloading Instagram and adding a Gmail account. She enters a single phone number to her contact list but doesn't call anyone yet. She doesn't send any text messages either. Maybe she's waiting for when she's alone.

"What about your phone number?" Hannah asks. "And Cassie's too?"

I hand over my device so she can forward our contacts.

At the Verizon store, the sales rep asked if Hannah had an Apple ID that he could pair with her previous account, but she shook her head, no, and said, "I'm going to start off fresh." She passed me a knowing look. "A new place, new phone, and new contacts. Just in case, right?"

"All of your old pictures will be lost," he said.

And that made me stop for a second. What about photos of her mom? The last ones Hannah may have taken of Beth before she died, their memories together? I might want to see them too. But Hannah said, "I didn't take many. And what I do have is backed up to Amazon Photos. I can access them there."

She and the sales rep created Hannah's new account from scratch.

My niece heads for her room, her backpack in one hand and her brand-new phone in the other. She's about to shut the bedroom door when she says, "Thank you again, Aunt Tara. I can't wait until Cassie sees her surprise."

I know my daughter will be thrilled, but that doesn't stop me from downloading the Life360 tracking app and immediately connecting it to my daughter's phone. Next, I send a Life360 notification to Hannah, and she accepts the invitation immediately. Good, now I can see where both girls are with their devices at all times.

A text flashes across my screen, and I think it's coming from Hannah. She's sending me a text while she's in her room. I grin that she's already having fun.

But the message reads: *Package received.* It's Detective Gillespie.

*When will you know something?* I ask.

*We're checking for fingerprints.*

*Are you going to call Rick Joffrey back in?*

*Yes.*

*When? Today?*

But the detective must be already typing his response because his message comes in quickly.

*There's a chance Rick Joffrey lied about being out of town.*

And I squeeze my phone, waiting for what he will say next.

The detective says, *Someone may have seen him going to your sister's house.*


"How soon can I have an alarm set up?" I ask over the phone. "I need one for my house."

The salesperson hums while she types. She's searching for the next available technician and tells me they can have someone out tomorrow at 9 a.m.

With that settled, I reassure myself I'll pay for this hefty expense with the money Beth left us, the money that I will use for taking care of Hannah.

Inspecting every smoke alarm, I test to find out which ones need new batteries and which ones are duds when I hear Hannah talking on the phone.

I tread toward her door. This is her first phone call home

and I'm curious as to who it is. Is it a best friend? Someone from homeschool?

I stand to one side, not wanting Hannah to spot the shadow of my feet beneath the doorway.

"It's okay," Hannah says. "I mean, it's good. Yes... they're nice. They seem to care... I know, it's strange. She's not what I expected. She's not at all like I thought she would be. The stories I heard."

My pulse quickens.

"You think she's putting up a front?" Hannah asks. "No way." Another pause. "I mean, I hope not. She seems pretty genuine. I understand. But I have to live here now so I hope that it's not true. I mean, I guess I could find out. I already said something to her about it. Yeah... that didn't go over so well."

My eyes drop to the floor.

*What you did to Grandma and Grandpa.*

"Oh, Cassie?" she says. "She's great. A really cool kid. Her mom got her a phone today so she's going to flip out when she sees it." The squeak of the mattress, and it must be Hannah rising from the bed, a rattling sound as she pulls open the blinds to look out the window.

"It's okay. Don't be sad. I know... I miss you too. We'll figure everything out. The fire, it was horrible, and I was scared, but that's over now. I'm here and everything will be fine." After a moment, she lowers the blinds, and they drop to the windowsill with a thud. "Don't worry," she repeats. "We'll see each other again."

I step away, not wanting to eavesdrop any longer, and certainly not wanting to get caught. How would I explain to her that I trust her while I'm also standing outside her door? While I'm comforted she has someone she can talk to, I'm also saddened by the fact they've been taken away from each other. Separated. Maybe I should plan a trip? Not now, of course, but maybe in a few months' time? Hannah will want to see her friends, and there will be a gravesite for Beth where we can pay our respects.

I'm in the living room when I notice that Hannah is no longer talking. I assume she's ended the call, but she's crying. It's a long, mournful cry that stretches from her room.

"Mo-o-o-m..."

I return to her door and hover outside. The girl is hiccupping she's crying so hard. Her voice is muffled like she's pressing her face against a pillow.

I tap on the door. "Hannah?" Another tap when there's no response. "Hannah, I'm coming in." I open the door and she's returned to the bed, curled on one side with tears running down her face. The front of her new sweatshirt is soaked.

"Oh, Hannah," I say, and sit beside her.

She releases more cries and I lean over to hug her shoulders. I rub her back. She sits up, and with the most anguished expression, she folds herself into my arms. With her head pressed against my chest, she heaves, every cry causing her delicate shoulders to rise and shake.

I hush her and rock her. I do my best to console her, the way I would if this was Cassie.

"I miss her," Hannah wails, and she grips me tight. "I want her back. I want my mom back now."

"I know, sweet girl." I'm crying also, the ache in my throat forming a knot.

I should have expected this, how the grief will hit Hannah in waves. It hasn't yet been a week and she is only just beginning to mourn. That phone call and whoever she spoke to from home must have caused her emotions to come flooding back.

"It was so scary," she says. "That fire..."

And I embrace her. "It's over now. Don't worry," I say, and stroke her hair.

Her ears are pierced, and I hadn't noticed that before. But she's not wearing any earrings. She brought nothing with her.

She ran screaming from her house with nothing but the clothes on her back.

"Mom..." she whimpers, "oh my God, she must have been so scared." A shudder runs through her body. "Did she know what was happening? Did she know she was about to die?" Her agony cuts deep, and I can do nothing but rock her. I don't know what else to do to take away her pain.

"Everything is going to be all right," I whisper. Eventually, Hannah's cries slow, and her breaths quiet. Her body relaxes. She's no longer as tense as she was in my arms.

She rubs at her eyes and catches her breath. Her nose is running, and I'm sniffling too.

She releases another sigh and pulls away. We sit quietly, the two of us, until I say, "I'm so sorry this happened, Hannah. I really am."

She stares at her bare feet. Her ballet flats have been kicked to one side. Her legs hang off the side of the bed.

"I just don't get it. What happened."

"The police will figure it out," I insist. *They'll find fingerprints. You don't know about the card yet, Hannah, and I don't want to scare you about that, but they're going to track down whoever did this. We'll find out who this is.* "Detective Gillespie is working the case non-stop. They'll make an arrest soon."

Hannah rubs at her nose. She looks at me warily. "No, I mean what happened between you and my mom. What you did." She hauls another breath. "What you did to my family."

I pull back, my breath caught in my throat.

*What you did to my family.*

*Her* family, not ours. I'm still the outsider. She may never forgive me.

"Hannah, it wasn't like that. It's not what you think."

"I just don't get it," she repeats. "After all this time, I finally see you again and you seem great. It's not at all like what my mom said, how I thought you were going to be. But then... I don't know what to believe. I'm so confused. You don't seem like you would..."

"Hannah, please—"

"I want to love you, Aunt Tara, I really do. I want to be happy here and feel safe. But I'm scared." Her chin wobbles. "And it's not just about what happened to Grandma and Grandpa, either."

"I didn't—"

She blows out her breath. "Mom told me that you killed someone else. That you lied to everyone about it. That's why you left Louisville. That's the real reason you left home."

My heart beats like a sledgehammer. *She knows.*

I try not to clench my fists in front of my niece. I try my best not to show my anger.

It's pretty clear: my sister lied to her.

# TWELVE

My phone rings. I expect to see a Louisville area code, and I'm hoping it's the detective or Mr. Fredericks with an update, but the Caller ID says *Unknown*. I answer despite the pounding ache in my temples. The pain from my conversation with Hannah storms through my chest.

When I answer, there's only silence.

I stare at the phone. The timer is ticking so it's not a dropped call. Someone is waiting on the end of the line and choosing not to say a word.

"Who is this?"

No response.

"What do you want?"

Still no answer.

"You have the wrong number." And I end the call.

A telemarketer? A robocall that needed a few extra seconds to reboot and play?

But my phone rings again, and *Unknown* reappears on my screen.

"Hello?" I say. But again, there's nothing. I hang up.

After leaving Hannah's room, I'm sitting at the kitchen

table. She asked me to go, saying she wanted some time alone, when my phone rings again.

Damn this person, and I don't bother answering. I press *end* as quickly as I can with my finger.

And now another phone rings, but this time it's coming from Hannah's room. She hasn't selected her ring tone and it defaults to the standard factory setting. She sniffles before she answers with a tentative, "Hello?"

My ears perk.

Is that her friend calling her back? Or is it someone else?

But she doesn't speak. The moment drags on until I'm almost certain she's hung up.

Her phone rings again. "Hello? Who's calling?"

I practically run to her room.

"Who is this?" she repeats. "*Hel-lo?*" she adds with the heightened aggravation of a teenager.

I push open the door, and she swings her head, looking surprised to see me again so quickly.

"Is everything okay?" she asks. I was about to ask her the same thing.

"That phone call. Who was that?"

"I have no idea. There was no one talking." She frowns when she checks her screen. "You think it's because I have a new number or something?"

"What did the Caller ID say?"

"*Unknown.*" I wince, but she doesn't see my face. She looks down. She shrugs as if annoyed. "This is going to be a real pain if I have someone's old number and they keep calling thinking I'm someone else."

But her phone stays silent. Her screen remains dark, and so does mine.

I bite my lip. Did we get put on some list when I added Hannah to my phone plan? But that's something the major phone companies would never allow. Also, Hannah's line was only activated a few hours ago.

I hesitate a moment longer before I say, "Okay," and I slowly back out of her room.

She cocks her head. Her face is puffy from tears, her eyes swollen, but she says, "Did you need something, Aunt Tara?"

"What? No, I was just... I was just checking on you."

"Okay." She peers at me curiously.

I return to the kitchen and immediately retrieve Cassie's phone—has someone been calling her also? I expect to find multiple missed calls, but there's nothing. It's only Hannah and me that someone wants to bother.


About an hour later, my niece emerges from her room. Her eyes are no longer red, but she keeps her gaze lowered to the floor. She's sheepish, as if embarrassed by what she said to me earlier. Her trepidation hangs in the air.

I'm finding it hard to look at her too. I'm ashamed by what she thinks I've done, what Beth has told her. Is she frightened of me? I try my best to appear normal, but my chest weighs as if someone has placed a five-ton brick on it. She carefully skirts around me.

Hannah asks when Cassie will be home. "About a half hour," I answer since Cassie is getting a ride home from another parent. We usually take turns.

She asks if she can help surprise Cassie with her new phone and suggests we wrap it with a bow. It's a great way to pass the time, a strange moment where we pretend that my niece basically didn't just accuse me of murder.


As soon as Cassie enters the house, she spots the gift box on the kitchen table and squeals. And it's such an ear-piercing scream that I have to laugh out loud. She tears open the wrapping paper to find what's inside.

She holds the phone to her chin and says, "*Oh my gosh.* My own phone! Really?" She wraps her arms around my neck. "Thank you so much."

"Well, with your cousin living here, we need to do a lot more coordinating. We should keep in touch."

What I want to say is, *This phone will be your life beacon if you need it.*

"Yes, absolutely." She runs to Hannah next. "I love the case. I love everything about it."

"Hannah picked it out for you," I tell her.

Cassie throws her arms around her next. "I love it."

"We set up most of it for you." I show her the passcode and email app. "It's all right there."

"Thanks, Mom," she says and flips through the apps. "Does this mean I can have Instagram now?"

"Yes," I answer cautiously.

Hannah tosses me a look. "I'll show her how to set up her privacy settings, Aunt Tara. Don't worry. It's what my mom showed me too. I have my own phone set up that way." She crooks a finger at Cassie. "Come on. I'll show you everything."

I watch them go, the bedroom door closing behind them, but this time it's with a louder click. Cassie is squealing again.

I'm too exhausted to make dinner. I'm running on fumes. My body aches, the knots pinching tight around my shoulders.

I order delivery on my phone. It's a splurge and something we don't indulge in often as the delivery fees are enough to make me balk and pick up the food myself. But I am physically, mentally, and emotionally wiped out, and it's too easy to click a few buttons and press *order*. In thirty minutes or less, dinner will be served.

I order from the Greek place Cassie loves so much: chicken skewers as well as hummus, fresh veggies, and pita chips.

Tonight, I'll make myself eat something. It's important to keep my strength up. With what Hannah told me, we're in new territory now.

With the food order placed, I root around the fridge and find a beer, something to temper my nerves. I take a sip, and then another before I realize how quiet the house has become. The girls are no longer talking. They're not laughing about funny videos I assume they would be watching on YouTube or commenting about what is on Instagram.

The door to Hannah's room isn't shut all the way—it's cracked a few inches—and I stand still in the hall. The lights are turned off, but a light glows from inside and flickers against the walls.

I find the girls sitting on the edge of Hannah's bed. Their faces are lowered, their eyes wide open, as if they're mesmerized —transfixed, really—by the candlelight. But the girls aren't just staring at one candle; it's a whole stack of candles they've lined up on the bedside table. Every jar and metal tin Hannah picked out at the mall is burning at once.

The hairs on my arms rise, and I tell myself this is nothing more than Hannah showing Cassie what she bought. Several of the candlesticks I recognize from my kitchen cabinet—long, tapered white candlesticks, as well as glass jars they pulled from the pantry. The candles are stuck inside a jar, their wicks alight. When did Hannah grab those and how did I not see them before? Cassie must have shown her where they're kept.

The scent of lemongrass, sage, and something acidic, possibly grapefruit, fills the air. But the most overwhelming scent is vanilla bean, Beth's favorite, and it's the largest candle that's set out front. It's the flame that Hannah is the most fixated with.

The sight of the girls and the glow of the candles is at once beautiful and strange, and also deeply alarming. Goosebumps cover my skin, my mouth dropping open as I watch Hannah lean toward the flame. She peers close, like she's waiting for a secret to be revealed, something within the flame that only she will be able to see.

The flame—it's too close to her hair, and I need her to back up. I don't want her to get burned.

And then there's my daughter. Cassie leans forward too, her eyes in a semi-hypnotic state. Just like her cousin, she leans as close as possible without singeing her eyelashes. She doesn't blink, just like Hannah.

I step forward. "Cassie?"

But my daughter doesn't look at me, only leans closer, the light from the candles warming her cheeks in an amber glow. The flames bob and weave on the wick. A pop and hiss releases from each one.

"Cassie," I say again, and this time, louder. I flip on the overhead lights, and Hannah finally raises her head.

"Oh, hi, Aunt Tara."

But Cassie doesn't look at me.

"*Cassie,*" I repeat. It takes her another second before she pulls away her gaze to stare at me.

"What?" she asks.

My face blanches. *What do you mean what?*

"Are you okay, sweetheart? You were just sitting there, zoned out."

"I wasn't zoned out. I was studying it."

"Studying what?"

"It's pretty cool, huh?" Hannah says with a grin.

I bounce a look between them. "What's cool?"

"The flame," Cassie says. "It's something Hannah told me about, but I've never noticed it before. If you look real close, it's like the flames are dancing. They're *dancing*, Mom, and it's so pretty. Have you noticed that before? Do you want to see?"

I don't move.

It's just candles. But all those flames... the fire that burned down my sister's house and killed Beth. It seems odd that Hannah would do such a thing, that she would want to light up her room after what happened to her less than a week ago.

The girls gaze at me with impish grins, and I shiver. Moments ago, this place resembled a teenagers' séance.

"It's too many candles," I tell them, and blow out the first one, the largest candle out front. The vanilla bean, Beth's favorite scent. "It's a fire hazard. We need to be careful."

Cassie frowns, and she gives Hannah a look.

My daughter blows out the rest of the candles while Hannah watches us. The room reeks of smoke, and I wave my hands in front of my face before I gather the glass jars in my arms. "These are going back in the kitchen."

Hannah says, "Have you ever tried?" And her words stop me in my tracks. "Aunt Tara, have you ever looked into the flame?"

I shake my head. I've heard that before. The echo of a memory rings in my ear.

I shake my head. "No, that's something I've never done before."

# THIRTEEN

Thursday

The morning is a rush of excitement and nerves because today is the first day that Hannah will attend her new school.

My daughter wakes early and hits the shower first. And then there is movement from Hannah's room. She's slow, almost dragging her feet.

I'm mindful of the time, knowing we need to leave earlier than usual if I'm to drop off Cassie before I bring Hannah.

My niece is on edge—it's obvious, and she's trying not to show it. But it's there, her apprehension. She walks slowly to the kitchen table and manages a few bites of toast, half a cup of coffee, before I tell them it's time to go. With their lunches packed, I usher them out the door.

"This is going to be great," Cassie says. "Don't worry, Hannah. You're going to be fine. You'll meet new friends." I catch my daughter slipping her phone into her pocket.

"Don't take that out in the middle of class," I warn her. "Your teachers will confiscate it, and I do not want a phone call to come and pick it up."

"I won't," she says, but I don't believe her, especially when I catch her grinning at Hannah. The temptation will be too strong, the phones too new, and they'll want to send messages to each other throughout the day. Cassie will want to check on her cousin.

My daughter jumped from the car when we pulled up to the junior high, and now it's Hannah's turn. Her chin drops and she stares at the backpack shoved at her feet.

"I put money in your lunch account in case you need to buy anything extra," I say. "If there are other forms I need to sign, let me know. If you have any problems, call me or go see Mrs. Carlisle."

"I'll be fine." But she does a poor job of hiding the shake in her voice.

"Someone should show you to your locker, and your homeroom too. Just ask the front desk."

She doesn't say anything.

"Do you have your class schedule?"

"I printed an extra copy."

"Good girl." This earns me a weak smile.

We pull into the parking lot, but today, and at this hour, we're stuck at the end of the car line. A stream of students spill from their own cars and move toward the building, some in tight groups of threes or fours, others walking by themselves and yawning. I check the rearview mirror as a bus pulls up behind us.

"That reminds me. Since I'm home the rest of the week, I'll pick you up from school today, Cassie too. You can wait for me in the pickup line."

We pull up to the front entrance and Hannah steadies herself before she lifts her backpack. "Well, here goes nothing," she says, and the corners of her eyes pinch. I'm not sure if she slept much last night either.

I place my hand on her arm. "You're going to do great, Hannah. Remember what Mrs. Carlisle said. You're a bright girl and you're going to pass your classes with flying colors. You'll meet new friends. It's exciting."

She nods, and then she's out of the car, her glossy black hair and backpack disappearing into the crowd along with the rest of the students. I crane my neck for another glimpse of her. She's somewhere in the crowd filing through the double doors.

I pull away but butterflies knock around in my stomach. It's like I'm dropping off Cassie for her first day of kindergarten, the heightened nerves of a parent. *Please let her have a good day.*

I remember high school and how rough it can be, the students, the bullying. But I had a big sister who looked out for me. She kept an eye on me. Hannah doesn't have the same.

The alarm technician parks the van in front of my house right on time, which is great that I don't have to wait around all morning. "We guarantee our arrivals," he says when I thank him. "We know how important home security is for our customers."

*If you only knew.*

About an hour later, and with several holes drilled and multiple devices beeping as he tests the system, I now have two control panels attached to my wall: one at the front door and one at the back. I also have sensors installed on each of my windows. When the technician places a call to ensure the system is connected, he gives me a thumbs-up before he walks me through the instructions.

It's simple, really. There's the go-to button: the panic button —the biggest button that I can reach for in case of an emergency. Plus, a quick two-step process for setting up the passcode. I know exactly the four numbers I will choose.

I thank him when he's done and rub my arms to ease my worry. On the panel, the green light flashes, which is reassuring. With a touch of a button, we can call for help. The police will arrive in minutes. I can sleep at night without the fear of someone breaking in without us knowing it. The girls, if needed, can push the panic button too.

My fingers hover over the control panel. Do I set the alarm system now? Do I lock myself in even though it's the middle of the day?

I'm about to press *set* when a car pulls to a stop in front of my house. The door slams loudly.

Cynthia? But she would have let me know if she was coming over.

I peek through the blinds and spot a gray four-door sedan parked behind my car. For now, the person's face is obscured. Seconds later a woman steps around the front of the vehicle and stops to peer at my house. She pulls at her suit jacket; it's tight at the hips, but the suit is attractive, modest, and burgundy in color with the skirt hitting just above her knees. She looks down at her phone, possibly to verify the address. She carries her purse and a red folder.

I open the door before she has a chance to knock. She smiles at me in greeting, but I tense immediately. Everything about her seems formal, official.

A weight drops in my stomach. Did Detective Gillespie contact the local police? Has something else happened?

She extends her hand and I shake it tentatively. "I'm Morgan Elstein," she says. "I'm with Child Services regarding your niece, Hannah Higgins."

My heart lifts. Yes, of course. Child Services.

"May I come in?"

I flush, realizing that I've momentarily lost my manners. I back away from the door and gather my thoughts. "Yes. The attorney told me to expect you."

She enters my house and makes a wide, and not so subtle, sweep of the living room. She takes in the beige couch and the accompanying loveseat, the sofa that sags a bit in the middle, and the open-floor layout that includes the kitchen with its Formica counter tops that I will never upgrade to granite. She peeks down the hall at the bedrooms before her eyes circle back around. Through the window it's easy to see our simple patio furniture and the slab of concrete that isn't spruced up with planters. I've had other things on my mind.

I suddenly feel self-conscious about what she thinks. Is my home suitable? Clean enough? What does she think of the sparse amount of furniture?

She presses her lips together into a half-smile and tilts her head as if she might be listening for something, a cry from someone—but what she's listening for, I have no idea. She glances in the direction of the bedrooms.

The woman's gaze returns to me, and she nods. I seem to have passed a test, which is good, and I release my shoulders. Our home is modest, and you can pretty much take in everything from where we're standing, but it's tidy enough. I haven't vacuumed in God knows how long, but our garbage isn't piled up in the corner. The floors aren't covered in filth. I'm sober and sane—well, as sane as I can be with everything that's going on. I keep a steady job.

"I took time off from work," I explain, feeling the need to explain my presence at home in the middle of the day. But she did make a house call, didn't she? She showed up as if she already knew I would be here. I add, "I took off all week to be with Hannah, to make sure she was settling in."

She studies me with her large, brown eyes. They're pretty, even beneath eyelashes that are globbed thick with coats of mascara. "That's great," she says. "I'm so glad you were able to do that."

"But Hannah isn't here. She started school today so if you want to talk to her, it will have to be later this afternoon."

She smiles. "That's okay. This is an initial visit, a way to establish myself with you first. An introduction, so to speak." Her smile grows broader; she shows a little more teeth. "And, my goodness, back to school already? I'm impressed." She gazes at the coffee table where Cassie has left out her drink bottle along with a hair tie and a dirty plate. But there's nothing else. As Ms. Elstein can clearly see, this is a safe and stable home for any child.

"That's good she went back to school, Ms. Jenkins," she reiterates. "This will help her get acclimated so quickly."

My shoulders relax another notch.

"Well, it's Hannah who is really leading the way," I tell her. "She's very brave." I motion to the couch and ask her to sit. "Would you like something to drink? Coffee, tea?"

"No, I'm good. I won't take too much of your time, Ms. Jenkins. Like I said, this is only an initial visit." We sit on the sofa, but she's careful to maintain a wide berth between us. The red folder and handbag are placed between us too.

"So..." I clasp my hands together, waiting for the next part, ready to get this over with.

But Ms. Elstein doesn't launch into a series of questions, and she doesn't pull out a check list from that red folder of hers either. Instead, she sits quietly and appraises me. She's in no rush, even though she said this wouldn't take long. It's like we're two friends chatting over coffee, except that neither of us are speaking, and I have no idea what this woman wants.

She smiles, and I smile back, but my smile is waning, the silence becoming awkward with each passing second. Is this another test to see if I'll grow antsy? To see if I'll crack in front of her?

I run my hands through my hair.

"So, do you want to take a look around?" I ask. "I could show you Hannah's room?"

"You do have a lovely home," she says. "Have you lived here long?"

"About ten years."

She gazes out the window. "It seems like a really nice neighborhood. Safe and calm. A good place to raise kids, right?"

"Oh, yes." I nod. "There are lots of kids. It's a great neighborhood. My daughter loves it here."

She studies me again—I'm talking too fast—and my hand reaches for the collar of my blouse. I straighten it even though it doesn't need straightening. I cross my feet, cringing that I'm not wearing any shoes and my toenail polish has seen better days.

She peers at the picture frame on the mantel. "Is that your daughter?"

"Yes. Cassie. She's twelve."

"She's beautiful."

"Thank you."

"Black hair like her mom." She nods. "So similar to Hannah too. And now your daughter has an older cousin living with her. How is she handling having someone in the house?"

"Really well," I tell her. "She's excited, actually. They've gotten pretty close in just a short amount of time. I think it's been helpful for Hannah to have someone near her age."

"Yes, that must be very helpful. And what about you?" she asks. "How are you handling things?"

"Me?" I laugh nervously. "I'm taking it day by day. As you can imagine, it's been devastating to find out what happened to my sister."

Her voice softens. "I am truly sorry."

"Thank you."

"I understand that you and your sister were estranged?"

I nod slowly. "It was a sad situation, and I regret it deeply. I'm sure Beth did too. But in the end, she must have known that if anything were to happen to her, I should take care of Hannah. After what Hannah has been through, escaping and surviving the fire herself, I'm so glad my niece can be here with us. We can take care of her."

"That is very good to hear," Ms. Elstein says. "Truly. Not everyone is able to do that. It's a lot to take on, bringing in another child."

"Well, lucky for us, we're doing great. Cassie and I want very much to make this work. We want Hannah to be happy, and Hannah is adjusting." I fold my hands in my lap.

"Your sister would be so happy knowing that Hannah is cared for. Is she in need of any counselling, do you think? Anything that you've observed in the last few days where you think Hannah should talk to someone?"

I think of the sobs in Hannah's bedroom, her distrust in not knowing whether to feel safe in this house, and especially with me. The ongoing police investigation into her mother's death. Last night with the candles.

"Yes, I think therapy would be a good idea," I tell her.

"There are at least two therapists in the area who are qualified with Hannah's situation. I'll send you their contact info, if you'd like."

"That would be great."

"Understandably, Hannah is going through a traumatic experience. There's no telling the emotional rollercoaster she's grappling with and how she'll respond as each day goes by. Has there been any anger? Any outbursts?"

"She's cried several times."

"What about any unusual behavior?"

"I think she's taking it day by day."

She looks to the side, her eyes landing on the alarm panel beside the front door. "Is that new?"

"Yes. We just had it installed." I look at her curiously. "How did you know?"

"I saw a van for an alarm company passing me on the street. A lucky guess." She tilts her head. "Is there something you need to tell me? Anything that worried you to install an alarm?"

"My sister dying in a house fire was frightening enough." She gives me an apologizing look.

"Yes," she says. "I can understand that. Ms. Jenkins, like I said, I am so sorry about the circumstances surrounding your sister's death, the tragedy that has caused her daughter to live with you. For what you and your family are going through, you have my condolences. I do hope they catch whoever did this. I hope that brings you peace."

I blink back the tears.

"Hannah's safety is of our utmost concern," she continues, "as well as her ability to live in a home with a family where she feels safe and cared for. And I'll be honest, it appears that you're doing just that. You're doing a tremendous job, Ms. Jenkins. Hannah is very lucky."

I let out my breath. "Thank you. I hope so. I worry sometimes, you know?"

She looks again at the alarm panel. "You would tell me if something happened, right?"

My back stiffens. I don't want to tell her about the threat that came in the mail. I don't want her to flag our home and deem it unsafe. They'll take Hannah away from here, and we just got her. We haven't had enough time together.

"The detective in charge of my sister's case is keeping me informed," I answer. "But it still makes me nervous. Until they find who did this to Beth, it's hard to feel safe."

"Ms. Jenkins, from what I've been told, the fire and what happened to your sister was an isolated incident. Tragic and horrendous, but isolated. Whoever did this was targeting your sister, and your sister only. So, Hannah is safe. And you and your daughter are safe too." She clocks another look at the alarm. "But it's good to have extra security in place. When do you plan on setting the alarm? At night? Or during the day when you're at work?"

"I'm not sure yet." And I hesitate. "At night mostly. I need the sleep."

"If anything happens, you'll tell the police, right? We have to be mindful of Hannah."

"Of course." But my pulse quickens.

"Have you had any strange people come by?" she asks. "Has anyone made Hannah feel uncomfortable? Or any strange phone calls?"

My breath catches in my throat. "What's going on, Ms. Elstein? Do you know something I don't?"

She lifts her hands to calm me. "No, it's nothing like that. But when we are made aware of the tragic circumstances surrounding the death of a child's mother, and then that child is placed in a home where the family members are shaken up and taking precautions—they install a new alarm system, for example—I need to ask certain questions."

I fall silent.

"Okay," she says and pats her hands on her knees. She lifts her belongings. "Thank you for your time. I told you this wouldn't last long." She extends her hand for another hand-shake. "I appreciate you seeing me when we didn't have a scheduled appointment. Drop-by visits are important too, I hope you understand."

"Yes," I answer. "And what about Hannah? Should we schedule a time for her after school?"

She checks her watch. "I'll get in touch and set something up. Is that all right?"

I hold the door open for her.

"You're a good one, Ms. Jenkins. Thank you for taking care of this child."

"I can't imagine not," I tell her, meaning it.

"Okay. I'll be in touch. If you need me, you can contact me any time."

She's halfway down the sidewalk when I call out, "And you'll send the names of those therapists, right? The ones for Hannah?"

She waves her phone. "Yes, I'll be in touch."

I watch Ms. Elstein settle inside her car and start the engine. She reverses out of the drive and waves once again before she takes off down the street.

It's only when she turns the corner that I realize she never opened that red folder. She never showed me what was inside even though I have to imagine it's Hannah's case file.

But why did she seem so interested in the alarm? And how did she know to ask about strange phone calls?

She said I could contact her any time. But she hasn't left a business card. She didn't leave me with any of her information. I never asked her to show me an I.D. badge.

# FOURTEEN

My phone rings and I'm anxious to see that it's Detective Gillespie.

"Are you talking to Child Services?" I ask.

"What's that?"

"Is there something you told Child Services, but haven't shared with me?"

"That's a whole other department."

"She knows about my sister's case."

"Why? Did someone come by today?"

"Yes."

"Well, that's something to expect. Hannah's situation is much more sensitive than others. Child Services would have been given preliminary information about her mother's murder investigation."

"She said she was checking on Hannah, but..." I struggle with the words, "but the more I think about it, the whole visit... it seemed odd. She was interested in my house alarm."

"You got an alarm? That's good."

"She seemed way too interested in when I would be setting it. I thought that was strange."

"It's a good idea to have an alarm no matter what."

"Does she know about the threat I received? Is there a chance she'll think Hannah is unsafe and will take her away?"

"No, she wouldn't know anything about that. Why? Did you tell her?"

"No, but she asked me about strange phone calls."

He pauses. "What strange phone calls?"

"Someone called us a couple of times. Yesterday. They were marked *Unknown*. Not hang-ups, just silent, empty air like someone was waiting for us to talk first. Hannah received a couple of calls too."

"Who has Hannah's number?"

"Hardly anyone. That's the thing. She just got a new phone and number yesterday."

"And no one spoke?"

"Not a word."

"Has it happened today too?"

"No. Not yet to me, at least. But I can check with Hannah when she gets home."

"Okay, so strange phone calls yesterday, and the note card in the mail the day before."

My voice tremors. "Yes."

"And Child Services this morning."

"Except..."

"You don't think it was Child Services."

I stop in my tracks. That wasn't what I was going to say out loud, or was it? It seems preposterous now that he's voiced the concern. I'm already afraid I'm losing it, and I don't need him to think that way about me too. But can he blame me? Someone mailed me a threat. They threatened us with fire.

My heart races. *I let this person who claimed to be Child Services into my house.*

"I'll check and see who in your county is making home visits," Detective Gillespie says. "What's her name?"

"Morgan Elstein."

"I'm sure it's legit. It's illegal to impersonate someone from Child Services, and what would be the point anyway? But I'll look into it and let you know."

I'm hardly listening to him. "Do you think she was trying to case my house? She was getting a good look around. She kept checking the hallway." My voice hitches. I think about how she could have been counting the number of doors and remembering every window. Hannah escaped from a window herself.

"Someone casing your house?" the detective asks. "I don't think so." But my hands white-knuckle around my phone. "Ms. Jenkins," he says, "you still think that someone is coming after you, don't you?"

I stare at my kitchen floor.

"The first time we spoke, you said, *They're coming after me next. First Beth, then me.* I didn't know what to think about it at the time, and I didn't push it. But with everything that's been happening, the note, and now these phone calls, your concerns about this woman showing up at your house... you think someone is out to get you, am I right?" Another pause. "Why do you think that's happening?"

"I... I don't know..."

"What aren't you telling me?"

I sit down. My knees are wobbly and the blood rushes to my head. Shame fills my chest too, and fear encroaches my lungs, the emotions easily interchangeable with each passing day.

*Tick tock, Tara.* You knew this was coming.

I don't say anything.

"Ms. Jenkins, we've been focusing on Rick Joffrey because of the messages he sent to your sister. We've been considering this an isolated incident where only your sister was targeted. Some sort of vicious rage from this man." *Isolated incident.* That's what Ms. Elstein said too. "But as you can see, things are getting more complicated. And if it's *not* Rick Joffrey, he's not who we should be looking at, and this is connected to someone else, then you need to tell me. You need to tell me now."

I focus on my breaths. Nice and easy... in and out... like all the other times I've had to calm myself. I can do this.

"The note card talks about flames. A match. A fire. The same way your sister died. And you knew it was coming to you, didn't you? You knew a threat was coming before you even saw what was in your mailbox. So, let me ask you this: is someone targeting your family?"

My body shakes, my knees quaking.

*We never wanted to get caught, Beth. We promised each other.*

We stood on the side of the road and she told me this was the only way to make things stop. It was the only way to punish him, that I would be protected now. But it was only the beginning.

"Ms. Jenkins," he says. "I know I haven't been forthcoming with you about everything, and that's been frustrating, and I apologize. But it's never been my intention to harm you and keep you in the dark. We have to be sensitive about these cases because there's only so much information I can share, and that includes sharing it with family members—especially family members. They want to help us catch the killer, but there's a chance they will tell someone and that person can leak it to the press. Critical details that only the police should know are now out for public knowledge. Just like that." And he snaps his fingers so loudly that I jolt in place.

"So, no holding back, Ms. Jenkins. You know that hiding details won't solve who did this to your sister. If anything, it could make things worse. It could lead to obstruction—to a crime—if that's what this is." The heat rises at my neck. "We don't want that, now do we?"

I steady my voice. "I didn't realize I was under investigation."

"You're not. But we're investigating your sister's case here. In Louisville, in Kentucky. And until now, I've had no reason to drag you across state lines and question you. I haven't involved Alabama police. But should I? Is that what I need to do?"

My eyes focus on an ant crawling along the floor. I could stretch out my foot and squash it. It would be so easy.

I say, "I can tell you right now you'd be wasting your time looking at me."

"I've been looking into your family, Ms. Jenkins. Your past. Your sister's background. Yours especially. I must say, a few things piqued my interest." The heat in my neck spreads between my shoulder blades. "I've been making calls and talking to people. People who knew you and your family. There are several things that are causing me to rethink what happened."

My chest contracts. My thoughts race. I need more time— I'm not ready to launch into these details yet. My past, or my sister's.

"So, what did you find with the fingerprints?" I ask. "What's on the note card?"

It's a curveball question, and he knows it. But the detective plays along.

"Your prints turned up as well as another set which we traced to a postal worker. Additional prints matched who delivered your mail. But nothing else. They must have used a sponge to seal the envelope and the stamp is a sticker. The type of card is sold in packs of twenty in stores around the country so it would be difficult to track. And the ink? Nothing specific. It could be anyone's ballpoint pen for all we know. The card was stamped and dropped in a mailbox without anyone going inside a post office. There is no camera footage. We have no way of knowing who this person is right now."

I was expecting this, wasn't I? People are smart these days. They can watch enough episodes of *Law & Order* to figure out how to disguise a mailing. There are plenty of thriller books to show them the ropes too.

"So, your fingerprints," the detective asks. "Aren't you curious as to how I was able to find them in the system?"

This makes me stop. "I'm pretty sure you already know the answer."

"Confirm a few facts with me, please."

I rub my forehead. A dull ache throbs pain against my temples. "My parents had the police arrest me for breaking into the house."

"And?"

"But it was *our* house."

"But you didn't live there anymore. They asked you to leave. Why is that, Ms. Jenkins? Why did they do that?"

My face flares hot. It's not just with the detective's line of questioning, but also the memories he's bringing up, the sting of humiliation that riddles its way into my stomach, my mother's voice once again echoing in my head: *You shamed us, Tara.*

"There was an accident," I tell him. "Months earlier. It wasn't... there was someone..."

It wasn't my fault. How many times do I have to tell people that? It wasn't what anyone thought. It was *him*—not me. Never me.

But there were flames, and Beth made me stay on the side of the road. She's the one who told me when it was safe to go.

And then there was the night my parents died. I shouldn't have been there either. I told Hannah the truth. No one understands what my father was thinking.

White splotches shine bright behind my eyelids, the splotches flickering, and I'm dizzy. Overwhelmed. The pain in my skull intensifies, and I brace myself for the migraine that could be coming.

I search for a glass—I need water—but there isn't one on the table and I'm not sure if my legs are strong enough to move me across the floor to the sink. It hurts too much to look up.

The pain... A sharp pulse wraps around my skull.

Detective Gillespie is talking again, but I tune him out. He might be asking me the same question, over and over, but I don't care. He's growing impatient, and I don't care about that either.

"Ms. Jenkins?" But his voice sounds as if he's talking to me through a stack of cotton. Everything is muffled, and I want his voice to drift farther away, for him to leave me alone. But he doesn't. He speaks louder, clearer. "Ms. Jenkins," he says, "talk to me. What kind of an accident? What does that have to do with your parents having you arrested?"

I mumble, "You already know this."

"What accident?" he repeats.

"You already know this. You know *all* of it." I lower my head.

"Tell me what happened—"

And I break. My voice comes out as a snarl, my words shooting at him like cannonballs. "Don't play games with me, Detective. Stop jerking me around."

He falls silent, and I close my eyes waiting for the outcome.

I lift my hand to my head. *Shit.* I shouldn't have said that. I shouldn't have talked to him that way either.

My emotions have taken over, and they're revealing a side of me I'd rather keep hidden. I've tried to bury that girl away. I want to stop being so frightened.

*Tick tock...*

I wipe the sweat at my brow. *Tara*, comes a voice inside my head. *You're blowing it.*

"What?" the detective asks. "What did you say?"

I rub my neck, not realizing that I said anything out loud.

"Are you all right, Ms. Jenkins?"

The pain won't go away. I've got to pull myself together and show Detective Gillespie that I'm in control.

"I'm fine," I answer, and to my relief, the flatness in my voice has disappeared, the anger dissipated.

*First Beth, then me...* my mind scrambles.

"I'm sorry," I tell him. "I've been under a lot of stress. This has been... it's been a lot. I'm not sleeping."

His next words tell me he doesn't believe me. He hasn't believed me for days.

"Ms. Jenkins," he says, "what are you trying to hide?"

# FIFTEEN

Wiping my hand against my mouth, sweat pools above my lip.

"I'll tell you everything. But only after you tell me more about Rick Joffrey."

"This will only delay things..."

"I need to see if I can rule him out first."

"That's *my* job," he says.

"But it's *my* life," I fire back. "And the safety of my girls."

A shift in his breath. He's giving in, and he's smart if he doesn't want to lose this thread with me. "We asked that he return for more questioning, and he obliged," the detective explains. "He denies sending you the card. The handwriting sample he provided didn't match up either, but the truth is, it's not a definitive way to rule someone out so we still have questions."

"And what about the other part?" I ask, the critical piece of information I've been waiting for. "You said that someone might have been seen going to my sister's house."

"Yes. The Chandlers, the neighbors. They remember a car, silver in color, passing by their home the morning of the fire. Rick Joffrey owns a Chevy Malibu, metallic gray. It's not silver, but it's pretty darn close. When we showed the Chandlers a photo, they couldn't be sure. They don't remember the exact make and type, and whoever was driving was going too fast for them to recall anything. The tires kicked up quite a lot of dust on the road."

"Yes," I answer. "They're right about that."

That was one of the biggest problems about Route 30, the paved, two-lane highway that snakes its way through the rolling hills of Kentucky before it reaches our more remote location, the asphalt turning to gravel the last few miles before it comes to a dead end with our home and surrounding farm. Behind every car, dust follows like a storm cloud.

"The reason the Chandlers noted a car at all," the detective continues, "is because there hasn't been much traffic. The last time they saw anyone go to your sister's place it was a truck for a grocery delivery, and that was weeks ago, and nothing else. As I understand, your sister had become a recluse, is that right?"

I chew on my thumbnail.

"Whoever visited headed back out about thirty minutes later. The Chandlers missed seeing them on their way out. They only heard the engine. But the problem is, the timeframe doesn't match up. Whoever this was left long before the smoke started and at least two hours before the Chandlers called nine-one-one about the fire."

"So, even if it was, or wasn't Rick Joffrey, you don't think they're the ones who did it?"

"We're looking at other entry points just in case. We're searching the area. Now, look, Ms. Jenkins, I'm sharing this information with you so we can be on the same page, do you understand? We need to work together. Because when I'm done talking, it's your turn. You need to tell me everything. You got it?"

I pause before answering. "Yes."

"We found tire tracks belonging to Rick Joffrey's car, but it was on the other side of the farm—*way* on the other side of the farm. It appears he pulled over on County Line Road and sat for a bit. Are you still familiar with that area?"

"Yes." It's not hard when I've driven that road a hundred times or more. County Line isn't the main thoroughfare for going to town, but it's the route to take if you're heading to the national parks or for a day of picnics and hiking. Several times I took off in that direction, a particular place where I would sneak to, but he doesn't need to know that.

"The problem," the detective continues, "is we can't determine which day it was when he left those tracks. We can't confirm it was on Friday either. We can only guess."

"And what did Rick Joffrey say about that?"

"That he found her address and went out there the day before. He wanted to talk to your sister, and since she didn't respond to any of his messages, he wanted to see her face to face. But he got lost. He got turned around, and he headed back."

"He doesn't have GPS?" I scoff.

"Either that, or he's lying."

*Of course*, I think.

"Do you think he went out there to confront her?" I ask. "She didn't answer the door, or she told him to leave, and he torched the house?"

"That's what we're checking. But it's also why I need to know if I'm heading in the right direction. Because if he did park his car somewhere else, he could have cut through those fields."

My spine tingles. He ran to the farm. That would explain why Hannah didn't hear anyone pull up to the house. But what about the car the Chandlers saw approaching that morning? Hannah never mentioned someone else visiting.

"Hannah didn't hear a car," I remind him. "The one the Chandlers mentioned."

"She was sleeping."

"Okay, so let me get this straight. Rick Joffrey denies going to my sister's house, but the neighbors saw a car. Maybe it was his car or someone else's, we don't know. His tracks aren't found in my sister's driveway but instead on County Line, which is way in the opposite direction. He claims it was the day before."

"Yes, or he's lying about everything."

"To cut through those fields, you'd have to walk miles," I tell him. "There's the Richmond farm, the Hutchesons' farm, the water tank. Pens full of sheep and livestock and corn fields."

"It would take almost an hour," he says. "We timed it."

Those fields, and when I close my eyes, I picture them clear as day. The beautiful region of Kentucky that was our happy place, the place where we grew up. The time before when it wasn't marred with death. It was tranquil.

Miles of farmland exist between County Line Road and the start of our property, the rolling hills and pastures, including the fence that Dad was always repairing, the same fence Beth would have had to maintain after they were gone.

There's the stream where we fished each summer, carp and striped bass that Mom would cook on a skillet. Pies made from apples we handpicked from the orchard. Beth and I would fly kites on a breezy day, something we started doing every fourth of July, and it became a tradition. We'd gotten quite good at it too, running past hay bales, the bales towering high above our heads as we ran to keep up with one another, our kites flapping and swooping in the wind. Mine was a ladybug and Beth's was a butterfly, bright green in color. Mom would watch us with occasional shouts for us not to tangle our lines.

She assembled picnics for us too, Mom would be carrying jugs of lemonade from the house, blankets also. We'd find our favorite spot beside the stream and lie on our backs, barefoot, our tummies full, and we'd stare at the clouds and guess their shapes. Dad would join us whenever he could, and our family of four would while away the afternoon until the sun set and the mosquitos swarmed around our legs. At night, we'd run through the fields and chase fireflies we kept in jars.

Those had been some of the best times. Happier times. I don't understand how everything became so broken.

*The fire spread quickly*, the detective said.

Whoever killed my sister, did this person really trudge through those fields, cursing and pushing stalks from his face with thoughts of murder on his mind? Did he storm across the stream where we loved to fish, the places where Beth and I would run and play, and approach the house, cutting through the apple orchard where Hannah once spent time with her puppy?

He set the blaze in the living room. He knew that's where Beth painted and maybe he hoped that would pain her. And then he ran. He escaped through the fields back to his car, sweating and panicking—or maybe not panicking at all, but satisfied, triumphant, a sick and twisted redemption in what he'd done—while our family home burned to the ground, my sister trapped inside, my niece the only one to break free.

Did this person—if it really is Rick Joffrey—do such a thing?

"Where is he now?" I ask.

"We're keeping him here for more questions. But time is running out. We won't be able to hold him much longer, not without concrete evidence. He hasn't asked for a lawyer which is either interesting on his part or he doesn't have anything to hide. The messages he sent to your sister don't make him look good, but it doesn't necessarily make him a killer. He denies everything."

I grapple with the details, the sweat returning to my palms.

"Ms. Jenkins," he says, "we need someone who can place his car on the side of the road, or for someone to tell us they saw a man matching Rick Joffrey's description cut through that land before he raced back out again. Until then, we don't have much, and there's no way to pin that note card on him either. We'll keep digging, but I need your help. Is there something about this man I need to know? Is there someone else we should be considering?"

*Tick tock...* the reminder strikes at me again.

How much do I tell him? How much can I afford to tell him?

"Has anyone threatened you or your sister in the past? With everything that happened to you years ago, is there someone who wants to hurt you, the rest of your family? Is there a chance it could be more than one person who's doing this?"

*More than one person...* he's asked the question. It's what I've been considering too.

My hands run slick with sweat. My fingers smudge the back of my phone case.

"There's someone angry enough to kill your sister in a fire," the detective says. "The same person who might have sent you that note. They threatened you. What if they go after Hannah again?"

*No.* Not Hannah. Never Hannah. She was too young back then. Yes, she may have heard things, seen things, but she was only three. How much does anyone recall from the age of three anyway? We've always depended on her not remembering anything. That's what Beth said, at least.

The memories bubble their way back up again. I need to find a way to push them back down.

*Strike the match and the flames get closer.*

The message is clear enough.

"Ms. Jenkins," the detective says, "it's your turn to tell me everything."

# SIXTEEN

Thirteen years ago

Beth reaches her hand and blasts the car horn. "Tara, let's go! We're late."

"I'm coming!" I run down the porch steps, my feet hitting the gravel drive next.

Today is a big day with Hannah's birthday. She's turning three and we're throwing her a party this afternoon at our parents' farm.

We spent the morning decorating the patio with pink streamers and balloons. Later, the kids will bob for apples after picking them from the orchard themselves. I'm hoping they'll get a kick out of that, and I'm already imagining their tiny mouths and little teeth biting into the red skin, the kids' faces wet with ponytails dropping into the water, the front of the boys' shirts soaked. I hope my sister has extra towels, plus cameras. We'll want to take a lot of pictures.

I clamber behind the driver's seat while Beth pushes crumpled food bags and receipts to the floor, an extra pair of my shoes she tosses to the backseat. "Your car is a wreck," she says with an annoyed laugh. "And my God, you're so slow. What took you so long?"

"I couldn't find my shoes."

"These shoes?" She points to the ones she threw in the back.

"No, another pair."

But the truth is, I was in my room reading something. The latest text message.

*Tonight. Let's meet. Same place, same time. And don't worry, no one knows anything.*

I hit delete. There's no way I'm listening to him.

Beth rummages around in my center console. The area is sticky from the sloshed remains of yesterday's slushie. "What is all this stuff?" She picks up a pair of scissors and a spool of ribbon.

"It's to help decorate your daughter's birthday party."

"You didn't think Mom would have all of this stuff already?"

"I wanted to help. Make an attempt."

"You're sweet," she says, then gestures for me to start the car. "Let's go. We're wasting daylight here."

I take off down the drive, the dust and gravel spewing behind us.

I see Beth scrunching her face. It's not unusual. She hates my driving and always thinks my car smells, and it probably does. There's a half-eaten sandwich tossed somewhere in the back-seat plus the stench of mud from an outdoor music festival a group of us went to last weekend. I smile with the memory. Two of those girls will soon be my roommates.

We zip down Route 30 as my sister clutches the arm rest.

"What?" I grin. "You told me we're going to be late."

"Yes, but I don't want to die on our way to pick up my daughter's birthday cake."

I wink. "We'll be fine."

We race past the Chandlers' home. I don't see them standing outside, but I wave anyway out of habit. You never know when they could be working in the garden or they're peering out the window as we come and go.

I tap my hands against the steering wheel and hum to the music. Beth does also, something from Today's Greatest Hits, KISS FM, while my little car roars along. It's going strong despite years of my heavy foot and need for speed when I can punch eighty, then ninety, nearing a hundred, as I tear down these long farmland roads. But I'm not crazy, and fingers crossed, I've never been in an accident. I slow down when I see another car. I watch out for cops.

My parents gave me this Toyota Corolla hand-me-down in high school, and I couldn't wait to take off as soon as I earned my driver's license. This hunk of metal has made it through college, my first job, my second, and the one I currently have which, double fingers crossed, could lead to a promising promotion.

Beth has suggested more than once that I buy a new car, and with what money? I ask. My latest job in hotel reception is decent, and it's a day shift so I don't have to deal with the late-night guests, but it's not enough. But management is considering me for an event planning position which would not only be an increase in pay, but something I can add to my résumé. Real experience where I can help plan weddings and fundraisers.

But for now, I'm still holding onto every dollar. And I make enough to cover my expenses, my gas, my food and clothes whenever I can afford them since we're required to look nice at work, but that's about it. It's one of the main reasons I moved back in with my parents after college.

But that's about to change. Within a month I'll be sharing an apartment with two friends and I can leave the family farm-house. I punch down on the accelerator. I can't wait to get out of there.

At twenty-four, I should have my own apartment without my parents, Mom mostly, getting on to me about dishes and clothes on the bedroom floor.

Beth, on the other hand, is married with a child—well, she was married, but her husband, Alex, died last year, and it's as brutal as it sounds. They were too young to get married anyway, Beth was only twenty-two, and then along came our sweet, beloved Hannah. But one day, and out of the blue, Alex decided he didn't want the family life anymore and he walked out. He said he was going on tour with his rock band, that it was *his calling*, if you can believe that. But the band was horrible, and I couldn't imagine anyone paying to see them. To make matters worse, he brought his new girlfriend. He didn't hide her from anyone, including my sister.

The band members died one night when their van flipped on an interstate outside of Atlanta. Their lead bassist was behind the wheel, and he'd either fallen asleep or he was drunk from their last gig.

It's sad, and I hate to admit it, but good riddance when it comes to Alex. Who leaves their young wife and child? Who brings their girlfriend on tour and flaunts her around, not caring that his wife is alone with their kid? My sister is the kindest person I know, and she would never hurt anyone unless it was warranted. When she married Alex, my sister deserved so much more, but instead, she ended up with a spineless wannabe musi-cian with wandering eyes.

But I'm proud of Beth and how far she's come. She's earning her own money from her art sales and is showing a few pieces in galleries around town. They're mostly landscapes and farm scenes since doesn't everyone love a painting of a happy brown cow?

Painting is also helping Beth with her grief, her conflicting feelings of anger and shame. Most everyone around here heard about how Alex died—it was all over the local news—and that his girlfriend died alongside him. People talk about how Alex abandoned them.

Mom has been begging Beth to move home where she can help take care of Hannah. She says that if Beth is to keep painting, that someone should watch over the little one so she doesn't get into any of the paint supplies. "That stuff is toxic," Mom said, and she offered to turn their front living room into an art studio. Over time, and after multiple requests, I think my sister is considering it. She knows she needs the help. The promise of a home-cooked meal and free childcare is tempting too.

So, my big sister will be moving back home while I will be heading out.

"We need to pick up the cake," Beth says. "We'll go straight home so it doesn't melt. We'll check on Hannah and make sure she's doing okay with the puppy." She shoots me a look. "Can you believe Mom got her one? She didn't even ask me."

"It's total bargaining power." I smirk. "She wants you home so badly."

"But now I have to take care of Hannah *and* potty-train a dog."

"All the more reason Mom is pulling the strings to have you move back in. She'll do everything for you. You know she will."

"She does things for you too."

"Well, now she'll be focusing on Hannah."

First thing this morning, there had been ear-piercing shrieks that shook me from bed, and my heart slammed. I shot straight up, assuming that something terrible was happening, but when

I stumbled downstairs, I saw what all the commotion was about. Mom and Dad had gifted Hannah a cocker spaniel, and he's a gorgeous little thing, caramel in color.

Hannah jumped up and down until I thought the dog was going to pee on himself, he was so skittish. Beth had to wrap her arms around her daughter to calm her down. "I know it's exciting, sweet girl. But you need to take it down a notch. You're scaring him."

"A puppy!" Hannah squealed. "I'm going to name him Roger." And everyone laughed at the commonality of the name, how quickly the three-year-old was to name him. Even I had to chuckle as I rubbed the sleep from my eyes.

"Isn't he cute, Auntie Tawa?" she asked, cuddling him.

Beth rummages through her purse. "It's going to be a full house," she says. "All of us living together. And now with a dog."

"I found an apartment." I glance at her. "I've been meaning to tell you. I'm moving out next month."

Beth stops rummaging. A huge smile stretches across her face. "Good for you," she says.

I glance at her again. "The timing works out. It was only a matter of time before Mom will have you and Hannah back home. And you're right, it would be a lot of us together."

She smiles, and my stomach unclenches that she truly is happy for me. "So where is this place?"

"Near Clarksville, closer to the hotel."

"And you have roommates?"

"Two. They work at the hotel also."

"It sounds perfect."

"You know, Mom is going to be glad to be rid of me. She'd much rather have you."

"No," Beth says with a laugh, "who she really wants is Hannah."

My eyes tick to her. "And you."

"You're the baby. She worries about you all the time."

"Well, I think I've worn out the welcome mat."

"And I think it's great you'll have your own place." She roots again at the bottom of her purse. "Found it." She pulls out a piece of gum.

Several miles later, I reduce my speed as we approach town. Traffic lights and brake lights flash red in front of me.

"Up here," Beth says, and points to a building on the left. The words *Emma's Cakes* are painted in bright pink swirls on a wooden sign.

"Isn't this where you got her birthday cake last year?"

"They're the best."


We get out of the car and I can already smell the deliciousness of baked goods wafting from the ovens. Bakeries are my kryptonite, cupcakes especially. My dream event would be to serve small portions of every kind of dessert imaginable so that people could try a little bit of everything, like a dessert sampler. In Kentucky, we offer whiskey flights, so why not dessert flights on a tray?

If I get that event planning job, I'll mention this to the next group that's hosting a fundraiser. Maybe they can pick up on the concept.

A bell jingles above our heads as we enter the shop. My mouth waters as I take in everything: the sweet, piped frosting of cinnamon rolls from the oven, the rows of strawberry cake and chocolate chip cookies that are on display.

I fall into line with my sister. It's a Saturday and the place is busy. Beth chomps her gum as we wait. She rocks side-to-side, something she does when she's pensive. She's focused with her check list of what still needs to be done before the party.

I'm about to tease her about how much she's chomping her gum when I see who is standing ahead of us. His dark hair is thinning on the sides, and he's wearing a black windbreaker. He waits patiently with those squared-off shoulders of his, his hands casually hanging by his sides.

I drop my gaze.

The person at the counter motions for him to step up. He reaches for his order, a white box with a paper receipt taped on the top. When he hands her a wad of cash, he waves off the change, saying it's the tip, and she smiles widely. He turns around and sees us, his eyes shining—piercing green eyes that will soon take in that I'm not alone.

Beth says, "Well, hi, Mr. Robash. Fancy seeing you here." She leans into him for a hug, and he awkwardly embraces her while he juggles the dessert box. "How are you?" she asks.

I keep my eyes rooted to the floor. We've known Hank Robash since we were kids. He works for our dad.

He clears his throat. "What are you girls up to?"

"Picking up a cake," Beth tells him.

His hair is cut shorter than the last time we saw each other, which was only a few days ago. He's handsome with a tanned face, the result of weekends spent at the golf course, the faintest of lines etched beside his eyes.

Here's what I know: Hank and his wife waited years before having kids and, once they did, the two of them have brought their sons to the farmhouse. Dad likes to host barbecues and office parties. He even dressed up as Santa one year and the boys giggled when they sat on his knee. But with the age difference, Beth and I never hung out with them much and the Robash boys would play on the tire swing while we feigned boredom and asked when we could meet with friends. Eli and Patrick are in high school now.

Here's what I also know: I don't want to see Hank Robash again. We should have cut things off a long time ago.

Beth glances at the pastry box in his hands. "What have you got there?"

"Donuts for the boys. They made honor roll again." He puffs out his chest. He's always been so proud of them.

"That's fantastic," Beth says. "They're so smart."

"Just like their mom," he chuckles.

Beth laughs too, and of course she does. She's kind to everyone in that way.

I watch as the people in front of us step toward the counter. We're next, which is great, because we can get this small-talk charade over with. I'm sick to my stomach for every second that we stand here.

I don't meet his eyes, but the heat of his stare is undeniable. He slides his gaze to me before he turns it to my sister. "So what are the two of you getting up to today? Something fun, I hope?"

"We're picking up a birthday cake for Hannah," Beth says. "We're having a party for her this afternoon. Our parents will be there. Say..."

*No. Don't you do it, Beth. Don't you dare.*

"You guys should come." And the heat rushes to my neck. "The boys may not be interested, a three-year-old's birthday party and all, but what about you and Mrs. Robash? Our parents would love to see you." She turns to me. "Wouldn't that be nice, Tara? Don't you think Mom and Dad would love to have friends at the party?"

I don't respond. What I want to do is find the nearest hole and disappear into the ground.

"Oh, I don't know," he says. "I saw your dad all week at work. He's probably sick of me."

But Beth insists. "Please come. You've been so good to us all these years and Hannah adores you. That beautiful gift you gave to her when she was born, it was so kind." She tilts her head. "Plus, it would be good to see Mrs. Robash again. Our mom would love that."

I want to die right there on the spot. I will melt into a puddle and sink through the creases of this floor tile.

The woman at the counter motions for us with her hand, and I move quickly, practically jumping while I yank my sister's arm.

"The party starts at four," Beth says. "Please say you'll join us, Mr. Robash?"

I hold my breath. He's going to say no, right? Any person in their right mind would say no, and he'll come up with an excuse. He'll say they have another commitment. They're meeting another couple for dinner, or Mrs. Robash isn't feeling well. There are a million things he can tell her.

But Hank *nods*—he actually nods and accepts the invitation.

"Well, okay, then. We'll be there," he says. "Four o'clock?" She nods, and he tips his head to her. "Thank you for including us."

"Great," Beth says, and she turns her attention to the woman at the counter.

Hank moves to leave. But before he goes, he steps in beside me. He's too close. I cringe at the mulled spice of his aftershave, a smell I used to enjoy—I used to comment about it, the detergent his wife uses to wash his clothes too. She always uses too much fabric softener.

"I guess I'll see you later," he says, and brushes against my shoulder. The shock of his touch reaches inside my bones.

# SEVENTEEN

Thirteen years ago

We're playing with fire. It's the best way to describe what we've been doing. Hank's decision to show up at our parents' house—along with his wife—is another insane, brazen risk that I can't believe he's taking.

Is he really that bored, or that ballsy? Maybe he has nothing else to do this weekend than attend the birthday party of his *boss's granddaughter*? He will mill about and make small talk while he dares to put me in close proximity to his wife. His former mistress, even though he would prefer it not to be that way.

But I also think that Hank likes the danger. The drama. He might even be getting off on it.

When they arrive, his wife, Gloria, bears her own gifts, something giftwrapped for Hannah along with bottles of lager that she tells everyone Hank brewed at home. "He's so clever," she says, as she pours our parents a glass. She also has a platter of what she calls her *world-famous deviled eggs*. I hate deviled eggs.

Watching them on the back patio, my stomach plunges. Everything about this is wrong. Their presence here is wrong. Everything is about to get worse.

Meanwhile, Hannah's puppy, Roger, is going berserk with every newcomer and sound. There's too much chatter with overly excited toddlers amped up on sugar and wanting to hug him. They stroke his soft fur. I'm afraid one of the kids will squeeze him too hard, or a grownup will trip with Roger prancing at their heels.

My money's on Hank. He's so self-absorbed he won't see where he's going. He'll have his eyes on me, and not on his wife, and certainly not on the dog.

Hank greets everyone with a hug, and my dad is surprised most of all by his visit. Just like Beth said, he's thrilled to have a friend present. "Let's kick back and drink that beer you brought." He claps Hank hard on his back.

"It was so sweet of Beth to invite us," Mrs. Robash says, and she air kisses my mom before she looks for a place to set down her deviled eggs. Mom makes room on the table while Mrs. Robash—Gloria—arranges the platter.

Beth chats with several parents who are either dropping their kids off while others linger, beers in their hands too. Dad and Hank settle into lawn chairs beside each other. Their cups are filled to the brim with Hank's dark lager, and Dad takes a sip and smacks his lips. "This is really good." Hank releases a smile.

"Thanks, boss," he tells him.

I squirm. *Boss*. It's so gross, it's so outrageous, and I want to scream. What was I thinking?

It was different before when we didn't have to be around family and we could keep it separate. Hank said he could help me. He could spot me some cash and also offered to talk to hotel management about that job, saying they're friends of his.

But this... attending my niece's birthday party and spending time with his wife only steps away? It's too much.

Everyone is laughing and talking, delightful conversation on this beautiful Saturday afternoon, except me. If anyone is wondering why I remain on the far end of the table, they haven't asked. I pretend my number one job is to collect gifts and restock snacks.

But I keep my eye on Hank, my insides queasy at what he's up to. I suppose that when he didn't hear back from me, he doubted that we would meet up tonight. This is his way of changing things. He'll convince me. He'll make another excuse to his wife.

*Gloria, I need to pick up a few things at the store.*

How many times can one man forget and have to go back to the store? She has to suspect something, and I eye her cautiously—all the more reason to end things.

Mom and Gloria sit beside one another and chat. Hank tells my dad a joke and he laughs, a big hearty laugh as Hank refills their cups.

I set out more snacks and juice boxes. Beth breaks away from the guests to thank me for helping, and I grimace. If only she knew.

I head to the kitchen in search of something else to load onto a tray when I stop at the kitchen sink and look out the window. Hank and my dad are talking seriously now, their heads close together. They lean back and roar with laughter. Hank must have told him another joke and my dad slaps his knee. Even Mom and Gloria are giggling at how much fun they're having.


Hank stands up and says something about going to the bathroom. He sways a little, and no one seems to notice, but I do.

Sweat beads cross my forehead. He's coming inside the house.

Hank smiles the moment he sees me. And with his eyes—those damn piercing green eyes of his—he makes a wide sweep of the house to make sure we're alone. And we are. The party guests remain outside. His eyes roam up and down my body.

"Nice party," Hank says, and steps closer.

I move away from the window so that no one can see us. But this only encourages him to step forward again.

I press my back against the counter. "You shouldn't be here, Hank. This is crazy."

"Oh, come on. It's just a little party."

"What were you thinking?" I hiss. "You should have told Beth you had other plans, that you were busy. You didn't have to bring Gloria."

I step to one side, and so does he. He releases another grin. He likes this game. He wants to keep playing.

And I realize that's all it is. I'm just another young woman that Hank has been able to dangle money in front of. *I can get you that job*, he's told me more than once, and I'm stupid for falling for it. I've never hated myself more than in that moment.

I lean away, wanting to put distance between myself and Hank, especially from the beer stench on his breath. My eyes race to the patio door, and it remains closed. No one is coming in, but I'm on high alert.

"This is too risky," I warn him. "I don't want this anymore."

"No one knows a thing," he hushes me. "I told you that. How many times do I have to keep telling you that?" He winks. "They could never guess about you and me in a million years." He sways as he holds his beer.

I push him away, but this only makes him lean closer.

"So," he says, his eyebrow cocked, "are we hanging out later tonight or not?"

"No."

"Come on now, sugar." I hate it when he calls me that. "Don't you want to see me? It'll be nice and quiet..." He presses against my body until I force my head away. "Come on now," he whispers. "Tell Mr. Hank you want to see him." He lifts his hand to tuck my hair behind my ear.

And that's when I hear a gasp, someone choking on their scream.

A hushed shriek. "What in the hell are you doing, Hank?"

It's Gloria. Oh, my God, *it's Gloria.*


Hank whirls around to face her, and I push him. He stumbles with his footing.

"Nothing, honey. I'm just chatting with Tara." But he slurs when he says this, his cheeks reddening.

There's something devastating in her look, the way her lips tremble, her eyes narrowing, that tells me she's not surprised, that she's been expecting this. She suspected this with Hank and someone else—maybe she's been aware of plenty of other women.

I should leave. I should remove myself from the kitchen and go outside. I'll get into my car and never come back.

But I don't move. And Gloria glares with such hate in her eyes. "You make me sick," she says.

"It's not like that, honey." He gives his beer a little shake. "I just had too much to drink, that's all."

"And with Tara?" she shrieks and glares at me. "And, *Tara?* What the hell were you thinking?"

I'm sick, and I can barely meet her eyes. This is unbearable. I stare at the floor like a shamed child. I have no idea what I was thinking either. *I didn't mean any of it... I didn't mean to hurt you, Mrs. Robash.*

"Are you crazy?" Gloria continues. "*Your boss's daughter?* Someone half your age?" She shakes her hands at him. "We've known Tara since she was a child. Since Hannah's age." She cries harder. "You're despicable, Hank. You've been a despicable person for such a long, long time."

Her glare returns to me. "And you, Tara? What's going to happen when your dad finds out? What will your family say?"

My chest heaves, the consequences I will soon be facing. The blame that I absolutely deserve.

But fear burns up my chest. She's not going to tell my dad, is she? She wouldn't risk Hank's job in that way. She wouldn't blow up both of our families.

"It's not what you think," Hank says, and I shake my head with disgust. It's so cliched, it's sickening. The empty excuse that someone will give every time.

Gloria storms over to her purse. "I don't want to hear it." She pulls out her car keys. "I don't give a shit how you get home, Hank. I really don't. Figure it out yourself because I'm leaving." She walks to the front of the house and flings open the door, slamming it behind her.

Hank passes me a look, but then his eyes startle. He's looking at someone else—someone standing behind me.

In the commotion, I didn't hear my sister. I didn't know she stepped into the kitchen. And I'm not sure how much Beth has heard, but it's enough because she stares at us with hurt and disbelief.


Hank sets his beer on the counter and leans against the granite to steady himself.

"Get him out of here," Beth says. "I'll tell Mom and Dad they had to go home, that something came up. Just..." She looks at me pointedly. "We'll talk about this later, okay? But I need you take him. He can't stay here in front of everyone, all these kids. Take him home and then come straight back. Do you understand me, Tara?"

I do exactly what she says, knowing that she's right. He's way too drunk and this is too explosive a situation to unleash in front of a bunch of guests.

"I am in *sooo* much trouble..." Hank says with a slur.

She folds her arms. "Take him now," she repeats.

I'm crying, tears slipping down my cheeks, my anger rising at the sheer stupidity of Hank, me also. But I have no choice. I do what my sister says, and I help him stumble down the front steps toward my car. I'll drop him off as fast as I can. I don't care if Gloria locks him out, that's not my problem. I'll come straight home like Beth told me.

I'll talk to my sister tonight, after Hannah and our parents go to bed. I'll explain my mistake, how this was only supposed to be a short-term thing, a stop-gap while Hank helped me out. I didn't mean for it to get this far, and I'm ashamed. *But, yes, Beth, Hank Robash is not the family friend we thought he was. I have not been the sister you hoped I was either.*


We drive silently down Route 30, and while I'm despising having Hank in my car, I remind myself that it won't be much longer. Another fifteen minutes, and then I can kick him out for good.

"Well, this is going to be tough," he says, and hiccups, which makes me grip the steering wheel. "Gloria's going to be so upset, but I'll figure out something. I'll get her to calm down. I'll tell her that she was imagining things, that we were only talking." He slides his eyes to me. "I mean, that's all it was, right? She doesn't have to know. We were just in the kitchen."

"You had your body pressed against mine," I tell him. "You were tucking my hair behind my ear." I shoot him a look. "She's not stupid, Hank. The way she reacted, I'm pretty sure this isn't the first time she's suspected you of something." I slam my hand against the wheel. "I'm such an idiot."

"Well, I guess this means we won't be meeting up later tonight, huh?"

My jaw drops. I could punch him.

I crank the air conditioning until it's on high and flip every vent toward me so the air can blast in my face. What was I thinking? What is the matter with me?

Hank grumbles, "What's your problem, anyway? Why are you getting so bent out of shape? *I'm* the one who has to deal with Gloria, not you. Going home, facing her and all her bitching, and now I have to deal with *you* and your anger too? Give me a break. You're being all sulky. Acting all..." His words slow as he lets out a sigh. "You girls are all the same. Every one of you. So much work. So much effort. Such bitches."

And his words fly all over my face, and I yank at the wheel so hard the car swerves before I have a chance to correct. I tug the wheel again, but the car fishtails.

*We're all the same.*

"What the hell is the matter with you?" Hank shouts. "Are you trying to get us killed?"

I increase my speed, my little car rattling forward as I stomp on the gas.

*Such bitches.*

Is that what you think, Hank? We're all toys for you until you no longer find us entertaining? We're worthless the moment your wife finds out.

He stares at me, then at the road as I increase my speed. I take a look at the speedometer—we're approaching eighty, then eighty-five, topping ninety.

"Slow down!" he roars.

How could I do this to Gloria, and with someone who works for my dad? Someone my dad trusted for years. My parents will never forgive me. And Beth? She's still at the party trying to make small talk while also struggling to understand what I've done. She will be beyond disappointed.

The Robash boys are only teenagers. What will they think of their dad? What will they think of me, the older friend who used to let them play on the tire swing? It will be devastating if their mom kicks him out for good.

We near the intersection of County Line Road, but I decide not to go that way. I turn on Dug Hill Road, and it's a bit of a detour and a longer route for reaching town, but at the speed I'm going, I don't want to beat Gloria to her driveway. I don't want her to pull up and we have to face each other all over again.

The road curves to the right and I keep accelerating.

"Slow down," Hank says. This time, he reaches for the steering wheel as if to stop me.

I startle. I panic. One of my hands flies up to be rid of Hank's arm, his disgusting, slimy fingers, his beer-stench breath, while my other hand fights to maintain control of the car.

*I'll give you the money you need.*

*I know the management team at the hotel. That job is yours.*

Then how come I still haven't heard back from them, Hank? Why am I still waiting on a phone call?

I shove his hand away, but he's stronger than me. He grabs at the steering wheel again, and he pulls hard. I swipe at him as we screech back and forth across the road.

"Don't touch me!"

"I told you to *slow down!*" Hank shouts.

But I don't release my foot. I don't slow down—I don't want to. I never want to listen to Hank Robash again.

# EIGHTEEN

Thirteen years ago

Hank lets go of the steering wheel, but when he does, his arm clocks me right in the jaw. The pain is instant, and it shoots to the back of my head, a sharp ache radiating in my skull.

I let out a shriek and my eyes go black, then it's dark, stars exploding across my vision. I open my eyes and blink repeatedly, trying to focus so we don't crash.

But it's difficult, and I'm losing control. My hands are knocked free from the steering wheel and the car fishtails once more. The pain is too much and I'm dizzy, the asphalt becoming an endless black ribbon until there is no more road, only grass and trees, then a giant pothole that we crash straight through, the undercarriage of the car bottoming out with a *bang*. The pothole slows us down, but only a little, because we hit something, and we hit it hard. We sideswipe it.

We hurtle forward, our bodies thrown forward, then back, our seatbelts locked tight against our chests. The airbags burst in our faces and the smack of plastic is against my face, the shock of the airbag stinging my cheeks.

The car rocks violently before it comes to a stop, and I realize that I'm screaming. I've been screaming this whole time and didn't realize it. And now I hear myself, along with the sound of crunching metal and shattered glass that falls to the ground. The engine rattles and shakes. The radiator hisses.

I collapse into my seat, thankful that I'm alive and can move my arms and legs. I push against the airbag, clearing as much of the plastic out of my face as I cough and choke from the debris.

It's gotten quiet, except for the steady tick of the engine. Another piece of the car breaks off somewhere in the back and it clatters to the ground. There is no sound from Hank.

I look in the rearview mirror and see that it's a telephone pole we sideswiped. It was on Hank's side of the car and the passenger door is crumpled against him.

Hank isn't moving. And now my anger from him hitting me, what we've done, turns into fear. With the airbags deployed, I can't see much of his face. I can't tell if he's breathing either, and I reach over.

"Hank?" I shake him. His body rocks but there's no response. "Hank! Wake up."

I scramble to get out of the car and race to the passenger side but it's difficult. We're on the side of a hill. After we hit the telephone pole, the car reached sloped ground that pitches about thirty feet below before it evens out and reaches the woods. A row of trees waits for us at the bottom.

I lean against the passenger door to keep my balance, but my shoes slip, and I try not to fall. "Hank!" I scream, but he still isn't moving.

I push against the airbag until I can finally see his face. He's bloodied and banged-up. And then he moans, his eyelids fluttering open.

I release my breath. Our sordid affair and what we have is over—he is a total sleaze—but I don't want him to die. I cannot watch him die like this.

I rush around to the driver's side and try to locate my phone. I need to call 9-1-1. But as I do, the car shifts forward, dirt and gravel coming loose beneath the tires until it begins to move. My car pitches forward. The tires lose traction on the downward slope, and the car is about to slide.

I step out of the way just as my beloved Toyota hurtles down the hill, carrying Hank with it. I scream, and I'm pretty sure he screams, and then my car grinds to a stop, missing the trees by only a few feet. I look around. But with the car below, no one will be able to see us from the road. A passerby might not be able to determine there's been an accident.

I scurry down the hill, my shoes slipping until I fall flat on my butt. I scramble back up again. It's difficult to open the passenger door, but I finally manage so that I can check on Hank. He's moaning. I search the backseat but can't find my phone.

Hank licks blood from his lips. He presses a hand to his head, but when our eyes meet, he laughs, a delirious laugh that causes every cell in my brain to boil with anger. He's drunk, and he's not taking this seriously. In some deranged way, he still thinks this is fun.

I tell myself I will call 9-1-1 because it's the right thing to do. I do not want Hank's death on my conscience. I do not want his boys to grow up without their father.

I search the floor, but there is still no phone—only junk, loose change, fast-food bags, and the shoes that Beth threw out of the way earlier. The spool of ribbon I thought we would use to wrap Hannah's present with has come loose. The scissors I brought are wedged into my center console.

Hank lets out another laugh. "You crazy girl." He wipes his nose as more blood trickles to his chin. I want to punch him in the jaw the same way he hit me.

It's the first time I check myself, and I rub my hands along my face, my body. My head hurts, I will have whiplash in the morning, and my jaw stings. But I will be okay, despite the bruise that will form where Hank hit me.

"What the hell did you do?" he asks.

"Hank, where is your phone?" I pat his pockets. "Do you have it on you?"

"My phone...? I don't know." His head rolls to one side as I dig at his jeans. He grins. "Ooh, watch it there. I might like that."

I pull back my hands.

He sighs. "Gloria has it in her purse. She keeps it when we go anywhere, says that I have a habit of losing it. But I think she just wants to snoop through my messages."

I grit my teeth. *I wonder why.*

I should run back up the hill. Flag someone down or look for my phone. Maybe it flew out of the window and it's on the grass somewhere.

Hank chuckles again. "You're a crazy bitch, you know that? Crazy, crazy Tara."

I bite so hard on my tongue until I taste blood. "It's over, Hank. You and me, what we were doing. I don't want it anymore. It's a good thing your wife found out, and I hate that it happened that way, but it needed to. You need to stop doing this to her."

He jerks forward and grabs my wrist, and the movement is so sudden, it catches me off guard. His green eyes turn dark as he says, "You don't get to end things with me, you got that? You don't have a say. That's not how this works—that's not how this has *ever* worked." He grips me tight as I whimper. "You know what I can do? I'll take back the deposit money for your apartment. I'll have your lease torn up. I'll tell the hotel to get rid of you too so you can forget about that promotion. If you mess things up with me, you won't have a job with anyone. Not if I can do anything about it." He leans closer. "Don't mess with me, Tara. You know better than that. *I'm* the one who calls the shots. I always have."

He twists until my wrist burns, the skin turning raw. I fight to free myself, to get away, but he's too strong.

He yanks me again as I clamber with my other hand to reach for the door, the steering wheel, anything I can wrap my fingers around and pull. I beat my hand against the horn, and it blares repeatedly, but it's no use. We're in the middle of nowhere, and even if someone hears us, it will take them a while to find us at the bottom of the hill.

"Let go of me!" I scream, and my legs flail out behind me. I kick and push, desperately trying to find leverage so I can heave myself out of the car. But the more I twist, the stronger his grip becomes, and his fingers wrap tighter.

"What is it with you girls?" Hank snarls. "You're always so good in the beginning, so pleasing, so appreciative. But then you change your minds. You think you can just end things whenever you feel like it. Well, that's never going to happen." Spit gathers at his mouth. His saliva dots my face, and I pull away with revulsion.

"I said, let me go!"

With my other hand, I reach for anything I can hold onto, something I can hit him with. And then my hand closes around the plastic handle of the scissors, and I tug. The sharp end is lodged in the center console from the crash, but it wriggles free. With my arm reared back, I plunge the scissors forward.

The metal sinks into flesh, and it's a disgusting sound, like the popping of a carved pumpkin. The scissors puncture Hank's shirt and slice into the fleshy part of his chest, and I tremble—I've missed his heart by inches.

He lets go, and I'm screaming at the blood that pours out and seeps into the blue cotton of his shirt. The blood blossoms into a bright red patch, and the patch grows larger. I'm going to be sick.

His expression twists, and I fall out of the car. My back lands hard on the grass, the breath knocked out of me, as he screams again.

I stand up. The scissors are stuck in his chest and blood drips down his belly. I don't think the wound is enough to kill him, but he's definitely hurt.

I stagger, my insides woozy. *I just stabbed a man.*

I hunch forward, my hands on my knees as I dry heave onto the grass. *I stabbed Hank.*

I'm crying and shrieking, every inch of my body trembling as his eyes bulge open and he glares at me, then looks down at the scissors.

"What in the hell did you do?" he screams. "You will not get away with this, Tara."

And I take off running. I clamber up the hill, sobbing, searching for my phone, my hands grappling at the grass and pulling at strands. I cut my finger on a piece of glass.

My hand trickles with blood, but I don't care because among the broken pieces of metal I find my phone. It's face-down and I lunge toward it, grasping it with both hands. I collapse on the side of the hill and think about what to do. I can make out the outline of Hank's head inside the car. He's still moaning, but he's also cursing. He's swearing and screaming the most horrendous things, and it's all about me. The rage explodes inside my head.

I should call 9-1-1, but I dial a different number instead. It was a huge mistake. I thought this would help. I thought things would turn out differently, but that's not what happened at all.

# NINETEEN

"A car accident," I tell the detective as I stare at the kitchen floor. "It was a long time ago. That man, he worked for my dad. It was the day of my niece's birthday party and he'd had too much to drink. He ran off the road."

That was Beth's idea: telling everyone that Hank insisted on driving instead of me.

"He died, is that correct?" the detective asks.

"Yes."

"He died when the car caught on fire?"

*Fire...* and I shut my eyes. "Yes, that's correct too."

"The police report states that his wife went home and you offered to drive Mr. Robash. But he never made it."

"He was a lot drunker than I thought. I should have never let him get behind the wheel."

"But the report said you weren't involved with the crash. He left you on the side of the road."

My breaths grow shallow. That part of the story was one of Beth's ideas also.

"He left you stranded."

"Yes."

He pauses. "What I don't understand is why his wife, Gloria Robash, blames you for the accident. If you weren't in the car, why would she think that you killed him?"

Because she saw something she shouldn't have. Because she started to suspect, but I can't tell him that. I can never tell him that. I can never admit that to anyone.

Thirteen years ago

Beth is the one I called. I needed her to help. At the very least, she could pick me up and take me away from here.

Beth was stunned when I screamed into the phone, her words rushing back just as frantic. "Wait... slow down. You were in a wreck?" A door closes, and I think she's slipped inside the house. The children's laughter disappears. "Are you okay? Are you hurt?"

I wince at the bruise on my jaw. "I'm okay. But Hank..."

"What happened?"

I start to cry.

She's breathless. "Tara, you're scaring me. Have you called nine-one-one?" The distinct jingle of keys is heard next, and I imagine she's swiped our dad's car keys. "Where are you?"

"But what about Hannah's birthday party?"

"Are you kidding? Don't worry about that. Mom and Dad can take over. A lot of the kids have already left. I'll tell them I need to pick something up for Hannah."

"Okay," I whisper.

"Where are you?" she repeats. "What did he do? I thought you were driving."

"I was."

"Where is he?"

"He's still in the car."

"Is he okay?"

"He's banged up. But I did something, Beth. I did something bad."

The slam of the door comes next. "Stay put, Tara. Don't do anything until I get there. Do you hear me?"

I tell her my location, or the approximate location because I don't see any landmarks or mile markers. I'm too afraid to stand in the middle of the road in case anyone drives by. "You won't be able to see the wreck," I tell her. "We're at the bottom of a hill. But watch out for a telephone pole. We slammed against it. I'll look out for you too."

"Okay. Hold tight."

I collapse against the grass, my tears streaming down my cheeks, my thoughts repeating over and over... *I stabbed a man...*

When Hank recovers, he will come after me like he said. He'll wait for my next shift to end at the hotel. He'll make me pay.


It takes about ten or fifteen minutes for Beth to find us, but to me, it's an eternity. She spots the broken-off pieces of headlight and a chunk of my front bumper that cracked off. The paint of my Toyota Corolla has streaked across the side of the telephone pole.

I stay low until I know she's the one approaching. No other vehicle has driven past and I'm grateful. When she sees me, she gasps, and I must look horrific. My hair is a tangled mess and my jaw is swelling like a balloon. I cup my hand to my chin and wince again with the pain.

Her mouth opens at the sight of my mangled-up car at the bottom of the hill. Hank is still inside. In the last few minutes, he's become quiet and the worry grips me. He might be more injured than I thought.

"What happened?" she asks, and helps me move down the hill. We try not to slip as we sidestep pieces of metal.

She reaches the passenger side, but I don't step further. I don't want to go anywhere near him.

Beth taps at his shoulder. "Hank?" But her hand flies over her mouth. "What...?" She jumps from the car. "There are *scissors* in his chest." Her eyes widen. "Why are there scissors in his chest, Tara?"

I can't speak.

She looks at him again. "He's bleeding, but he's still alive. Have you called nine-one-one?"

I stammer. "N-no. I thought you were."

"I thought *you* were."

"I wanted to call you first," I sob. "I didn't know what else to do. I stabbed him... how do I explain that I stabbed him?"

Beth reaches for my shoulders. She looks at me long and hard. "Tara, tell me exactly what happened here."

"He wouldn't let me go." I show her my wrist, the skin that is raw and bloody. "He punched me."

"He did *what*?"

I tell her everything, about the affair, how I was ending things anyway, but Gloria found us in the kitchen. I tell her that Hank made promises and gave me money to help me out. He said he would secure that job for me at the hotel, and I believed him. I tell her what he said about women. How we're all the same.

"He was gripping my wrist, and I was so scared, Beth. I didn't think he would let me go. And then my hand found those scissors... and I didn't know... I didn't mean..."

My sister holds my stare.

"What am I going to do? They could arrest me. I could go to prison. I was the one driving—"

"No," she says. "That is *not* going to happen. I will *not* let that happen to you." The expression on her face hardens. "That man is an asshole. He used you. He took advantage of you, and he bribed you. He's sick. A grown man." Her face blanches. "My God, the party, and I didn't know. I invited him and you didn't say anything. You should have—"

"I didn't want anyone to know, Beth. I'm scared. He said he'll get back at me, that he'll find me." And I'm trembling now, full body shakes that extend to my fingers. "What if he hurts me?"

"He won't."

I stare at the car. "What if the scissors went deeper than I thought and he's bleeding out? I'll be charged with *murder*, Beth. Vehicular homicide. I assaulted him."

"No," she repeats. "He assaulted you. Look at your face. He *punched* you. He wasn't going to let you out of that car, so you did what you had to do. It was self-defense."

"But the cops..." And my voice drifts. "The cops won't think that way. They'll try to pin this on me. *I* was the one who was driving. *I'm* the one who stabbed him."

"Not if I can help it."

And something on my sister's face breaks at that moment. "He's not going to get away with any of this," she says, and she returns to the car. She's mumbling and cursing and it's hard to understand what she's saying, but then I hear her. "He was driving, that's what we're going to tell them. *He's* the one who wrecked, not you. You never stabbed him with anything, you got that? No one ever has to know."

"But how? There are *scissors* in his chest. How do we explain that?

"You won't go down for this," she tells me. "I won't allow it." Her face storms black. "And to think we grew up with this man, that we trusted him. Dad trusted him." She hovers over Hank. "Help me move him. We need to move him now."

"W-what?"

"You heard me." She reaches into the car and yanks the scissors from Hank's chest. She tosses them to the floor and they clatter against broken glass. Blood gushes out, but she doesn't flinch. She repeats, "Help me move him."

I jolt into action.

Beth puts an arm behind his back and tries to heave him out. But Hank is heavy, and she can't get him to budge. My sister pants as she tries to drag his body out of the car. "Help me!" she shrieks.

I grab his legs and pull him to the ground. She lifts his shoulders while I wrap my hands around his ankles, and I'm no longer thinking, I'm no longer overanalyzing. I'm doing what my sister tells me. She's in charge. She will help me.

We slip, we shuffle, we cry, and we curse until we drag Hank's body around to the driver's side. Beth says we should put him behind the steering wheel.

The next task is far more difficult. Lifting and grunting, we shove his arms and legs until he's inside the car. His head bobs sickeningly, the blood from his head dripping to his neck. The blood from the stab wound also streaks to his stomach.

With him in place, we're covered in sweat. I'm crying, but Beth isn't. I'm not sure if she's teared up once. She's on a mission, and whatever else she has planned, she isn't finished yet.

I have a feeling this is no longer about Hank anymore. My sister's face tells me this is something else, something deeper. She's consumed with rage, not only about Hank, but about every man who's ever hurt her, every man who's hurt me too. And most of all, I think this is about Alex. The way he abandoned her for someone else and left her with a small child. What she's doing is revenge for everyone who has ever broken our hearts.

.  .  .

She tells me to wipe the blood from my hands, and I do what she says. She has blood smeared on her shirt from lifting Hank, and she takes it off, leaving her tank top on underneath. Tossing the shirt in the car, she pulls out a lighter from her pocket. It's the same lighter she used to light Hannah's birthday cake.

My breath freezes. "Beth, what are you doing?"

She pulls back with her thumb and the lighter ignites. It catches fire. She stares at the flame for a long, long time. She doesn't look at me, only stares at the flame. "Have you ever looked?" she asks. "Have you ever really looked at the flame? How it dances."

The numbness in my body takes over. I don't know what Beth plans to do, but I don't like it. I don't like where this is going.

In that moment, the look on my sister's face is livid. She's sick and tired of feeling this way, and most of all, she's tired of not being able to do anything about it—her life, what Alex did, more men that will come along like him, and Hank—and she wants revenge. She couldn't protect herself from being hurt, but she will do whatever she can to help me.

"I'm burning the car," she says.

"*What?*"

"Don't stop me."

"Beth. You can't." Hank slumps behind the steering wheel. He hasn't made a sound.

"He's going to die anyway. His injuries. He's bleeding out as we speak."

"You don't know that. We have time. We can get help." I pull out my phone. "We can call nine-one-one."

"And then what?" she asks, and releases her thumb. The flame goes out as quickly as it appeared. "He'll go after you, isn't that what he said? And not only that but, yes, Tara, you were driving. You stabbed him. We can claim self-defense, but to what extent? You were having an affair with this man, and his wife caught you out less than an hour ago. You were both angry. You argued. The cops can say you wrecked so you could hurt him, maybe even kill him. And when that didn't work, you stabbed him in the chest. Hank will back up that story. The police will come up with all kinds of ways for blaming you, and I'm not going to let that happen."

"Beth... no..." I sob. "If we burn the car, he'll..."

"If he burns, they won't know about the stab wound." She pulls back her thumb and the lighter sparks back to life. The flame bobs as she steps forward.

She opens the back door and searches the floor for something. When she stands back, she brings the lighter to a piece of paper she's found. She holds it against a fast-food bag. She tosses the burning items onto the backseat.

The flames fill up the back of my car. It happens so fast, the smoke filling the interior until it seeps toward the sky.

"Beth... *what are you doing?*" I scream. But I don't move, and neither does she. She's transfixed by the blaze.

She lets out a laugh—an actual laugh—before she sobs. She's crying so hard and shaking so much that all I can do is hold her, the two of us watching my car on fire.

"Beth, we can still pull him out."

"No." She wipes her eyes. "Leave him."

The flames creep toward the front seat where Hank is sitting. The heat nears his face, and that's when we hear him moan.

It's low at first, and I tell myself I'm hearing things. But it's Hank and he's moaning. He's crying for help. He struggles to lift his chin.

*Oh my God*, he's not unconscious. He's coming around and the heat is intense on his back. The flames are gaining at his head, and it will be excruciating. The smoke billows around his face as he chokes. He's unable to get out of the car. He's too weak.

"*Beth!*" I scream. "We have to save him." I rush forward, but Beth pulls me back.

"I said, *no.*" And she lands on top of me and pins me to the ground. We kick and fight, the two of us rolling around until I stop. The truth is, I give up. It's too late; the flames are wrapping around Hank's head as he wails.

Hank Robash burns—he burns alive—and it's the most horrifying sight. It's my deepest, darkest nightmare and it has haunted me for years ever since, causing me to bolt upright in the middle of the night to search my room. I'm convinced there will be flames. I'm convinced I will end up in a fire just like him.

*First Hank, then Beth, then me.*

Hank's head disappears behind a wall of flames, and I can no longer watch. His screams pierce the air until I am screaming too.

"Don't look," Beth tells me.

I squeeze my eyes shut, but that doesn't block out the sounds Hank is making. They're animalistic, deep, painful screams, until the cries are literally burned from his throat. The flames erase everything and Hank falls silent.

# TWENTY

Beth orders me to get inside Dad's car. I'm numb. My legs and heart, my very soul have turned to soot and ash. We will, no doubt, go to hell for this.

Beth shoves me in the passenger seat before she scrambles around the front. She starts the engine and busts a U-turn as we haul back to our parents' house. The sun is setting, and it's funny how I remember this part: the sky's burned orange hue and distant blue haze, the approaching twilight... the gruesome heap of metal and charred flesh that we're leaving behind.

Those fields and that farmland... I will never be able to look at it the same way again.

Beth talks rapidly. She shifts her eyes to make sure that I'm keeping up, but it's hard. "It's critical we stick to the same story," she says more than once.

"I already told Mom and Dad that Hank had too much to drink," she continues. "You offered to drive him home. We'll say that he insisted on driving instead, but he got belligerent. You were frightened, especially when he punched you. You begged to be let out of the car. And since I was on my way to pick up something for Hannah, when you called and told me what happened, I came and got you. That's when I found you on the side of the road." She eyeballs me. "Are you hearing this, Tara? Are you hearing what I'm saying to you?"

I can't stop crying.

She drives almost as fast as I did earlier, her movements antsy, her eyes clocking the road, the time on the dash, and then back to me.

"He wrecked the car on his own. Okay, Tara? You weren't there. I already picked you up. We had no idea he was speeding like that. The car caught on fire from the crash."

I swallow and sniffle, my hands clutched against my chest.

I can't get the sound of Hank screaming out of my mind. I think I might throw up, and I crack open the window.

A car approaches ahead, and my body tightens. Beth's shoulders stiffen too when the driver waves their arm out the window.

Beth slows down. "You've got to be shitting me," she says.

It's Gloria—she's in her car approaching us—and now I'm certain that I will pass out. I will fall in the middle of the road or die in this car.

What is Gloria doing out here? Why isn't she home?

Beth lowers her window when Gloria does the same. My sister acts as if there is nothing wrong in the world. "Hi, Mrs. Robash. Is everything all right?"

The heat from Gloria's stare cuts a hole straight through me, and I turn my head. I can't look at this woman, not when she knows what Hank and I have done. Not when I know the heinous crime we have committed also.

"I was heading back to your parents' to pick up Hank. That asshole, he doesn't deserve it..." She's crying, and trying not to, especially not in front of me. "He was drinking, and I shouldn't have left him. But your parents said he's already gone."

My jaw runs slack. Everything inside of me wants to scream.

Beth says, "He took Tara's car. He shouldn't have, but he insisted on it. Tara went with him so she could get it back. She needs it for work tomorrow." She shoots me a pointed look. "But Tara got scared and told him she wanted to get out. He dropped her off on the side of the road."

"He dropped her off? What happened?" She scoffs. "Don't tell me. A lovers' quarrel."

I bite my lip, trying not to sob.

"Tara..." She glares. "You, and this mess. What you've done to my family. Everything that has been going on between the two of you. *None* of it is going away, do you hear me? I will never forgive the two of you for what you've done."

"Can we drop this right now, Mrs. Robash?" Beth pleads. "I need to get Tara home. I need to get back to my daughter's party. After all, it's pretty upsetting what he did, leaving my sister out here in the middle of nowhere."

Gloria says, "She'll be fine. But I was wondering what the two of you are doing out here anyway."

"I was going to ask you the same," Beth says coolly. "Route 30 is faster."

Gloria pauses. "Part of me doesn't want to see him crashed at an intersection. Or find the cops pulling him over for a D.U.I. I took the long way." She sniffles again, her jaw tightening.

But Beth is as calm as I've ever seen her. She motions at the road behind us, and I wince. Somewhere back there, smoke is spilling into the sky, Hank's body on fire. Gloria only has a few more miles to go before she'll come across the accident.

"I bet Mr. Robash is home by now," Beth says. "He's probably pulling into the drive. He made it safe and sound." She releases the brake and lets the car crawl forward. But then she stops. "Oh, and Mrs. Robash?" she adds. "When you see him, can you tell him that my sister needs her car back tomorrow? I hope he didn't do anything to mess it up."

And with that statement, we leave Gloria, my shock at my sister's boldness, while Gloria resumes in the opposite direction with no clue in the world as to what awaits her.


Gloria is the one who spotted the smoke. She found the debris on the side of the road and the car in flames. She called 9-1-1 and screamed at the operator.

It's unbearable to imagine Gloria sitting and waiting for the police to show up. She must have been sick to her stomach thinking that Hank might be a charred heap inside that vehicle.

Several hours passed before the police determined the car was registered in my name. It took another twenty-four hours to confirm the body inside was that of Hank Robash.

Our family was shocked when the police told us the news. Everyone also bought my side of the story: Hank dropping me off. They were horrified that he would punch me and leave me on the side of the road. By then, my jaw was swollen and the bruise radiated a deep purple toward my ear.

The police officers sat across from us in the living room, my parents trembling at the news that Hank was dead while my dad struggled to reconcile his feelings about his deceased employee. He was devastated that someone he considered a friend would strike his daughter, someone he spent time with and played golf with, that he would hurt me when I was simply trying to bring him home.

One of the officers said, "Thank goodness you weren't in the car, Tara. He would have crashed with both of you in it."

And just as Beth hoped, when Hank's body burned, any evidence of a skin puncture, of a pair of scissors lodged in his chest, was destroyed by the flames. He was so badly burned that it was difficult to determine every injury he sustained from the wreck. No one would know.

Like I said, the police bought our story, and lucky for us, there were no other witnesses. The ordeal should have been over with, and that's what we hoped.

But doubts swarmed something fierce inside Gloria's head, her suspicion and anger growing as she replayed the moments of that day. The fact she met us driving down the same exact road, how close we were to the wreck. Our conversation, and how antsy I must have appeared. There may have been a hitch in Beth's voice.

And then Gloria recalled one tiny detail: the blood she spotted on my shirt.

When I turned my head, that mere second when I met Gloria's eyes, she remembered seeing drops of blood on my sleeve. In our haste, Beth hadn't seen it either. It was Hank's blood.

But where Hank hit me, my lip didn't bust, and Gloria was convinced that something was wrong about our story. How could we have not heard the accident or known that Hank crashed? She told everyone that I must have been in the car with him when he slammed against the pole, and that's how I got the blood on my shirt. She told anyone who would listen that I was lying about the accident. I left Hank to die. She thinks my sister helped me.

Because somewhere in Gloria's grief, in her anger toward us —the fact that she would never be able to confront Hank about his affairs—she wanted someone to pay for what he'd done, and she embarked on a warpath against me. In her rage, she needed to point the anger at someone. I would be her target.

But I also think it was Gloria's way of not blaming herself. It was already bad enough that he got drunk at a child's birthday party and that she took off without him, the fact they argued, and she left him to drink and drive using my car. If she'd brought him home, he would still be alive.

She told the police about her suspicions, but by then, I no longer showed any signs of whiplash and I'd gotten rid of the shirt with Hank's blood. There was no way to determine if I'd been inside the vehicle when we crashed, especially when it was my word against his... and Hank... well, he was no longer speaking for himself.

Beth also stuck to the story—it was her story after all. She repeated that she picked me up and that I wasn't anywhere near the crash site.

The days dragged by. After Hank's funeral, which no one from our family attended, my sister and I started avoiding each other. It hurt, but it was difficult to make eye contact, especially when I was still stunned with our decision—haunted by it, really, that we would leave someone to die. The screams from Hank tormented my dreams. And my sister suffered too. I could see our guilt catching up with us, the torment of what we'd done, the secret we were keeping from everyone.

*We're not murderers*, Beth said, and it was more like she was trying to convince herself. *Don't ever tell, Tara. Promise me.*

I promised.

But my sister is the one who held that lighter. She's the one who set fire to the backseat and held me to the ground as we watched Hank burn. That day, I've never been more in awe of her, and never so frightened.

The distance between us grew. Beth claimed to be busy packing boxes for moving into Mom and Dad's house while I gathered up my things for moving out.

In a way, we must have thought that by not seeing each other and not talking about it, we could pretend that nothing

happened. We could make it disappear. But someone didn't
want things to disappear, and that was Gloria.

On a Sunday afternoon, she showed up at our parents'
house with her sons, the younger boy pale from what his mom
was saying and accusing us of, while the older boy stood in the
foyer, his hands clenched at his sides.

Gloria stabs her fingernail at me, her nails that were once
carefully manicured, but bitten off, and screams, "She's lying. I
know that Tara is lying. She was in that car when they wrecked.
She didn't get out before it happened. She doesn't want anyone
to know what she did."

I can hardly speak. The Robash family, what's left of them,
is in our home and facing off against us. My sister is there. She
stopped by earlier with Hannah and left her daughter to play in
the other room. She rushed to the front of the house when she
heard them arrive.

Beth's arm presses against me. It's reassurance. It's the
closest we've been to each other in weeks.

"Why would Tara do that?" Beth says. "Why would she lie?
You saw the state of the car. How could she be in a wreck like
that and only come out with a bruised jaw—a bruised jaw that
*your* husband gave to her, by the way. What kind of a monster
would do that to her?"

The older boy, Eli, hunches forward, but his mother holds
out her arm and warns him to stand back. Dad does the same to
Beth.

But the younger Robash son, the quieter one, Patrick,
cowers by the door. It's written all over his face that he's terrified, he doesn't want to be here, but they've forced him to come.
He's hurting too. He doesn't know what to believe.

Gloria throws a cold glance at my parents. "Did you know
that your daughter was fooling around with my husband for
months before he died? That she seduced him, that Hank gave

in to her?" she cries. "*Tara* did this to us. *He* did this to us. They broke our family apart."

A knot reaches my throat. Never did I think that Gloria would say this in front of my parents, let alone her own children. What the hell is she thinking? What could she possibly gain by doing this?

But Gloria is too full of hate. She's been betrayed, and there is no opportunity to make Hank suffer. She will make everyone else suffer instead.

"Mrs. Robash, that's not what happened..." I say, but I stop. Because that *is* what happened. I'm lying about everything.

I peer to my sister for help, but her eyes prompt me as if to say, *Tara, you've got to handle this part. I did the rest.*

"Mrs. Robash—" I begin.

"No." She raises her hand to me. "I don't want to hear it. The two of you, it makes me sick. It had been going on for months. And I caught you. I saw the two of you together and you didn't deny it. Neither of you did. You drove Hank."

"I didn't drive—"

"You knew that he wanted to end things, including the money. The money would stop, and you got angry. You wanted to punish him. You wrecked your car. You put him in the driver's seat, and that's when you left."

My mom gasps. My dad swings his eyes to me, then back to Gloria. But I'm spinning with what she just said. Gloria knows about the money.

She must have been digging. Since Hank's death, she's gone through their records, their bank accounts, and it turns out Hank wasn't as clever as he thought. There will be cash withdrawals she can't account for and the dates will curiously line up with all the times that Hank would suddenly announce he had to run errands.

Dad says, "Gloria, I know this is a lot, and we know you're upset. We're so sorry for your loss. For what happened to Hank.

But let's not forget what he did to my daughter. He punched her, and I don't care if it was because he was drunk. He abandoned her on the side of the road. He was out of his mind—"

"She deserved it!" Gloria shrieks. "She deserved all of it. She's sneaky." She jabs her finger again. My mom lets out a cry and grips my arm so tightly.

Gloria quiets now. "Isn't it strange, Tara, how the car caught on fire? You sideswiped a telephone pole and went down a hill, but that impact shouldn't have been enough for the car to burst into flames. They think Hank might have been alive before the flames hit. My God..." And she staggers when she says this. "Can you imagine? What was he thinking? How scared he must have been." She wipes at her eyes as she struggles to regain her composure. "I just don't understand how it happened. It doesn't make any sense. You didn't crash into a tree. The engine wasn't crumpled."

"We don't know," Dad tells her. "Tara's car was old. She had it since high school. Something happened."

"The car caught on fire, but Tara came out with hardly a scratch?"

"Which is all the more reason we know she wasn't in the wreck," Dad says.

"I don't believe it." She glares at me. "I never thought it would be you, Tara. I never would have guessed in a million years that he would sink so low. I mean, can you believe it?" She snaps her eyes to my parents. "And to think you had no clue either. They did this to us, and right under our noses. My Hank, and your daughter."

Dad drops his arm. "I think you need to leave, Gloria. Please go. Leave your sons out of this and take them home." He ushers them toward the door.

But Gloria removes a phone from her purse, and I'd recognize it anywhere—it's Hank's.

"I have every text message," she says. "Everything that was

sent between Hank and Tara, the lies they've told. The number of times they've met up. I've pulled everything from our phone records, and it's proof. Proof they were up to something."

"That's not true," Dad says. But when he looks at me, his eyes waver. "Tara would never."

"I wouldn't," I insist.

"You wouldn't do what, Tara?" Gloria asks. "Leave him to die? Or have an affair with a married man?" She waves the phone at my parents. "I can show you everything." She nods at her sons. "They've read every message. They know what they were up to and the things they said to each other." I shudder at what she's done to her sons, how she's exposed them to something they shouldn't have to know. She's dragging their father's name through the mud. She wants payback so badly.

"The amount of money Hank gave you," Gloria continues, "that's *our* money. The boys' money. You used him, Tara, and then you left him."

"No," I cry. "I wouldn't—"

"We're telling the cops." The older son, Eli, speaks up. His glare hasn't stopped since they entered the house, his jaw locked tight. He's grown so much over the years, they both have.

*Donuts for the boys*, Hank said. *They made honor roll again.*

He was always so proud of them.

Eli tells me, "We told the cops what you did. That you left him on purpose. They promised to look into it. This case isn't closed." He sneers at Beth. "And we know about you too, that you helped your sister, that you're covering up for her. You're also responsible."

Dad's voice booms. "I said that you need to leave. I will not stand here and listen to you say these things in our home."

The younger brother, Patrick, backs for the door.

But Eli says, "You have everyone fooled, Tara. But for not for much longer. I promise you that."

"I said, *leave*," Dad repeats.

They turn for the door, but Gloria says, "You will both pay for what you've done." She glares at my sister and me. "Mark my words." And she stomps down the porch, her sons trailing behind her, Patrick hanging his head while Eli shoots us a long, hateful look. He gets into the car and slams the door.

We listen to the spin-out of gravel as Gloria takes off down the road. I hold my breath and don't release it until I know they're gone.

No one moves. No one says a word.

My sister steals a glance to see how I'm holding up, but it's not good. I'm shaking, and I can't stop shaking. The tears roll down my face.

"What on earth just happened?" Mom asks. She looks at me, nervousness etched in her eyes. "What is she talking about?" She gazes at the floor, a spot on the rug, until she peers at me again. "What she said about you and Hank? It's not true, is it? It's not true, right, Tara?"

Just the fact that she asks, the sheer horror of what Gloria revealed to my parents, and I burst into tears. My shame is enough to provide my parents with an answer.

Mom turns away. She can't comprehend it—she doesn't want to comprehend it. She says something about checking on Hannah, and she leaves the room.

Dad turns away from us too. At the entrance of the hall, he slides me a look that's enough to kill me. The tears sting my eyes. I see it in his face: the very beginning of doubt.

When he reaches his office, Dad slams the door, just like Eli. And when he does, a family photo on the living wall crashes to the floor, the glass splitting a harsh line across the picture. The crack is so deep, it's impossible to see our faces.

# TWENTY-ONE

Present

Detective Gillespie allows me a moment to catch my breath. But he doesn't let me rest for long.

"It's a wild story," he says. "What Gloria Robash claimed. But it never held up, did it? The police said that Hank died when he crashed your car."

"That's right."

"I know this is difficult and it's a lot to dig back up, but there's something else that you and I need to talk about. It's what I mentioned earlier. About finding your fingerprints in the system."

It was only a matter of time before we would come back to that.

"Like you mentioned, your parents pressed charges about you breaking into their house. Your parents no longer wanted you living there, so why is that, Ms. Jenkins? Why didn't they want you in the house?"

"I was moving into an apartment."

"But they didn't want you to visit."

"It was complicated."

"It appears a lot about your life is complicated."

I bristle with his comment, and he tries again.

"What did you do that made them change their locks?"

My eyes lift to the ceiling.

"Did you find what you were looking for?"

His question is way too close to home, and I tell myself not to answer.

"Ms. Jenkins," he says, "it's time we talk about your parents. The night they died. You have got to tell me what happened."

Thirteen years ago

After Gloria's visit with her sons, our family went through a dark time. The suspicion was more than enough already, but Gloria was on a rampage and she went so far as to print every one of our text messages with logged times of our calls. She left them in a manila folder for my parents to find on their doorstep. There was no denying the affair now.

I went off the deep end for a while. Guilt will do that to a person. A desperate need for money will have a huge effect on a person too.

I lost my job at the hotel. I was having trouble sleeping—waking constantly to nightmares of Hank screaming, the car on fire, the look in my sister's eyes as she held that lighter—and I was late to work one too many times before they let me go. And there went that promotion. To this day, I still don't know if Hank planned on speaking to management. He probably lied about that from the beginning.

I found a job waiting tables at a diner that mostly served farmers and truckers passing through the area. The tips were measly, the coffee always smelled burned, and I hated every second of it. But I couldn't pull myself together to find anything else, and I was falling way behind on rent. I was weeks away from my roommates telling me they could no longer front me the money, and I couldn't blame them. I would have to move out, but to where? I ended up crashing on friends' couches instead.

Dad had a difficult time talking to me. It must have been excruciating to show up to work every day, at the office he ran, while word got about Hank being with his daughter. The car accident, my involvement with him, including the rumors that Gloria kept spreading.

Mom didn't know what to think. She asked me to stay away from the house for a while. *Just until things calm down*, she said. Her request that morning was devastating in itself.

I slunk away... and in time, I got desperate. Incredibly tight on cash, and with the weight of the world seemingly against me, the accusation in other people's eyes when they saw me, I was reckless. I created my own downward spiral, my own worst enemy.

Whether or not Beth struggled as much as I did, she didn't let it show, at least not to me. She said she was busy with art commissions and was finishing packing up the house.

And then came the phone call—several phone calls, to be exact. I had no idea if my parents and sister received the same calls too, but I should have guessed. I should have asked. My parents could have explained things, a warning that would have removed the ridiculous idea from my head. But as it turns out, I was the only one in our family to fall for it, what the person on the other end of the line was asking. I was the only one to sink so low as to consider their proposal. I was the only one that desperate.

And it seemed harmless at first. They said they were from a commercial development company and wanted me to find a specific document. Perhaps it was in my dad's home office, they prodded, and would I take a look around and send them a copy?

It would be easy, they said, and the result would earn me a cash reward. That was pretty much all I needed to hear.

I went to my parents' house on a day when I knew they wouldn't be home. But to my surprise, they came back early. They caught me digging around in Dad's office.

After my parents pressed charges, Beth was the one who bailed me out. But she told me not to come home, that our parents were too upset and planned on changing the locks. They were appalled that I would consider taking the deed to our parents' farm and would send it to someone with possibly disastrous motives. They didn't think I would put our family in such jeopardy.

If I thought that was the moment I hit rock bottom, I was wrong. Because it got much worse.

I was sitting at a bar, belly up to the counter, and feeling sorry for myself as I accepted one too many Fireball shots from someone—to be fair, he offered, and the least I could do was accept the free liquor. With his wallet held out and his attempts at sweet talk, he thought he could score. But I had other plans, and I told him I wanted to go home. I would go home alone.

By then, I'd scraped together enough money for a second-hand truck. It was a stick-shift that I had trouble driving, which was only made worse when I was drunk. But I had to get to work every day and my beloved Toyota was a melted heap smashed into a cube somewhere in a junkyard.

I was drunk and I must have been on autopilot because when I left the bar, I turned on Route 30 like I'd done a thousand times before. I drove to the end of the road, my foot pressed hard on the accelerator until I reached my parents' driveway.

But that's where my memory ends. I don't remember a thing that came after.

·  ·  ·

Hours later, I woke up outside, flat on my face and in the middle of my parents' front yard. The sun was out, and an oppressive heat blanketed me, the dirt beneath me, as the sweat seeped into my shirt. My mouth felt like it had been filled with sand.

Paramedics hovered as I blinked slowly, my head foggy, while another team rushed inside the house to help my parents. They were still in their beds. My sister called emergency services around 8 a.m. when she couldn't get through to our mom. She needed her to take care of Hannah while she worked, but Beth was worried when no one answered and she called 9-1-1. Emergency responders reached the house before she did. And even though they were quick, there was nothing they could do to do help. The medical examiner said Mom and Dad had been dead for at least six hours.

My truck was left at the entrance to my parents' driveway. That's as far as I'd gotten because, apparently, I slammed into their mailbox, ditched the car, and ran for the house. But how did I get in? And how could I have unlocked the door when they'd replaced the locks? There was no sign of forced entry, and the paramedics found me passed out on the grass. The police said they didn't think I went inside.

But Beth does. To my horror, she accused me of breaking in and stumbling around. She thinks I walked back out, but not before I did something first.

With my truck wrecked, she thinks I went into our parents' garage and started the engine so I could take their car instead. But for whatever reason, I changed my mind, or forgot, or I was too drunk to know what I was doing, and I left. But when I did, I left the car running. And with our parents asleep and unaware of anything that was happening, they breathed in the carbon monoxide that filled the air, a silent, deadly killer that seeped from the garage and filled the house. Our parents never woke up.

That's what my sister told the police when they questioned her. The betrayal nearly destroyed me. Only months earlier, Beth stood by my side and asked me to cover up for what we did to Hank, something so vicious that it continues to haunt me in my dreams, our secret hanging over us like a black cloud. Our once sisterly bond broke and I never told a soul. I kept quiet like she asked me to. United in our fear, we told ourselves we could never go to prison, that no one could ever know what we did.

But as much as I hated Hank, I would have saved him. I would have pulled him out of that car. I would have called for the paramedics and waited for them to arrive. When Beth set the fire, I would have pulled him from the vehicle if she hadn't tackled me to the ground.

But it was my sister's idea not to move, and we watched him burn.

And after all that, Beth turned on me. With the death of our parents and the guilt she must have felt after Hank's death, she fell into some sort of despair—a despair she disguised from everyone. And in my anguish, I watched her do a complete one-eighty in her emotions toward me. She blamed me for our parents' deaths. And in the days and weeks that followed, her reaction became eerily similar to the way Gloria Robash was blaming me for Hank's death too.

I've tried to understand. And over the years, I've learned that grief can make people say and do the most horrendous things. Their reactions become unhinged, unexplainable. They are desperately trying to make sense when nothing in the world does anymore. And in order to protect themselves, to not face what they have done, they will point their anger on someone else. I think it's easier that way. *No, I'm not the monster. You are.*

I was still drunk when they tested my blood alcohol content and the doctors said that explained my blackout. I didn't have a key to the house and the police determined that my parents were asleep and never let me in.

So who started the car? Who let the engine run in our parents' garage?

Paramedics found Dad in bed with his shoes on—not house slippers but the brown leather Oxfords he wore to work. He was also wearing a dress shirt that he had buttoned to the top. It was as if he'd gotten up in the middle of the night and thought he was heading to the office. But despite the dress shirt and shoes, he kept his pajama pants on. Meanwhile, they don't think our mother stirred and slept through everything.

One of Mom's friends came forward several days later and said that Mom had been getting increasingly worried about our dad. He had been sleepwalking again, and it's something I remember him doing when we were kids—going to the kitchen to make coffee at 3 a.m. or standing in the hall and having a conversation to no one on the phone but a dial tone.

There were other instances too, and Mom would usher Dad back to bed every time, not wanting to frighten us. As we got older, his sleepwalking episodes reduced until they had pretty much stopped, and my parents thought that was the end of it. But in the weeks following Hank's death, with the stress surrounding everything that was happening, and the rumors about me, Dad's sleep disruptions must have returned.

Mom said that Dad was sleepwalking once or twice a week, sometimes more. She would find him outside staring aimlessly at the sky, or he'd be searching the house for his car keys and wallet.

The police said that Dad was sleepwalking, he got himself half-dressed, went to the garage, started the engine, but returned to bed. He kept his dress shoes on and settled himself beneath the covers, not realizing the house was filling with poisonous gas fumes that would kill them both.

Our parents' deaths were ruled a tragedy, and their funeral was massive. People from all over town came to pay their respects, including Dad's employees from work. My sister and I sat in the same pew at the church, but not together. If anyone noticed how much Beth was avoiding me, they didn't say anything. The wake was a blur with people coming up to us, a slow-motion roll of mournful faces, friends and neighbors clutching our hands and telling us how sorry they were. Everyone showed up to the service except for the Robashes, but I doubt anyone could blame them. I certainly didn't want to see them there either.

By that point, I could hardly stand to be in the same room as my sister, and she could scarcely be around me either. The words she uttered, the accusation in her voice about me being so drunk that I would hurt our parents, and I was devastated.

When Mr. Fredericks read our parents' will a few days later, Beth flinched, but didn't seem at all surprised. It was like she'd already been given a heads-up, either by our parents when they updated their wills months earlier, or the attorney had told her in advance. It was our parents' wish to protect the farm and surrounding property, and that by taking certain precautions they would protect it from me. Everything would be entrusted to my sister.

Beth didn't apologize for our parents' decision. Even worse, she said she would uphold their wishes. Cast off, and cut off, I returned to the farm days later and begged for Beth's forgiveness. I asked if there was a way we could work things out, and explained repeatedly that I hadn't gone inside that house. It was impossible for me to enter.

She and Hannah had already moved in, and I watched Hannah play on the front porch. But my sister wouldn't listen. She didn't want to talk. When she opened the door and asked me to leave, she said, *Both of us have done enough.*

It's taken me years to think about the words my sister said to me, the way Beth had phrased it. *Both of us.*

It's only now that I realize what she meant. She always included herself in the blame too.

. . .

It takes a while for me to say anything else to Detective Gillespie.

His voice returns, a distant echo. "Ms. Jenkins, are you all right?"

*No, I'm not all right,* I want to tell him. I'm devastated, and I can't stop crying. He's made me relive a part of my past that I've tried hard not to think about.

"I appreciate what you shared with me, Ms. Jenkins. I really do. I know that was a lot to go through. And I'm truly sorry about what happened to your parents. It was a tragedy. A horrible accident." He pauses. "But I've also uncovered details regarding other activities that were going on around the same time. It was before your parents died. The phone calls you received. It wasn't just you, but the phone calls were made to everyone in your family."

I know that, but I stay silent.

"Your parents listed the reason for why you broke into their home. They said you weren't able to grab a certain document, but they didn't want to take any chances, so they changed the locks."

"I wasn't planning on doing whatever it was they think I was doing," I mumble. "I wouldn't have let it get that far."

"But you were curious."

"Yes, I was curious."

"It's interesting," he says, "how the Robashes are playing back into all of this, don't you think? All these years later?" My breath cuts short. "They may have tried to get back at your family at the time... and now they're possibly trying again? Why didn't you tell me any of this before?" he asks.

"Which part?"

"About the Robashes."

"You know about the Robashes."

"No, I mean, everything else that happened. Should I be looking into Gloria Robash surrounding your sister's death?"

The blood rushes to my ears... to hear him say her name and anything that has to do with Beth has me dizzy.

"Do you think it's possible she sent you that note card?" he repeats. "Ms. Jenkins?"

"No, I don't think that will be necessary," I tell him.

"And why is that?"

"Because Gloria Robash is dead."

# TWENTY-TWO

Gloria Robash died of a heart attack three years ago while playing golf at a retirement community somewhere outside of Hilton Head, North Carolina. She was wearing a white visor and her friends said she seemed to be fine, but at the tenth hole, she collapsed. Her heart gave out. I don't know why I hang onto those details, but I do. On her Facebook page, where her settings are left open to the public, I read the outpouring of condolences after her death, the tributes that kept on coming, how much everyone loved her. She'd only moved from Louisville the year before.

Gloria Robash is gone. But two other family members remain: her sons, Eli and Patrick.

The detective ends the call telling me he will look up whatever information he can find on the Robash sons. I'm completely drained, but I force myself to return to Facebook. It's time I look up Eli Robash's account.

He's still living in Louisville, Kentucky, and it doesn't appear that much has changed since the last time I checked his profile even though that was several years ago. Naively, I thought the threat was over and time had moved on. But how naïve it was of me to assume that Eli would have forgotten. Rage over a loved one's death can burn for a very long time, and trust me, I know.

Eli is older now, and his hair has darkened over the years. He's not the blond I remember from high school, that last time I saw him at our house. But he still has those piercing green eyes, and in each picture, he smiles in that same cocky way like his father.

Eli's latest post features him at a cocktail party alongside his wife. She's dressed nicely, despite the gaudy bauble jewelry she wears around her neck, and he's wearing a suit and tie. I've learned that Eli is successful, and so is his younger brother. The two of them went into business together after college and they run a construction company with a strong interest in buying and selling land for future development. Hank would have been so proud of his boys.

Eli has a son and a daughter himself, both toddlers based on the photos he uploaded last weekend. He must have his hands full running a full-time business while raising a family, but he seems confident enough, happy enough. His grin says he's someone who yearns to be important, who wants so much to be a promising and effective business leader while he can also make a difference. But I see right through him: he wants to make boatloads of money too.

As for Patrick, I still don't find much about him since he doesn't post on social media and he seems to keep to himself. Smart man. What little I find is always company-related, and even then, he prefers to remain in the background, and that sounds about right. From what I remember, Patrick was always the quieter, more reserved sibling while his older brother was louder and more brash. More threatening too.

Eli harassed us for weeks after his father died. Even after his mom dropped off that packet to my parents with our printed text messages, Eli wanted to go further. It wasn't enough, and he wanted to frighten me, Beth too. He became the Robash family henchman.

Eli showed up once at the diner where I worked, and I nearly dropped the food tray. He said, "What goes around, comes around," while Patrick tugged on his arm and begged him to leave. He told him they could eat somewhere else, and he pulled his brother out the door.

At the end of my shift, I would spot Eli waiting for me in the parking lot. But he always stayed in his car. Presence known, his intimidation received. It was effective. Another time, he watched me walk up and down the aisles of the grocery store as he leaned against his shopping cart. When I finally gathered the nerve to confront him, his cart was abandoned in the produce section.

Beth said he was doing the same thing to her, and that she would simply glare back. But when he waited outside a park where Hannah was playing, that rattled her at how close he was to her daughter, the lengths he would go to intimidate them.

Eli Robash. All these years later, is he the one who burned down Beth's house?

*Strike a match and the flames get closer.*

The words he said to me at the diner: *What goes around, comes around.*

Karma. Revenge. The words are interchangeable depending on your perspective, however you want to justify things.

Eli still believes that I killed his father, that I left him to die. He believes that Beth helped me too. Does this mean he went after my sister first? She was closer. She was in Louisville and would have been a much easier target. After the fire, he sent that card in the mail to let me know I was next.

It's time to pick up the girls from school, and I'm exhausted. Thank you, Detective Gillespie, for putting me through the ringer and reopening years of painful wounds.

I knock back two Tylenol and, just in case, an ibuprofen before I head out the door.


I collect Cassie first, and she's in the backseat, halfway through a story about a fight that went down at recess, but I'm half-listening. I'm unable to stop thinking about what the detective said and trying not to let my daughter see my hands shake.

We pick up Hannah next and seeing her after her first day of school fills me with nervous anticipation. Did she do okay? Did she get lost among a sea of students? Does she absolutely hate it here?

We find her standing alone. She's on the phone. Her head is turned away and she doesn't see us coming.

We wait patiently. I don't want to honk—that would mortify her, Cassie too—so we wait. I hope she'll eventually turn and see my car, and she does, pocketing her phone and walking toward us.

"Everything okay?"

"A friend of mine from home." She climbs into the front seat.

"Any weird calls?"

"What weird calls?" Cassie asks.

"It's nothing, sweetheart. Just these *Unknown* numbers that came in after we activated Hannah's phone." I don't mention that I received the same calls too.

"No other calls," Hannah answers.

We pull away from the parking lot. "So? How was it?"

She shrugs. "It was okay, I guess?" But it's more like a question, and I wait to see if she'll say anything else. "I found my classes okay. They assigned me a student aide which was awkward at first, but it eventually helped. At least I know one person in school."

"You'll meet more," I tell her. "Just give it time."

"What did you think of the cafeteria?" Cassie pipes up. "Isn't it massive? I told you it would be massive." I swear that's all my daughter thinks about when it comes to high school: the meal plan and the soccer program.

"It is... big," Hannah says, and she giggles, which makes my daughter giggle too.

"Are your classes up to par with what you were doing with homeschool?" I ask.

"I think so. I mean, from what I can tell, at least. I've already missed the first two months of the semester so I'm trying to pick up where they are. It's different from what I was doing. But we'll see."

"Okay," I say. "It'll sync up, I'm sure."

"We'll see," she repeats with another nonchalant shrug. She falls quiet before she says, "Hey, Cassie, I was listening to people talk about the sports teams. I might try out for soccer in the spring." She turns to Cassie. "Maybe I could give it another shot?"

Cassie's face lights up. "That would be awesome. We can watch your games and cheer you on and—"

"I doubt I'll start," Hannah says. "It's been a while and I'm really out of shape."

"So? You never know. It'll be fun either way. Oh, I can't wait." Cassie talks the rest of the way home, providing Hannah with a rundown on the team uniforms, what she's heard about the coach, the tournaments and practice schedule. They can work out in preparation for tryouts, and she is so psyched by this that it warms my heart to see Hannah smiling in response.

This is progress and Hannah could really be starting to enjoy it here. She'll meet new friends and maybe earn a spot on the team. Things could go well for us.

As soon as we're home the girls, once again, disappear to Hannah's room. The soccer conversation hasn't let up, and the door closes, their voices muffled as I hear the squeak of the bed. They're in their private club again, their girls' club, which suits me fine because all I want to do is lie down on the couch and take a nap. I want to curl into a ball and sleep for a thousand years. I will lie here and close my eyes...

I must doze off because about an hour later, Cassie texts me from Hannah's room. The buzz in my pocket startles me awake and I pat at my jeans to pull out my phone.

*Mom, we're hungry. What's for dinner?*

And so it begins: we are texting to communicate with each other when I'm only down the hall.

I'm tempted to order delivery again, I'm that tired. But those damn delivery fees and the extra surcharges, and I force myself to rise from the couch.

Sandwiches perhaps? Or maybe a simple pasta? But even boiling water sounds overwhelming at the moment. I dig around the pantry, hoping to find something else, when I see a car moving past our house—their slow speed is what catches my attention. It's like they're searching for the right place, or they're casing us.

The hairs on my neck rise.

When I looked up Eli on Facebook, he posted that photo of himself and his wife, but that was earlier in the week. Since then, he's had time. He's had more than enough time to drive to Alabama.

I creep to the window and stand back, not wanting to be seen. I check out the car.

The vehicle is dark, maybe a charcoal gray, four-door. Some

type of sedan. The brake lights light up. They've gone too far and they're backing up. They back up slowly until they're in front of my house, and that's when I see an arm rise, the long sleeve of a burgundy suit. The driver, a woman, lifts her hand. She's holding a phone and taking a picture.

I stop in my tracks, and instantly jump to the side. She drives off.

The burgundy suit of Ms. Elstein from Child Services. Did she come back to meet Hannah? I told her she would be home after school.

But why didn't she stop? She has that single photo of my house.

# TWENTY-THREE

Friday

It's another day of the girls hurrying for school while I'm barely able to move through the motions. We sat down to a pasta dinner but only after I called Mr. Fredericks so he could confirm the name of the Child Services worker assigned to Hannah's case. There was no answer, and it was after hours, which meant everyone must have already left the office. To my frustration, I don't have his cell number.

Ms. Elstein is legit, I keep telling myself. She is real, there's no reason for her not to be. She took a photo because it's something to include in our file: the state of our home. Like she said, we live in a nice enough neighborhood and it's safe for kids.

But what about the burned mark on the sidewalk outside? The evidence of a fire? The fear this must have caused for Hannah.

Before we went to bed, I showed the girls how to set the alarm. I could tell Cassie wanted to ask questions, but she took her cue from Hannah and nodded. They listened carefully.

I thought the alarm would buy me some peace, but it hasn't.

Not even the sleep meds I down each night stop me from getting up countless times to check the alarm. The light glows red. No one has tampered with it.

In the morning, the first thing I notice is Cassie's hair. She's wearing it down, which is something she doesn't normally do. At the kitchen table, she chews quickly through a Clif Bar, her glass of juice in hand. But long gone is the high ponytail and black rubber band. With her hair past her shoulders, she looks so much like Hannah.

I also catch a whiff of the Victoria's Secret perfume Hannah bought at the mall. The scent is undeniable, the sticky sweetness that encapsulates teen youth. The scent layers in my mouth like tufts of cotton candy. My daughter's lips are glossy too, not overly done, but a sign she has used her cousin's lip gloss. She is careful not to waste any on the glass of juice she brings to her mouth.

The coffee pot steams, and I'm finally able to pour a mug and head to the privacy of my room. Retrieving my phone, I dial the detective's number, but my call goes straight to voicemail. I leave a message and ask for confirmation about Child Services. I don't mention the drive-by from Ms. Elstein yet.

I know I'm being paranoid. I'm sleep deprived. I convince myself that Ms. Elstein will contact me later today and set up an appointment with Hannah. I'm worrying over nothing.

I text Cynthia next. It's been far too long, and I should have already told her what's happening. She's called several times to check on me, and while I wanted to tell her about Hannah and the latest on the police investigation, something else has been on my mind. Something critical.

*Will you come by later today? I need to see you.*

Her response returns almost immediately. *You know I will. I'll bring wine.*

I decide to tell her about Hannah via text. It's not fair that I'm unloading this to her in such a way, but it's the best I can muster right now. I need to give her the heads-up for when she arrives, for when she will see Hannah. After that, we can go over every detail.

*I'm taking care of my niece, Hannah. I have full custody now.*

It takes Cynthia a full thirty seconds to respond. The three dots dance across the screen before disappearing, then returning. I'm almost positive she wants to dial my number and get to the heart of what's going on—this is life-changing news. But Cynthia doesn't push. She never pushes, and that's one of the things I love most about her.

*I'll see you this afternoon*, she responds. *I'll bring two bottles.*

I spend the next few hours in a haze. With the girls dropped off at school, I sit on the couch and wait for either Detective Gillespie or Mr. Fredericks to return my calls. I consider going to the office to check up on work, but my efforts would be wasted there. I can't focus; my mind is too all over the place, not to mention I look like a wreck.

I'm so jumpy that I actually cry out when a notification dings on my phone. It's an incoming email from Carl Fredericks' office with a note from one of his staff members that Mr. Fredericks apologizes for not returning my calls. He has a busy day lined up in court. They ask that I see the message that has been forwarded from Child Services.

The email is from Ms. Morgan Elstein, and it's a follow-up to Mr. Fredericks based on her home visit with me. She's keeping the attorney in the loop, which seems odd, and I'm not sure if that's standard protocol, but it's a relief to know that she's real. This is confirmation that she's legit. She's not casing our house. She hasn't been hired by Eli Robash to take us out.

To my extended relief, she also mentions that she took photos of our neighborhood and exterior of our home to include in the file, a way to demonstrate the safe environment where Hannah is living. I scroll through the rest of the email thread and find where Ms. Elstein initially included Hannah's school transcript. She said that she would be reaching out to me, which she has.

I sink into the sofa. For the first time in days, my heartbeat calms a little—but only a little—because Detective Gillespie is returning my call.

"I looked into Gloria Robash," he says. "She's deceased, like you said. I also looked into her sons, but they have alibis for Friday. They were attending a conference in Louisville. The younger brother, Patrick, was leading a panel discussion at the time the fire was set."

"And Eli?"

"That's what's interesting. Eli Robash showed up to the panel discussion late. His car was caught on security video leaving the hotel, the location of the conference. He returned hours later."

*What goes around, comes around*, Eli said.

"He claims he had another meeting. We have confirmation that it took place at a downtown coffee shop, but there's a two-hour window after that where we haven't been able to lock down his location. He says he drove around for a while before he returned to the conference. He was checking on other properties, but that hasn't been confirmed. The hotel security camera shows him returning to the garage just as his brother's presentation was beginning."

"That two-hour window," I ask, "is that when my sister's fire could have been set?"

"Yes, we think so."

"So you've spoken to him? Eli Robash is still in town?"

"Yes."

The knots in my stomach release somewhat. It's a relief to know he's there, and not closing in on Alabama.

"And he talked to you willingly?" I ask.

"He cooperated with us, if that's what you mean. But again, I'm sharing these details with you because I need you to be aware. I want us to work together. So, tell me, Ms. Jenkins. Do you think there's a chance Eli Robash would leave the conference and set fire to your sister's house? Could he be behind all this?"

"Yes," I answer him, finally. "There is the possibility."

"We'll need proof, of course, but that's the direction my investigation is starting to head also. We've asked him to come back and answer a few more questions."

Eli Robash... and I cower with the thought of Eli, now a grown man, driving to my sister's house to avenge his dead father. Why did he wait thirteen years to get back at us for what we've done? Something new must have prompted him.

"There's something else," the detective says. "That meeting that Eli went to, the one at the coffee shop? He was meeting with Mr. Chandler."

I sit straight up. That's very interesting.

That night, Hannah ran to the Chandlers for help, and they cared for her. They offered to drive her to Decatur so she could be with me. They've always been so kind.

When Mr. Chandler sat down for that meeting, did he know what Eli Robash was thinking? Did he have any idea he would go to my sister's place and set it on fire?

*It's what the Chandlers told me*, Hannah said.

They think it's my fault what happened to her grandparents. Just like the Robashes, the Chandlers have spent years blaming me too.

. . .

The school car pickup line is different today. Hannah is no longer standing alone, but she has Mrs. Carlisle, the school registrar, beside her. My first thought is that something has happened. My second thought is, but wouldn't I have already received a phone call?

When I pull up, Mrs. Carlisle motions for me to roll down the window. "Do you mind parking?" she asks. On her face she wears a smile, but it's tight. Her eyes slide to Hannah before they return to me.

I crane my neck to get a read of Hannah's face, but her expression is blank.

I find a parking spot and Mrs. Carlisle crosses the pedestrian path to meet us. But Hannah remains on the sidewalk. She doesn't follow, and I can't tell if it's because the school registrar told her to remain put, or she simply doesn't want to hear whatever is about to be repeated.

Cassie pops her head up from the backseat, but Mrs. Carlisle asks if I can step out of the car so that we can speak privately. The pit in my stomach grows bigger.

"What's going on?" Cassie asks.

"Give me a sec." I unbuckle my seatbelt.

Mrs. Carlisle stands away from the car, and it's enough distance to ensure that Cassie won't overhear us. She also keeps her back to Hannah.

"Ms. Jenkins, I'm sorry to talk to you like this but I thought it best that we speak in person." She glances over her shoulder at my niece. "We caught Hannah smoking in the girls' bathroom."

"What?" That is not at all what I imagined Mrs. Carlisle was about to say.

Hannah... smoking? But I haven't detected anything in her behavior to make me suspect this. And where did she get the cigarette? My niece stares sheepishly at the ground.

"Other girls," Mrs. Carlisle explains. "Hannah tells me she was trying to make new friends and they offered her one in the bathroom. All the girls are in trouble, it's not just Hannah. They were sent to silent lunch and in-class detention. And, of course, we have to notify their parents." She frowns. "But the reason we didn't call you is because there's something else."

And now I'm really worried. Hannah must have had an outburst. She cried in class. She was thinking about her mother. I've pushed her too hard and going back to school this soon was a mistake. Even Ms. Elstein from Child Services had seemed surprised.

But that's not what Mrs. Carlisle says. "She's doing poorly in her classes. I know it's only the second day, but I checked in with the teachers, and they're baffled as to her level of understanding. For as advanced as her classes were in homeschool, she doesn't seem to understand the material at all. She doesn't know where to begin."

Confusion makes its way across my forehead. "What do you mean?"

"Hannah doesn't have the first clue in honors chemistry. And I'm not saying that she was overwhelmed or couldn't pick up where they were in class, but it's as if the material is foreign to her, like she's never taken an honors class in her life, and that's the same in her advanced trigonometry class too."

I slide a look at Hannah, who continues to stare at the ground.

"She was unable to work in the lab," Mrs. Carlisle continues. "She turned in a blank page with nothing answered. She said she didn't understand the material." She stops and studies me for a moment. "Are we sure her school records are accurate?"

I laugh at the absurdity. She's kidding, right?

I also shrink at what she's implying.

"Wait, you think they're fake?"

She appears flustered. "No. I think that would be a very difficult thing to do. The homeschool association keeps exceptional records so it would be impossible for them to send something that had been doctored. They'd have no reason to pad her grades. But... that doesn't mean that her documents weren't altered at home. They could have been altered by the student... or a parent, let's say..." She raises her eyebrows.

The heat flushes to my cheeks. "Are you trying to tell me that my sister and niece cheated and turned in somebody else's work?"

Mrs. Carlisle lifts her hands. "Look, I'm only thinking out loud here. It's just that she's not performing the way her records implied she would. She should know the material inside and out, Ms. Jenkins, and she does not."

I cross my arms. I'm defensive of my niece, but I'm also defensive about what Mrs. Carlisle is suggesting about my sister.

I shake my head. "No, you've got this all wrong. Hannah needs time. She's been through a lot, and everything is new and overwhelming."

"Absolutely. And I agree with you, it's early days. We understand that Hannah is going through severe trauma, something that none of us could comprehend. Perhaps she's not ready? Perhaps a counselor would help? I don't believe our in-house counselor could—"

"No, it's okay. Child Services is putting me in touch with a therapist who specializes in cases like hers. And you're right. She's endured trauma that none of us could understand, let alone cope with. Maybe her mind has gone blank. It's going to take some time, and a lot of healing." I lift my eyes. "But there *is* some good news. Something she mentioned yesterday."

"Oh?"

"She used to play soccer with her homeschool. She mentioned maybe trying out for the high school team, and I think that's a good sign, don't you? She wants so badly to acclimate, and that may explain the cigarettes. She wants to fit in. But let's hope the therapy helps and she can settle in better. I think what she really needs is time."

"Absolutely," Mrs. Carlisle repeats. "And that's exactly what we hope for too. If she wants to try out for extracurriculars, that sounds wonderful. But regarding her schoolwork, let's move her to traditional classes for the time being, okay? In a few weeks, we can reassess and consider moving her back. What do you think?"

I steal another glance at my niece. She looks so small standing there on the sidewalk, alone with her head hanging. She will be devastated by this, embarrassed even. Or maybe it's the right call and we don't need to push her to take on such a difficult curriculum yet.

I nod my agreement. "Okay. That sounds good."

As soon as I say this, Mrs. Carlisle heads for the crosswalk. She waves for Hannah to leave and Hannah gives her a wan smile.

## TWENTY-FOUR

Cassie is at soccer practice when I knock on Hannah's door.

Her voice is quiet. "You can come in, Aunt Tara."

I find her lying on the bed, her thumbs tapping away on her phone. She locks the screen and places it face-down when I sit beside her.

"Can we talk about today? About what Mrs. Carlisle said?" I ask.

"Which part?"

"The smoking first."

She sighs and lifts herself to a sitting position. "I know, it was stupid. I don't know what I was thinking. I was trying to make friends... I didn't want to say no."

"It's a gross habit. Not to mention you got into trouble at school."

"I know," she says again, and tucks her hair behind her ears. "It won't happen again, I promise."

"Okay, that's good. And now, the other part, about your classes. What Mrs. Carlisle told me. Are you doing okay? Do you need more time?"

"No, it's just..." She looks around, flailing for an answer.

"It's just that everything is different. I didn't think it would be, but it is. It's not at all like homeschool. It's not my kitchen table at home, you know? And it's not with Mom. It's all these teachers I don't know, and everyone is so loud. They're halfway through a lesson and I'm trying to catch up. I feel lost right now."

I nod and squeeze her hand, knowing this is absolutely understandable. "Mrs. Carlisle wants to give you some time," I explain. "You're going to drop back to traditional classes for a little while."

"I know." She wipes her eyes. "She already told me. I'll try better next week, Aunt Tara. I really will. You'll see."

"I know you will. No pressure, okay?"

Cynthia sends a text to let me know she's on her way. She's already dropped off her boys at lacrosse practice and has about an hour before she needs to pick them up, but it's enough. It will give me enough time to get through the question I want to ask her.

I fall into her arms as soon as I open the door, and she hugs me tight. How stupid of me not to share everything with her sooner, to think I could handle everything on my own when I didn't have to.

She juggles two bottles of wine in her hands. "I can't drink all of this, especially when I've got to pick up the boys from practice. But I have a feeling you need this more than I do."

I take the bottles from her and usher her inside. She's looking around the living room—she's looking for Hannah, and when she doesn't see her, she drops her voice to a whisper. "Is she here? Is everything okay?"

I suggest we move to the kitchen.

Cynthia wears a blazer over a silk blouse, her lavender skirt flared at the knees. She always looks stylish, especially at work, but today, her face is riddled with concern. Surprise too.

"Why didn't you tell me?" she says, still whispering. "This is a lot, T. You should have let me know."

"I know. It is a lot. But we don't have to whisper."

"Sorry, it's just... I don't want to talk about her if she's in the next room."

"It's okay. She's probably on her phone."

Cynthia doesn't look convinced, and I pour us a glass of wine. We sit at the table where I tell her about Hannah. I explain how I went years without seeing my niece and my sister, and that yet, Beth updated her will to include me as her legal guardian. As horrifying as her death was, I now have a second chance to know Hannah, but I gloss over the details about the police investigation—I'm not ready to go into all of that right now, especially if Hannah is able to overhear us. She doesn't know about the threat that came in the mail or anything about the Robashes.

When I finish, Cynthia remains silent. She hasn't touched her wine, but I have been taking more than enough sips in between my sentences to make up for it. Already, my edges have softened and the warmth spreads to my stomach.

I'm finally ready to ask my friend one of the most important questions of my life.

"Cynthia, if anything were to happen to me, if there was an accident and I was to die, would you... would you take care of the girls?" Her eyes widen as I press on. "I'm redrafting my will, and it's nothing fancy, just a template I found online, but after what happened to my sister, the steps she took to ensure Hannah would be cared for, I know that I need to do the same. I need to list someone for the girls, just in case."

"Yes, of course," she says. "Of course we'll take care of them."

Her answer is a relief, but it doesn't come as a surprise.

Cynthia understands since she has children of her own. She knows that I don't have anyone else.

"Do you want to talk to Erik about it first?" I think about her husband. "You can discuss it first and then get back to me?"

"No. He'll agree, absolutely. He's been worried about you all week. And now with Hannah coming to live with you..." She looks once again to the hall as if Hannah will appear at any second. "We will absolutely do this. But it's not going to be necessary, okay? Nothing is going to happen to you."

Well, that's what Beth thought too.

A rush of air releases from my mouth. "Thank you."

Cynthia's answer, her willingness and understanding about our situation, takes a five-ton weight off my chest, and I feel as if I can breathe again. If anything happens to me, the girls will be okay.

I wonder if it's the same feeling Beth experienced when she updated her will. The peace of mind in knowing she had a backup plan, that it wouldn't be left a mystery with Hannah not knowing where she could go. It's the *just in case* part.

Because the girls are everything to me now. And I am all they have too.

I'm getting ready to pick up Cassie from practice, my hand hovering over the alarm panel, ready to lock Hannah inside, when Cassie sends a text asking if Hannah can join me in the car. She suggests that we do something fun.

*To cheer Hannah up*, she says. *Something happened at school but she doesn't want to talk about it.*

I knock on Hannah's door. Cynthia is gone after a half glass of wine and picking up her boys. I stopped myself from drinking too, knowing that I need to stay on alert. I also need to drive the girls.

Hannah answers with an overwhelming yes when I suggest

Cassie's idea for going out. She doesn't ask where but looks ready to be free from her room and to think about something else.

The girls decide on a visit to Sephora, the makeup store that I've been to once before, but don't shop often. Discount pharmacy makeup for me. The girls are giddy with excitement the moment we step inside, and they walk ahead, arm in arm. Cassie has already slipped her hair out of her ponytail from practice and lets it drop past her shoulders.

Music pumps from the speakers with a techno beat. The girls roam the perfume aisle first, taking turns to spritz fragrances on their wrists, before they find the makeup section. I follow, but not too closely, not wanting to cramp their style.

I hang out in an aisle filled with bath bombs and body scrubs, letting the girls enjoy a mini makeover from one of the saleswomen. Cassie looks as if she could burst from happiness as she studies the dizzying array of eyeshadows and lipsticks. She plucks a cotton ball to sample each color.

With the two of them side by side, they look like sisters. They're even acting like sisters. I wouldn't be surprised if someone assumes that Hannah is my daughter too.

The saleswoman dabs peach blush to Cassie's cheeks while Hannah applies liquid eyeliner to her lids. I step closer to watch. In one fluid motion, she applies the liner like a pro, something I've never been able to master especially when it comes to liquid eyeliner. But with Hannah, there is not a smudge to be seen, and at the corner of each eyelid, she has created a small wing.

"Impressive," the saleswoman says. "You're really good at that. If I'm not careful, you could take my job."

Hannah plays with some of the eyeshadow next, selecting a sheer color that she applies to the crease before she sweeps a highlighter shade at her brow. She admires herself as Cassie reaches for a cotton swab and tries something similar. But the cotton swab fumbles in her hand and she's pushing too hard. Hannah helps her instead.

"Seriously," the saleswoman says, "where did you learn to do all that?"

Hannah shrugs. "Instagram. I've watched a lot of makeup tutorials."

"Well, you're really good."

She's right. Hannah is a makeup pro. Which is strange since she said she barely wears any. All week with us she's worn the tiniest amount of lip gloss.

"There are lot of YouTube videos," Hannah explains. "I like to play around in my room. After you watch them enough times, it helps. I got the hang of it." She adds more blush to her cheeks.

Minutes later, with a shopping bag filled with makeup for Hannah, and extra samples the saleswoman threw in for Cassie's sake, we are paying at the counter, my credit card once again swiped as Cassie happily holds the bag for her cousin.

"Hannah, when we get home, can you teach me?" she asks. "I want a full makeover. That would be so fun."

They are chatting away as we leave the store. And for the first time since picking up Hannah from school, her face has come alive again. She's having fun. The school registrar's concerns and getting into trouble at school, temporarily forgotten.

# TWENTY-FIVE

The girls are in the bathroom, their new makeup tossed on the counter, when a number I don't recognize shows up on my phone. But it doesn't say *Unknown* and my shoulders relax a little.

The person calling is Mrs. Carlisle from school. "I'm sorry," she says as soon as I answer. "I hate to bother you so soon but there's something else I need to tell you."

My heart thumps. What could possibly be next?

"I contacted the Louisville Homeschool Association. After our conversation, I wanted to check on a few things. The woman I talked to was very kind, very knowledgeable. In fact, she remembers Hannah quite well and said she was one of their most promising students. She met her a few times and says she's delightful."

Okay, everything tracks so far.

"She said that it would be highly unlikely for Hannah to have altered her tests or have someone input her information for her. It would be incredibly unlikely that her mother would do this either. Your sister took your niece's education very seriously."

I say, "So that's settled, then?"

"Well, it does help," Mrs. Carlisle admits. "But I still believe it's a good idea to keep her in traditional classes for the next couple of weeks just until she gets used to the classroom setting. The different teaching styles. Our way of doing things."

"But something did give me pause," she adds. "I mentioned that Hannah was eager to make friends and is considering trying out for the soccer team. The woman I spoke to seemed very surprised."

"Why's that?"

"Apparently, Hannah was injured during a game in middle school. It wasn't enough for her to need surgery or anything serious, but she did go through several months of physical therapy. Unfortunately, it didn't help much and she walks with a limp sometimes."

My mind flips through the information Child Services shared with me. There was no mention of an injury, but I suppose without surgery, it wasn't enough to be included.

"From what I understand," Mrs. Carlisle says, "that's why Hannah stopped playing soccer. It was enough to keep her from trying out for other sports too, which is why the woman from homeschool seemed surprised that Hannah would try out again. She seemed quite against it when they sent the sports registration form each year."

I scrunch my face. Her injury was a long time ago, and she's healed. She's gotten better. She's ready to try again.

"Let's just give this girl a shot, okay?" I tell Mrs. Carlisle, but it comes out sharper than I intended. "My niece is doing the best she can. She's doing a hell of a lot better than any of us could if we were in her same situation. She's only a kid."

"Yes, Ms. Jenkins," Mrs. Carlisle says. "I just wanted you to know. We'll continue to keep an eye on her."

"You do that." I end the call.

Saturday

It's just before noon when the girls finally wake up. They stayed up late with Hannah completing Cassie's makeover and taking a dozen photos. I reminded them once again not to post anything on Instagram. *Just until everything calms down*, I told them.

The girls' giggles lasted past midnight, then quieted when they settled in the living room to watch a movie.

But I went to bed. With the house alarm set, I opted to forgo my sleep meds this time, wanting to be alert in case anything happened. Which means, all night, my ears pricked for any sounds. The sight of someone jumping over the fence and running toward the house.

By morning, I needed a third cup of coffee while I envied how the girls could sleep so soundly. But it's because they don't know anything, blissful ignorance. Cassie is in the shower first before it's Hannah's turn, a calm in our routine as it's the weekend.

I should be more relaxed too, but I'm not, especially when the detective sends a text.

*Do you have time to talk?*

I call him back, not wanting to waste any time. "What's happening?"

"I told you that we asked Eli Robash to return to the station and provide a handwriting sample. He agreed, and in fact, he was more than willing to help. But he never showed up. And now he's not answering his phone." My chest tightens. "His wife said he was called away for business early this morning. We're unable to locate him."

The coffee sloshes from my mug to the floor. I rush to the

window, my fingers peeling away at the blinds until I gain a full view of my street.

I look for anything, and anyone, that would indicate Eli's presence in my neighborhood. He's evading the police. He's running out of time. He wants to finish what he started before the police catch up with him. It's now or never.

A car drives by, and I hold my breath. But it's my neighbor pulling into her driveway.

Another car passes, but they turn at the stop sign.

I search the road. What am I expecting to see? Eli Robash standing in my front yard waiting to confront me? The man glaring at my house with those piercing green eyes of his, reminding me of his father. He'll brandish a gas canister and hold up a match, his head tilted back with laughter. I shiver.

I swallow, but it's not enough. I step away from the window.

"Ms. Jenkins?" the detective says.

I punch the alarm code, and the light shines red. The code is a combination of the two digits of Cassie's birthdate and Hannah's birthdate, a set of numbers I will never forget, numbers that have special meaning.

"Ms. Jenkins," Detective Gillespie repeats, "there's no reason to panic. He's more than likely on this business trip, and we'll hear back from him this afternoon. He'll stop at the police station."

"No. He's driving here."

I clock the time on my phone—it's nearly 1 p.m. He could have easily made the drive by now, especially if he left Louisville this morning. He's approaching our neighborhood. He could be in front of my house in minutes.

I back away from the door, the phone slipping from my ear. A cold sweat sweeps my neck. I am suddenly shivering in the middle of the day in the middle of my living room.

"Ms. Jenkins," Detective Gillespie says, "as a precaution, I will tell you this. I'm going to loop in the local police now.

There is no reason to panic, but I think it's time to notify someone closer to you."

I hold my hand to my stomach.

The local police. He *is* worried.

"It's a precaution," he reiterates. "But you're out of my jurisdiction, and it's time I catch local law enforcement up to speed."


"Mom," Cassie says. "What's going on?"

Her voice is distant.

"Mom? *Hello?* What's going on with you?"

I blink several times before I turn my eyes to her.

Cassie laughs, but it's a nervous one. She passes a glance to Hannah who watches me.

"Are you okay, Aunt Tara?"

"We should get out of here for a little while."

"What should we do?" Cassie says. "Catch a movie or something?"

"Or something," I respond, but my voice is flat, and Cassie throws another worried look in my direction.

"Let's drive around," Hannah suggests. "You can show me around town some more."

That's as good an idea as any. It will certainly get us out of the house.


We drive down the main street as Cassie points out the restaurants and boutiques, before we reach the river and turn west and we head past the more industrial section of Decatur. Looping back to the other side of town, we pass Point Mallard Water Park.

"It's a lot of fun," Cassie says. "And in the summer, the place is packed. There are a ton of water slides and a wave pool. We should go."

"That would be great." Hannah stares at the entrance to the water park.

Driving has helped. But I find myself checking the rearview mirror to see if anyone is tailing me, if there is a car that is following too close, if Eli Robash is sitting behind the wheel.

I looked him up on Facebook, which means he could easily find me too.

I don't pull over, I don't want to stop, but eventually, the girls ask if we can get food. We didn't have anything before we left the house and it's way past lunch.

"What about that new Korean place?" Cassie suggests.

At the restaurant, the girls do most of the talking while I push my food around, picking at the rice, a bulgogi bowl that I normally would have devoured in minutes, but my appetite has long disappeared, and I can't taste anything.

When someone enters, my eyes tear to the front door, but it's an older couple and they're with someone who could be their grandson. He wears a baseball cap and jersey, his once white pants streaked with dirt. The next to enter is a young family with the mother bouncing a toddler on her hip.

Hannah and Cassie finish everything on their plates. They occasionally pass glances to me to see if I'm okay, if I'm listening, but I'm definitely not. My eyes are glued to the door. And when I'm not studying who is coming and going, I'm checking my phone for another call from Detective Gillespie.

"Mom, you're freaking me out," Cassie says the moment Hannah heads for the bathroom. "What's going on?"

"I'm sorry. I'll be okay. I'm thinking about my sister, missing her."

"Well, you're starting to freak Hannah out. She said that whoever killed her mom might be coming after her too."

My body stiffens. "When did she tell you that?"

"Last night." Cassie looks down as if she's said too much.

"But don't tell her I told you that, okay? I think she feels like she can really talk to me."

*But this isn't about problems at school or an argument with friends, Cassie.* This is huge, especially if Hannah is worried about someone coming after her. Why does she think that? She doesn't know about the threatening message I received. She doesn't know a thing about the Robashes.

"That's not true, right, Mom?" Cassie asks. "They weren't trying to kill her in the fire, were they? No one is coming after her."

"No," I tell her. "Hannah is safe. Everyone is safe. The police are close to finding who did this and they'll make an arrest soon. You'll see."

She nods, changing the subject as soon as Hannah returns to the table.

"What should we do next?" Cassie asks. "It's early. We've got a whole night ahead of us."

"You talked about a movie earlier. Maybe something like that?" Hannah suggests.

The girls check online for tonight's listings as I pay the bill. We're walking to the car when Cassie spots something tucked beneath my windshield wiper. "What's this?"

It's a piece of paper that's been folded in half, a flyer, I think. But as soon as I look closer, my throat runs dry.

I should snatch this from my daughter's hands, tell her it's an ad for something, a discounted car wash—anything so the girls won't know what is written inside. But Cassie is quick, and she opens the note, her face paling.

"Mom... what is this?" The paper goes limp in her hands, her fingers trembling.

# TWENTY-SIX

I rip the note from my daughter's hands.

*I told you to watch out and now I'm coming for you.*

My hand tightens around the paper to crumple it, but I stop. This is evidence—another piece of critical evidence that I should show to the police.

My eyes sweep the rest of the parking lot. *He's here.*

He walked right up to my car and placed this on my windshield. He knows we were inside the restaurant, and he waited.

Or he's lurking inside one of these cars.

My heart slams. I'm searching, my breath coming out in spurts, when Hannah snatches the note from my hands next. Her eyes dart back and forth. I swear I see the blood drain from her face too.

She points at the most hideous part, the part I desperately wish I could erase. Below the cruelly written message, he's also drawn a picture.

It's an image of a house with flames shooting from the roof. In black pen and an orange marker, it's a crude drawing, an outline of a woman, her hair long and black, her face on fire. Her mouth twists in a tormented $O$ as she screams from the flames.

It's meant to be my sister, and I want to throw up. Beth is burning alive and they've recreated the scene.

Hannah chokes. She staggers, her legs giving out on her, and I hold her so she doesn't fall to the ground.

Hannah sobs, "What is this? *Who* did this?" She searches the parking lot too, and it hits me. We need to get moving. They could walk up to us at any second.

"Girls, get into the car *now*." We're too vulnerable standing out in the open.

I rip the card from Hannah's hands and unlock the doors. They scramble inside and buckle their seatbelts, but Cassie is crying, and so is Hannah. Cassie doesn't have a clue, but she knows something horrible is happening. She saw what was written on that piece of paper.

By keeping certain details away from the girls, I thought I was doing the right thing. I was protecting them. But all I've done is kept them in the dark. I've put them at risk by not warning them about everything I know.

How can they protect themselves when they aren't aware of a threat that is coming?

I slam the keys in the ignition and fire up the car. I'm to blame for this, and I must find a way to fix everything.

I reverse quickly out of the parking space and call Detective Gillespie. I don't wait for us to go somewhere to find a separate room, close the door, and speak to him in hushed tones. We don't have time for that anymore.

Bringing my eyes to the rearview mirror, I watch every car that pulls in behind us. Has anyone taken off from the parking lot and is following us? Are they trailing us right now?

Hannah must be thinking the same thing because she keeps turning around in her seat—she's monitoring every car and checking the drivers. When I change lanes, she watches if anyone changes also, but no one does. At least, not that we can tell. As soon as the light turns green, I gun it and head across the bridge.

Detective Gillespie answers.

"Another note card," I tell him. "But it was on my windshield. We were at a restaurant. He put it here which means he's here. I know he is."

"Okay. I'm putting you in touch with someone immediately. The local detective I mentioned."

"He drew a picture of my sister," I continue, wishing I didn't have to repeat this in front of the girls. "She was... they drew her on fire."

Cassie bursts into a sob in the backseat and I squeeze my eyes, my heart shattering. I keep driving—I don't know where we're going and what we're going to do, but we definitely won't be going home. I focus on the road.

"What are your plans?" the detective asks. "I need to tell Detective Haygood where to find you."

"I'm not sure yet. I just took off."

"Okay. But don't go too far. I need him to meet with you as soon as possible."

I change lanes again, and I'm painfully aware that when I do, I'm not slowing down. My speed is approaching eighty, then ninety, but I don't care. The farther we can get from Eli Robash the better.

Up ahead are signs for Interstate 65, and I contemplate on whether to take the exit. Do I veer north toward Nashville or head south to Birmingham? We could drive through the night and end up in Florida. We can find an airport where we can fly somewhere far away. We won't return until we know they've thrown Eli Robash behind bars.

*Don't go too far*, the detective said.

I pass the exit for the interstate and continue east. We'll find someplace to hide in Huntsville.

"We'll get a hotel," I tell him. "After we check in, I'll tell you where we are."

The girls are still crying when we hang up, but Hannah is also staring at me.

"You said *another* note card. What do you mean? What was the first one?"

I wince. Hannah's words, her fear, and it's as if she's carving my heart out with a spoon. Hannah is right to be upset that I've betrayed her by keeping this information.

"*What did it say?*" she asks, and this time she screams it. My hands loosen on the steering wheel, the sound of her wail punching into the air.

I apologize. I ramble a litany of excuses, but she doesn't want to hear it. "Who is doing this to us?" she says. "Why would they want to scare us like this?"

When I check Cassie in the rearview mirror, her face is white as a sheet. "Mom, please slow down. You're scaring me."

I release my foot from the pedal. I've got to get ahold of myself so we don't crash.

"I've been keeping the police informed," I explain to Hannah. "They know everything. They're chasing this person down."

"Is it that Rick Joffrey guy?"

"They don't think so anymore."

"Then who?" Hannah says. "*Who is it?*"

We pass the signs announcing the Huntsville International Airport. We speed past Cummings Research Park and approach the towering Saturn V Rocket, its red lights flashing in front of the U.S. Space and Rocket Center. Several hotels are up ahead.

"Aunt Tara!" Hannah says. "Talk to me."

"Does the name Eli Robash ring any bells? Did your mom ever mention him?"

"Eli Robash... the land developer guy?"

I flash her a look. "Yes. How do you know about him?"

"He used to call my mom. He kept asking about the farm. He wanted to buy it from her, but she kept telling him no. The Chandlers said they were holding out too even though he kept asking them about it."

"Did he ever get angry, Eli Robash? Did he yell at her?"

Her eyes widen. "I don't think so. But Mom didn't tell me a lot, just that she insisted on being a hold-out. The Chandlers too. They wouldn't sell."

"There's a chance the Chandlers might be reconsidering."

Her voice rises. "But they said they wouldn't. They told Mom they wouldn't." She gasps. "Wait, you think Eli Robash was so mad at Mom that he would kill her just to get some property? But that's insane. I mean, he was pretty relentless, and Mom eventually blocked his number. He showed up at the house one time."

My breath catches. "When?"

"Weeks ago. Maybe a month." She says, "I don't remember because I wasn't really paying attention. I didn't think it was that big a deal, boring property stuff and all. But he was there, and they talked. I got the impression he wasn't happy, and neither was she, and he left."

My eyes race toward her. "Did you hear what they said? Anything specific?"

"Not really. Like I said, I wasn't paying attention." She takes the note and stares at the hideously cruel drawing. "Oh my God. That shitbag killed my mom? He drew a picture of her *on fire?*" She checks the traffic on either side of us, the other speeding cars. "*He's here?*"

"We don't know that."

She waves the note in the air. "It sure as hell seems like it. This was on your car."

Cassie hunches over in the backseat. She hunkers down like she can hide back there.

Hannah shrieks, "He did this over some land? He killed my mom for some property?"

I'm sobbing too. The idea is appalling—the greed of it—the cold calculation. But it's so much more than that, I want to tell her, even when I know that won't make anything better. Hannah will never understand the secret I've kept with her mother, even when her mom stood up for me, protected me.

Because the truth is, the Robash family wants revenge. They've waited long enough. And the flames that Eli promised have gotten much closer.

I pick the first hotel we see. It has a wide, open parking lot and an on-ramp in case we need to make a quick escape to the interstate. I slide my credit card across the counter of the Drury Inn & Suites and the receptionist hands me a key card. I hustle the girls to the elevator, and we zip upstairs to the fifth floor.

Minutes later, I send Detective Gillespie our information.

*Hang tight*, he responds.

The girls remain in the sitting area. They don't know what else to do, and Hannah stares at the floor. There's a small sofa, a kitchen table, and a basic kitchenette made up of a counter and two cabinets. The suite includes two bedrooms. The girls will share one while I have the other.

Cassie sits on the edge of the sofa. She doesn't speak but twists the ends of her sleeves. Tired of sitting down, Hannah paces at the window. She yanks the curtain to one side and looks out.

"We'll stay here," I tell them. "Just a night or two. Until we know what's going on, until they can catch him. The detective is sending someone from the local police and they'll be coming here tonight. We're going to be okay."

Cassie whimpers. "Mom, this is crazy."

"I know, sweetheart. I'm so sorry. But we're going to be all right."

"I'm scared." Her lower lip trembles. I'm instantly beside her and clutch her hands.

We sit while Hannah maintains her watch at the window. Finally, I tell them, "Why don't you guys watch some TV? A movie or something? Something to distract you." I place the remote in Cassie's hand. "I need to make some calls in the other room."

Cassie nods, but she doesn't register the remote. She keeps her gaze on her frightened cousin instead.

I enter one of the bedrooms, keenly aware that we have brought nothing: no clothes, no pajamas, nothing to change into tomorrow. But at least there is shampoo and soap, and I can call the front desk and ask for toothpaste.

I sink on the edge of the bed and struggle to regain my composure. What have I done? How did I let everything get this far?

It's a few more minutes before I'm able to pull my phone from my pocket and call Cynthia.

As soon as she answers, I tell her, "I need your help."

The alarm in her voice is as acute as my own. "What's going on? Where are you?"

"Can you stop by my house? Tomorrow? I need you to pack some of our things."

"Pack your things?" Her panicked breath comes next. "Tara, what's happening?"

"We're in a hotel. We're going to be here a few nights... the police investigation... there's a chance— I don't know." My words are coming out in bits and pieces. My mind fractured. I take another breath to complete the next sentence. "There's a chance whoever did this to my sister could be targeting us too. And he might already be here in Alabama. I didn't tell you everything, Cynthia, and I should have. I'm sorry. A lot has been going on, and the detective thinks it's a good idea for us not to go home. That's why we're at a hotel."

Cynthia is busy processing the information, and I can tell by the way she's fallen silent. But she's also moving. She's racing from one room to the next looking for her car keys.

"You can't come here tonight," I tell her. "The detective is coming."

"Which hotel?" she asks.

"The Drury Inn in Huntsville. But it's no rush. I don't need our clothes until tomorrow. Don't risk going to my house tonight."

"Don't risk—? Jesus, T... you're scaring me."

I nod even though she can't see me. I'm scared enough for all of us.

"Tomorrow, okay? Please say you'll wait until tomorrow."

"Okay," she answers.

"I'll text you the code for the house alarm." I add, "And make sure Erik goes with you. I don't want you going into the house alone."

# TWENTY-SEVEN

Detective Gillespie notifies me that Detective Haywood is on his way. He's with the Huntsville Police Department and has been briefed on what is happening. *You're in good hands*, he tells me.

I wait until there is a knock on the door, and I jump. The girls jump too. They're finally watching TV and I've joined them on the sofa, but we haven't been paying attention. It's only background noise as Hannah continues to check the window.

With the detective here, I ask him to join me in one of the bedrooms where we can talk. Leaving the girls with the television, I make sure to shut the door behind us.

Detective Haygood sits at a small table near the window. He removes a notepad and pen and lays them out in front of him. He has dark hair, not as black as ours, but dark enough, and he's casual in his jeans and a white button-down shirt that he's rolled to his elbows. It's a Saturday evening and I have no clue what his work schedule is like or if I've interrupted his weekend, but he doesn't mention it, and it doesn't matter at this point. He's here and that's what matters. We need the help.

The detective asks for the message, the threat we've

received, and I slide it across the table. He doesn't touch it, but his eyes linger on the hideous drawing. He frowns, a glint of disgust.

When he lifts his eyes, he says, "We will do everything we can to find out who is doing this." And his voice, his very assurance, the presence of a detective in the room is enough to make me weep.

He removes a pair of blue gloves from his pocket and puts them on before he slides the note inside a paper bag. He seals it and marks it with a reference number.

"As you know, Ms. Jenkins, Detective Gillespie has filled me in on everything. He's leading the investigation in Louisville regarding your sister's death, but with these two threats you've received, it was wise of him to get me involved. I'll be taking over this part. From here on out, if anything happens, any suspicious activity, you contact me first." He hands me his business card. "And don't worry. I'll keep Detective Gillespie informed every step of the way."

I nod and clutch his business card like it's our lifeline.

"With Eli Robash's whereabouts still unknown at this point, he's moved much higher on the suspect list. Detective Gillespie's team has uncovered multiple emails between him and your sister, going back years and then really picking up speed the last couple of months. It might have been because he was getting close to the Chandler neighbors agreeing to sell. And if he could pressure your sister, then maybe she would finally sell too. He would make a lot more money if she did."

"My niece said that Eli Robash showed up to their house a few weeks ago. He may have argued with my sister."

"And let me guess? She refused to sell to him again?"

"We can only assume."

"It's enough to support motive. I will definitely let Detective Gillespie know." He scribbles something on his notepad. "I understand that you were approached to sell your parents' land also. It was years ago when you were still in Louisville."

I swallow. "That's right."

"They were pretty insistent, huh?"

"Yes. The phone calls kept coming, and it was tempting at first. The money, you know? I was young and dumb enough not to understand how it really worked, and I listened to them. They told me all I needed to do was send a copy of my parents' deed, but I couldn't find it, and my parents busted me for searching the house."

"That's when they pressed charges."

I nod again, and the flush finds its way to my neck. "As it turns out, I wouldn't have been able to do anything with it anyway. My parents had to agree to sell the property, not me, since it was in their names. But I think these people wanted to find a loophole, something in the family ownership they could dispute. After my parents found me in Dad's office, they got scared and thought I would be tempted again. They changed the locks. They updated their will and left everything to Beth. They knew my sister would never sell."

"And would you have done so?" he asks.

"No," I tell him without hesitation. "I know I wouldn't, and I knew it back then too. I was just curious. They duped me."

"But it wasn't the Robashes that were calling you back then. They were too young. They didn't have their company yet. But it's interesting that it's the Robashes who want to buy it now."

"They waited," I tell him simply.

"According to Detective Gillespie, Mr. Chandler met with Eli Robash last Friday about possibly selling the farm. The Robashes have been waving a pretty penny at them, and they admit they've been considering leaving the farm life and moving closer to their grandkids."

"I can understand that," I say sadly, although the thought of that area off Route 30 being cut out and shaped into an interstate or an enormous shopping center is enough to break my heart. I never thought the Chandlers would sell. I think our family always hoped one of their kids would move back and take over the farm.

"Mr. Chandler also said that Eli Robash discussed your sister's land situation when they met. He was frustrated that she kept turning him down and refusing to take his phone calls." He studies me. "I'm aware of the other instances, Ms. Jenkins. The car accident when Hank Robash, their father, was killed. It happened in your vehicle, is that correct?" He doesn't need an answer. "We're very aware there's a strong possibility this could be a lot more than a land dispute."

I drop my eyes. The image of my car on fire... Hank's body wrapped in flames...

The drawing of my sister's hair alight flashes in my mind too.

"This latest note?" he asks. "You think Eli Robash is in town and left it on your windshield?"

"Yes, I think he's here. But I also think he's turning his rage toward Hannah. With my sister dead, I still have no claim. Everything is in Hannah's name. She will take full ownership when she comes of age."

"I see." He thinks this over. "And if something were to happen to Hannah, then the family ownership could potentially stop there. The land could go up for auction instead... unless you're able to buy it."

"Which I can't. So if Hannah died..." and my voice shakes at the thought, "the Robash company could try to buy the land for themselves."

"Okay." He stands up. "I need to check with the restaurant and see if they have any security cameras. I'll ask around in case someone noticed someone near your car." He tucks the evidence bag under his arm and tells me they'll look for prints too.

"I'll be in touch," he says, and surveys the room, nodding. "Ms. Jenkins, you were smart to come to a hotel."

## Sunday

Just like me, the girls hardly sleep, and it's evident in the harsh lines on Cassie's face in the morning, Hannah's too. My daughter is increasingly restless about having to stay inside the hotel. To her, this feels like a prison. She's trapped. With every passing hour, she's getting angry.

Hannah is once again standing guard at the window. She knows what Eli Robash looks like and says she'll alert us if she sees anyone closely matching his description in the parking lot. I hope that doesn't happen.

We don't have anything to eat for breakfast and I'm flipping through the hotel book and considering ordering room service when Cynthia sends a text that she's downstairs.

Within minutes, she and her husband, Erik, are at the door. They have countless duffel bags, my travel suitcase, and dozens of groceries too. Cynthia is a bundle of nerves and talks to us a million miles a minute. A stricken look is on her face.

"I had no idea what you needed so I grabbed a little bit of everything. Sweatshirts, leggings, underwear, I just went through everyone's shelves and grabbed what I thought would work. I hope that's okay."

"That's great," I tell her. "It's exactly what we need."

She stops talking long enough to fold me in a hug, and Erik does the same. He hasn't said a word yet, but I can tell he's alarmed. He gives me a look that says we need to talk, and certainly out of the girls' earshot, but Cynthia starts up again. She rushes to my daughter next.

"Oh, Cassie. Are you okay?" She hugs her tightly, and my daughter manages a small shrug.

"And you must be Hannah," Cynthia says.

"Hi," she says with a peep, and Cynthia closes the gap between them and hugs her also.

When they break away, Cynthia faces me. "We brought food," she says, although that's fairly obvious. Erik places the bags in the kitchenette. "We didn't know what you'd like so we brought stuff you can microwave. A bunch of snacks." She works with Erik to remove every item and set them in the fridge or the cabinets.

I stand back, grateful for the help.

"Coffee," Cynthia says, and she waves a bag of dark roast at me.

"God love you."

"Plus, crackers, apples, cereal, milk. Lactose-free for Cassie," she adds. "I'm thinking you won't want to order food every night, so I bought stuff for you to cook too." My face blanches. "I know, you hate to cook. But there's stuff in here if you decide to." She places a package of flank steak and a small bottle of marinade in the fridge. On the counter, Erik sets down a bag of potatoes and some salt and pepper shakers. "Comfort food," she suggests.

Cynthia inspects the cooking pots and utensils and frowns at their wear, possibly a scuff mark or three. She also makes a face at the electric stove. It's basic at best, but it will have to do. "Do you want me to cook right now?" she asks. "I don't mind. You can eat now, or you can eat later."

Erik places a hand on her arm. "Honey, let's relax a little bit, okay? Let's take a breath."

She pauses, and sighs. "Okay."

Erik turns to me. "Let's talk."

I motion to the bedroom, where they follow and we sit at the same table where Detective Haygood sat the night before.

With the door shut, Erik says, "What's going on?"

I fill them in the best I can. It's exhausting, but I do it anyway, going through every detail that I've shared with the police: the two threatening note cards and my theory that Eli Robash is out to hurt Hannah. There's a chance he wants to hurt all of us, I tell them, but Hannah especially.

I don't talk about the car accident and the way Hank died. I can't go through that again, not right now while everything is terrifying enough.

When I'm done, Erik and Cynthia are speechless. I've been talking for such a long time that my voice is hoarse, and I need water. I fill one of the plastic cups from the bathroom sink and return to the table.

Cynthia watches me sit. "That's why you asked about the girls living with us, isn't it? You said that if anything happened to you, like your sister, you want them protected. Just in case..."

"Yes, just in case."

Erik says, "We'll take care of the girls, Tara. Don't worry. But that is *not* going to happen, okay? You're going to be safe. The police will track him down."

Tears spring to my eyes. "But he's here, I know he is. And they don't know where."

"They'll find him," he repeats.

"Did you notice anything at the house?" I ask. "When you were there, was anything different?"

"No, nothing," Cynthia says. "We looked around. We reset the alarm when we left too."

"Okay, good. Thank you."

Tears fill her eyes next. "I'm scared for you, T. I know I shouldn't be saying this, but I am. But I'm also hopeful, you know? Like Erik said, they're going to catch him. They'll put a stop to this. You won't have to hide forever."

"You're safe." Erik surveys the room. "He can't get to you at a hotel. I mean, what is he going to do? Torch the whole building down?"

# TWENTY-EIGHT

After Cynthia and Erik leave, I tell the girls they're not going to school tomorrow. They make sandwiches at the kitchen counter and dig into bags of chips when I explain about us keeping a low profile. They don't say a word.

But later, an alert pops up on Cassie's phone. "Mom, I have practice."

"When?" She stares at me, and my eyes widen. "Today?" I say. "No way. You're not going."

"But I can't miss practice."

My head pounds. I don't have the energy to argue with her, but I try again. "No, Cassie. We're staying here."

Her voice rises to a whine. "But if I miss practice, I can't start at the game. And if I don't start at the game, then Lauren will play instead of me, and you know that's how Coach is. She won't make exceptions."

"These are very different circumstances, Cassie. This is not because you're sick."

"But, Mom. I *can't* miss, okay? I *won't*." She folds her arms across her chest. "I am not going to sit around all day in this room. If I do, I'll go crazy." She springs from the couch. "This guy, whoever he is, is *not* going to do this. Frighten us. Keep us locked up in here."

*Oh, sweet girl, if you only knew what he's capable of. What we're all capable of.*

"Mom!" Cassie says.

"Cassie!" I shout back. "Take a look around. We're in a hotel because we're hiding. We're hiding from someone who put a threatening note on my car. He could be anywhere. He could be looking for us. This isn't some movie or a joke. This is serious."

"I know, but you know what you're letting him do? You're letting him call the shots. And we shouldn't. We're just supposed to hide in this room all day? And for how long? The police are already onto him. He'd be stupid to try anything else. I am *not* missing that game!"

I want my daughter to stop screaming. But I also don't want to hide in this room either. I'm sick and tired of being afraid. She's right—we're letting him call the shots. I've let this man terrorize me for years.

Hannah speaks softly. "Let her go, Aunt Tara. It will be all right. It's only for an hour. Seriously," Hannah says to me, calmly. "Just a short break. She could use getting out of here."

"See, Mom?" Cassie says.

Cassie reaches for her soccer bag that Cynthia brought along with the other bags from our house. She puts on her shin guards and socks, her mind made up, triumphant that her cousin is on her side. She rakes her hands furiously through her hair and pulls it into a ponytail.

I watch silently. Everything in my body is telling me this is a bad idea, that we shouldn't go. But Cassie is getting stir-crazy, and so am I. Her next game is Tuesday and she won't want to miss it. Knowing my daughter, she will march out that door and walk to practice if she has to. She'll hitchhike, and there's no way I'm letting her put herself in more danger.

I find my purse and keys, knowing I will need to drive her. It will take more than an hour with the extra drive in and out of Huntsville, but then we'll return. Cassie will be happy, for now.

Hannah must sense my hesitation because she says, "It's okay, Aunt Tara. I'll keep the door locked. You stay at practice and watch her. There will be a coach and a bunch of other kids so nothing bad can happen. Okay?"

She's kind to say this to me, and my niece's reassurance bolsters me enough that I'm able to head for the hotel lobby, my daughter in tow.

# TWENTY-NINE

I don't leave my daughter at practice. Instead, I remain in my car pressed up against the steering wheel and watch her like a hawk. My daughter, meanwhile, takes out her own fury. She kicks the ball like someone's face is plastered to the front of it, and I can only imagine what she's thinking. With her arms pumping, she runs up and down the field as if she's working every demon out of her core.

It would probably help for me to do the same thing, but my body remains rigid, knots taking shape down my back. Cassie's face is red when practice ends. She buckles herself in the seat and doesn't say a word, not needing to. She feels better, I can tell, although the idea of returning to the hotel weighs heavily on her mind.

When she pulls off her shin guards and socks, the dirt and grass float to the floor. It's crazy how only a few days ago, I watched her do the very same thing, and it was right before I announced that Hannah would be living with us. It was right before everything in our world turned upside down.

I'm anxious to head back. I'm eager to return to the hotel and make sure Hannah is safe. I've texted several times and she's responded with, *Everything is good.* I know I shouldn't worry, but still.

I tell her we're on our way soon, another thirty minutes, I calculate, based on the return trip to Huntsville, especially if there's traffic. But it's a Sunday afternoon and there is very little in terms of cars. With the roads clear and with my heavy foot, we speed over the bridge crossing the Tennessee River. We reach the interstate, then the hotel, the entrance to the parking lot a beacon of salvation as I swing into a parking space.

But as we exit, I check the other vehicles to make sure there's no one waiting, that no one is jumping out to get us.

I motion for Cassie to hurry up. We should get to our room as soon as possible. I need to lay eyes on my niece so I can feel better, so I know that she's secure.

But when we reach the room and open our hotel door, something is different—I notice it immediately.

It's the smell at first, but it's not the smell of something burning. It's not flames or smoke that's rushing to my face and causing me to shriek. It's the smell of red meat cooking. A delicious marinade.

It's the flank steak that Cynthia bought for us and it's sizzling in a pan on the kitchenette stove. To my delight, Hannah is cooking for us.

Cassie tosses her bag to the floor as I shut the door. The pan is sizzling, the meat browning, but there's no sign of my niece. She's not standing near the stove, she's not watching, and I need to tell her not to do that again. It's too dangerous. The smoke could set off the alarms, and she should never leave a hot stove unattended.

There's also a pot of mashed potatoes. On the counter, a plate has been left out that was used as a cutting board.

"Wow," Cassie says. "This looks great."

I'm impressed too. But there's still no sign of my niece, and my heart flickers with worry.

I turn down the heat on the stove and call for her, but she doesn't answer. Cassie calls her name too. The door to the girls' bathroom is closed, and the light is on. The light beams from underneath, a white strip glowing against the carpet.

"Hannah?" I say. "Are you in there?"

No answer.

"Thank you for making us dinner."

But there is still no response, and my shoulders rise. I don't hear a toilet flushing or the faucet running.

My stomach lurches—*is she okay?*

I tap on the door. It hasn't been pulled shut all the way, and my knuckles push the door open. I look inside. I see her.

My niece stands in front of the sink, but she has latex gloves on her hands. On the counter is a cardboard box and a plastic bottle. A puddle of black drips into the drain. Another smell hits my nostrils, and this one is different—ammonia. And it's undeniable, the metallic taste coating the back of my throat and stinging my nostrils.

But it's the sight of Hannah that troubles me the most. She sees me—I know she does—but she ignores me. She runs the latex gloves through her hair, the gloved white fingertips now coated in black dye.

I look again at the cardboard box, the words on the label slowly coming into focus: *L'Oréal hair dye. Color black.*

My niece is coloring her hair.

Why would she do that?

*Long, black hair like her mom*, the attorney said. *Like you too*, he added.

*Hannah?* I want to say, but her name doesn't form on my lips. No sound is coming from my mouth. I'm frozen, while somewhere behind me, Cassie is hanging out in the bedroom. She asks, "What's that smell?" But then flops on the bed to play with her phone.

I watch Hannah, a dozen questions storming through my

mind. I don't understand what's happening. My brain isn't computing fast enough.

My niece is dyeing her hair. Which means her hair isn't naturally black. It's a disguise. And a cold prickle sinks into my gut.

Hannah stares at my reflection. "Oh, hi, Aunt Tara." She drops her hands from her head and black dye drips to the floor. It doesn't soak into the towel she has draped around her shoulders. "It's okay, Aunt Tara. Don't be scared."

She turns away from the mirror and leans against the counter. There's not much room between us and the smell from the hair dye overpowers us both. I cover my mouth to keep from coughing.

"Hannah?" I whisper. "Why are you dyeing your hair?"

I want to reach out and touch it to make sure it's real, that I'm not imagining things. But her head is coated in a wet, sticky dye. More black dye splashes to the floor like squid ink.

Hannah pulls off her plastic gloves, one at a time, and keeps her eyes on me. She tosses the gloves in the sink, and they land with a *thwack*.

I wait for her to say, *It's no big deal*. A giggle, a shrug of the shoulders. But she doesn't do anything like that. Instead, the corners of her mouth peel up, revealing one tooth, and then another, until it's a full grin. This is unlike any smile I've seen on Hannah before.

"Hannah?" I whisper.

This is my sister's child. Beth's child. As a little girl, she was a mirror image of her mother. *My mini-me*, Beth used to call her.

When Hannah stands next to Cassie, they look like sisters. People would think she's my daughter. I noticed the resemblance as soon as we saw her at the airport.

"Hannah?" I repeat.

She pulls the towel from her shoulders and drops it to the floor. "I'm not Hannah. I'm Jodi."

I stagger back, one shockwave after another rippling through my body.

*Who in the hell is Jodi?*

I slam against the doorframe until it rattles. "Mom, are you okay?" Cassie asks. I hear her moving around on the bed. "What's going on in there?"

My mouth opens, but no words come out. I can't stop staring at Hannah—at *Jodi*—whoever this is—this girl who stands less than three feet away, while my daughter, my sweet, innocent daughter, remains in the next room.

The girl I knew as Hannah has suddenly disappeared.

Her lips curl again. "Had you fooled, didn't I?"

And I freeze.

I should yell at my daughter, tell her to get out of here and find help. But my voice is stuck in my windpipe and my feet are glued to the floor.

Cassie is suddenly beside me. "Hannah?" she says with a strange laugh. "What are you doing to your hair?"

But the girl doesn't look at her, only toys with the black strands, the dye coating her skin until she rubs it between her fingers. "I thought I'd have more time to finish." She glances at the box of dye. "Oops."

And now I pull my daughter back. But Cassie balks.

"Hannah? What are you doing?" She peers at me for an answer, but I don't know what to tell her. I keep my gaze on this woman—this *stranger*—who moves toward us.

"What does it look like I'm doing?" she says to Cassie with a smile. "I'm keeping my hair black, like yours." She reaches out her hand to flick the end of Cassie's ponytail, but I jerk my daughter away in response. "Black hair." She slides her gaze to me. "Like your mom. Like Beth."

*Like Beth.* She didn't call her Mom.

I shake my head. No, this can't be right. Something has snapped inside of my niece. The grief has overwhelmed her and we should have gotten her to see a counselor sooner. She's too young to comprehend what's happening: running from someone, hiding from someone—the crude drawing she saw of her mother on fire—and it's too much for any sixteen-year-old to bear.

What we're witnessing is some sort of a breakdown. In order to cope, Hannah's personality has split—I read about that somewhere. She's named this other personality Jodi. She's conjured up someone to protect herself. Hannah will hide within her own psyche until she is safe.

But my niece doesn't remove that eerie smile from her lips.

I peer at the face that I have grown to love and care for over the past few days. The real Hannah is in there, I know she is. It's not too late—we can still reach her. Behind those dark almond eyes that are shaped like mine, like my daughter's, Hannah will return to us. She has to.

But something still troubles me.

I ask, "Why isn't your hair black?"

"My dad." She shrugs. "It wasn't dark, so mine isn't either. Not like you guys."

I think of Alex, how his hair had been more of a dirty blond. But when Hannah was a toddler, her hair fell behind her in silky black strands. It was jet black like my sister's. It should not have lightened so much over time.

She tousles her wet hair as more ink smears on her fingers.

"When's your birthday?"

"September fourth," she answers.

"Why didn't you get your driver's license?"

"I didn't want to." She smiles again. "I didn't need to drive. Since I was in homeschool, I didn't go out very much, and no one has seen what I look like for a long time. Not even the Chandlers noticed a difference."

Why wouldn't the Chandlers notice a difference?

I take a heady breath. "You also don't limp."

"That soccer injury?" she scoffs. "It was no big deal." And she kicks out her leg. "I'm fine, as you can tell."

My head hurts, my thoughts ricocheting inside my brain.

"What was the name of your dog?"

She stops. "What dog?"

My voice cracks. "The one Grandma and Grandpa got you, remember? He was a cocker spaniel."

She rolls her eyes. "I don't know, and I really don't care."

My eyes brim with tears. "It was Roger, remember? You named him Roger." But there's no point in doing this anymore. My fears have bubbled all the way to the surface.

"Who gives a shit?" she says. "That dog is long gone. But I'm here. *Me!*" And she jabs a finger at her chest. "I'm Jodi."

Cassie cries, "Don't say that, Hannah."

But the girl screams, "I'm *not* Hannah. I've never been Hannah. I had you all fooled, didn't I? You believed everything I said, even the attorney." She laughs, and it's such a sharp, high-pitched sound that Cassie grabs my arm.

My mind spins. There's no photo of Hannah in the system, like she said. She never got a driver's license. There are no updated pictures in the yearbook from attending homeschool. The Chandlers haven't seen her in years.

I scroll over the last few days. The black coffee that is mostly preferred by adults. The expert way she applies makeup and the way the saleswoman joked that she could have her job. The fact she has no idea what to do in her honors classes.

With a trembling voice, I say, "You're really not Hannah."

Cassie says, "What's wrong with you, Mom? Of course that's her."

But my eyes well with tears. "No, Cassie, it isn't. She's telling us the truth. It was never Hannah in the first place."

The girl cocks a smile. "Bingo."

# THIRTY

My daughter staggers in her steps. She stares at the girl—at Jodi —and so do I. And then Cassie is cowering behind my back. She wants to hide and shield herself. We are looking at a stranger. I have no idea who we are sharing a hotel room with, and worst of all, I have no idea who's been staying in our house.

*Where is the real Hannah? What has she done to her?*

"My niece," I demand. "Where is she?"

"Who cares?" the girl says and moves closer.

I back up another step until we're almost to the door. Next is the sitting room, and then the main door to the hall. We have to be fast. We need to move quickly.

But Jodi smirks. "Don't even think about it, Aunt Tara."

I squeeze my eyes shut. I don't want her to call me that anymore.

I need to figure out a way to talk to this girl and calm her down. I need her to explain. I can distract her, and when the timing is right, I'll shove Cassie and tell her to run. I'll block Jodi, and Cassie can head for the elevator. She can find help.

"Who are you really?" I ask.

"Wouldn't you like to know?" She laughs. But as soon as she does, her eyes lower. The once full grin slips away. She looks almost sad. "You didn't know about me, did you?"

"Know about you? How would I...?"

Her face reddens, her eyes redden. "I don't know why I kept my hopes up, thinking she would tell you one day. But this shouldn't surprise me. I always wondered if Beth ever told you the truth."

"Told me what?"

My mind keeps spinning. *Beth. Jodi. Hannah.*

She sniffles, and her cheeks flush pink. She looks tiny again, so broken and hurt. "She kept me a secret all these years."

The phone rings and the sound startles us, the shrill piercing the room. But it's not a call from any of our cell phones. It's the hotel phone beside the sofa.

I think, *This is my chance.* I will push Jodi to one side and grab the phone. I'll scream for help and demand they notify the police.

But Jodi is faster than I am, and she lifts the receiver in one quick motion. "Hello?" she answers. I wait anxiously as she tips her head and listens to whoever is speaking.

Maybe it's Detective Haygood—he's calling to check in on us. He's downstairs and wants to update us about something. His timing couldn't be more perfect.

I hear Jodi say, "Come on up." But she leaves the phone off the hook.

Jodi turns to us with a smile. "Looks like we're going to have a guest."

The meat is sizzling. It will be burned to leather by the time we remove it from the stove. The burning smell, combined with Jodi's hair dye, is enough to make me want to retch, Cassie too, and my daughter keeps her hands gripped around my arm.

I stare at the door.

In minutes, Detective Haygood will be here. He can help us.

But why would Jodi tell him to come up? She wouldn't want the police here... unless he's not the one coming up to our room.

It's difficult to breathe. It's what I feared. He really is here. Jodi led a path straight to us.

The quickest of knocks sounds at the door, and her face lights up. She points at us. "Stay right there. Don't move."

With the phone still off the hook, she pushes it to the floor and out of reach. She tucks her hand around the bedroom door and pushes in the lock, then closes it. She locks the door to the second bedroom too. She's left us with no place to hide. We can't even hide in the bathrooms.

I search the sitting room for my purse, but it's on the floor against a wall. I peer out the window. We're on the fifth floor and it's too high up for anyone to notice us banging on the windows. No one will hear us from the parking lot either. But we could scream. We could scream until guests in a nearby room or someone heading to the elevator could hear our shouts. They could call for help and the police could be here in minutes.

But Jodi wags a finger. "I said, don't try anything." And taking a look at the stove, she frowns. "Oh, it's going to be so overcooked. And I wanted to make this dinner special." She pouts before she pats her hair, the strands still sticky. "And what a shame that I'm such a mess. I didn't want him to see me like this either." But she bolsters herself with a smile and reaches for the door.

Another squeal of delight as she ushers him into the room. "Look who it is!" she exclaims.

My eyes land on someone—my hope that it's Detective

Haygood disappeared moments ago, and I prepare myself for the hateful glare of Eli Robash. But it's not him either.

This man is blond with a slim build. His face is narrow, almost boyish, but it's his eyes that give him away—bright green, piercing eyes that stare at me and bring it all back, his eyes just like his father's.

I'm not staring at Eli Robash, but his younger brother, Patrick.

But Eli is the one who stood in our parents' house and left us with threats. He's the one who leered at us while Patrick, the quieter, more frightened brother, hovered by the door.

Eli confronted me at work while Patrick convinced him to leave me alone and pulled on his elbow. Patrick never once looked at me—he was too afraid. I thought he wanted nothing to do with our family argument.

Patrick is here... he's in this hotel room... so where does that leave Eli?

I half-expect to see him walk in the door next. Or he's in my front yard preparing to burn down our house. He sent his younger brother to do the rest of his dirty work.

My heart bangs—or does Eli have Hannah? He's keeping her under lock and key and has her trapped somewhere. We must find her, save her, get her out.

My eyes drift back to Jodi. Who exactly is this person, and why is she working with them? She's been pretending to be my sixteen-year-old niece.

She plants her hand on Patrick's chest and looks at him. "Hey, babe. You got here just in time." And she kisses him on the mouth. He kisses her back. I squirm at the sickening wet sound they make until they pull apart. She tosses me a playful look.

Patrick gives me a look also. "Hi, Ms. Jenkins. It's been a long time."

"Patrick, I'm so sorry... about everything. But let's talk,

okay? I don't know what's going on, but we can figure something out."

He shakes his head and wraps his arm around Jodi's waist, and it's confirmed absolutely that Jodi is not a teenage girl, but a young woman. Most likely, in her twenties. She's been pretending to be a teenager since the day my sister died.

Jodi has been playing a part. She must have stolen my niece's identity, and they hid Hannah somewhere. For the past week, she's been pulling off this charade and keeping everyone fooled like. Mr. Fredericks. The police. *Me*.

I stare at Jodi. She's working with the Robashes. For whatever reason, she's helping them to get my sister's land. They've convinced her to help them avenge their dad, her love for Patrick enough to make her take on this con and live with us. She would pretend to be Hannah so they could infiltrate our family. She was instrumental in pulling this entire thing off. She dyed her hair.

But why?

I consider what Jodi said. *You never knew about me, did you?*

"Everyone should sit down," Jodi says cheerfully, and she motions to the table. She pulls plates from the cabinet, and finds forks and knives before she scoops great helpings of flank steak and mashed potatoes onto the plates. "We can't let this food go to waste." And she wiggles her nose. "Again, I'm sorry. It's going to be overcooked." She laughs. "Let's just say I got a little distracted." And she touches her hair.

Patrick addresses me. "Sit down," he orders, and he glares at my daughter. The young, quiet teenager that I knew of Patrick is long gone. "I said, *sit down*," he insists.

"M-om?" Cassie whispers.

"It's going to be okay, Cassie, I promise." I plead to Patrick. "Let my daughter go. She has nothing to do with what happened. Back then or anything now." He doesn't budge, and I turn to Jodi next, my eyes filling with tears.

She must feel *some* compassion toward my daughter, right? After all, they were friends. Cousins. They spent evenings in Hannah's room, and Cassie adored her. She trusted her. My fury builds—*she loved her*. "She's terrified," I say. "Please, Hannah—Jodi. Please let Cassie go. It's me you want, not her."

But Jodi snaps, "You heard us," and she places the plates hard on the table. "I made everyone dinner."

We still don't move, and Patrick pulls a gun from his jacket pocket, and now it's my turn to cry out. The gun gleams with the bright, polished silver of a semi-automatic, and my shoulders jerk. Cassie trembles beside me.

Patrick points the gun at my head, then at her.

I lower Cassie to the table. We have no choice. Her feet drag and she nearly trips on herself, but we sit in the chairs. Her crying grows louder.

And my heart tears in two. I can't believe they would frighten her like this, Jodi especially. Just this morning, she and Cassie watched TV together. And yesterday, Hannah—Jodi—gave my daughter another makeover. They watched a movie.

I clench my fists. I could kill her for this. I could kill them both.

Jodi points at our food. "Go ahead, you guys. Eat up. We'll have dinner like we do at home."

*Home*, and she winks at me, and I swear to God, I will leap across this table and beat her if I get the chance. I clench my hands in my lap.

I look down at the plates. There is no way we are going to eat what she has cooked. It is a shriveled brown mass, the meat as tough as leather. We will not share a meal together as if this is the most normal thing in the world, as if there isn't a gun pointed to our heads. Especially with my daughter sobbing and the safety of my niece still unknown.

Patrick doesn't lower the gun. "Don't think about trying anything, Ms. Jenkins. Don't scream or make a run for it. You won't get very far. We're going to eat this nice meal that Jodi has prepared and then we're going to talk." He looks at the plate and pushes a lump of mashed potatoes around with his fork. "It's important we eat," he says. "We've got a long night ahead of us. Everyone needs their strength when we leave."

My stomach lurches. They plan on taking us somewhere.

Jodi sulks. "I'm sorry about the food, babe. I was dyeing my hair and time slipped away from me." She shoots us a look. "I didn't think they'd be back so soon."

Patrick stabs the flank steak with his fork, but it doesn't make much of a dent. He saws the meat until he's able to tear off a piece and put it in his mouth. He chews at it, for Jodi's benefit I can only imagine, before he manages to swallow it down.

He's trying not to cough, but all I can think is, *I hope you choke. Right here and now.* I hope you both choke at this table. I don't care if you die in front of my daughter. I want to be rid of both of you.

"We need something to drink, don't we?" Jodi says, and she finds glasses in the cabinet and fills them with water. She seems intent on playing the role of the happy hostess.

*Where is my niece?* How could I not have known the person living in my house was a stranger? I let them get to us. I invited them right through our front door.

There's a little bit of coffee left in the pot from this morning and she pours the remainder in a mug. She doesn't bother to heat it up. She reaches for her pocket and pulls out a pack of cigarettes. She lights one before she takes a deep drag. "Oh, I've missed this," she says, and lets out a long exhale. "Black coffee and a smoke is divine, don't you think? The best combination." She winks. "I've had to give this up all week just to be with you. It was a struggle, I want you to know, but it was worth it." She joins us at the table and smiles.

*We caught her smoking,* Mrs. Carlisle said. *It's like she doesn't know the material at all.*

Well, of course she doesn't. Chances are, Jodi doesn't know the first thing about honors physics. She may have never taken an advanced placement class in her life, and if she did, high school was years ago and a long enough time to forget.

A grown woman sat in those classrooms. She went to high school and pretended to be a teenager. She wore a backpack and carried a lunch tote and hung out with the other teens. She waited to be picked up in the car line and talked about music and favorite TV shows with Cassie, stuff kids her age would be into. She looks like a teenager. She talks like a teenager. We bought into her entire act.

I let this woman into my house. Worse—I left her alone with my daughter.

And to think I consoled her when she cried about my sister. She pretended to mourn for Beth. She made me believe she was my niece... Hannah... the girl I'd forgotten. The niece that I still don't have.

*Vanilla bean was her favorite,* she said.

*You remember the driveway? You could hear anyone drive up to the house.*

How does she know all these details? How did she gain so much background info about my sister and where they lived?

I glare at this imposter, this person that I want to beat into oblivion. But I can't hurt her—not yet, at least. We need to know where they're keeping Hannah.

Patrick continues to eat. How he's managing to chew is beyond my comprehension, but it's pleasing Jodi. No one wants to see her get upset because she appears to be the unhinged, loose cannon of the two while he is the quieter, more methodical planner. Along with Eli, they have constructed this entire operation.

My throat tightens. Wherever Eli is, I pray to God he's not hurting Hannah.

I ask Patrick, "You said we were going to talk, so let's talk. What did you do to my niece?"

He stabs at his food. "That part can wait."

"I need to know if she's okay."

"Just chill, Aunt Tara," Jodi says.

"Don't call me that."

She rolls her eyes.

"What do you want, Patrick? You and your brother? What do you want from us?"

He laughs. "Who says Eli has anything to do with this?"

I flinch.

"He's moved on." He waves his fork. "Well, he's mostly moved on. He's got a wife and kids now and he's super busy running the company. Trust me, he's still angry as hell about everything that happened. Don't think we didn't toast each other when your sister died, when the house burned down." He smirks.

"My brother has no idea what we did," he says. "Or what we're doing now." He slides his girlfriend a look. "He gave up on taking revenge years ago which was so disappointing. He was intent on it for such a long time, but after you moved away and Beth went underground for a while, he got quiet. He stopped thinking about it as much. But I never did." He glares. "I never forgot what you did to my dad."

"Patrick, it's not what—"

He slams his fist on the table. "I know that you slept with him, over and over, and that it broke my mom's heart. I know that you let him drive drunk and that's why he crashed the car. You could have pulled him out, but you didn't. You let him burn. Your sister was there too."

"No, that's not it. What happened was years ago."

"Years ago," he mocks. "Well, I want you to know that it's been years in the making for me too." He sneers. "How long I've waited to talk to you, Ms. Jenkins. See you again. How I've waited to introduce you to Jodi." He passes her a grin. "I think it's time you know how many people your family has hurt."

## THIRTY-ONE

I am crying and shaking. "I don't understand."

"My mom was good at lying, wasn't she?" Jodi says. She's back to calling her Mom. "She lied to so many of us." She stabs her fork. "She was *so* good at covering up stuff for years. Whatever was convenient to her, right?"

I peer at Jodi. "I don't know what this is about or who you are. I'm sorry."

"Beth," she says. "Your sister... *she's my mom.*"

"But how? That's impossible. She had Hannah. Hannah is sixteen. And you are—"

"Twenty-two. I'm her first kid."

I want to push back from the table. She's lying. There's no way Beth would have hidden something like this from us. It's too big a secret to have kept from Mom and Dad. Why would Beth have hidden her first child? We could have helped. We could have helped raise Jodi.

"There was an art program," Jodi explains. "When Mom was in college. You must remember. She was accepted her senior year and she went away."

Beth moved to an art school outside of Seattle. She'd been so excited with the opportunity and was gone for nearly a year. And then she returned, and everything seemed fine—I thought it was fine. She finished her studies and was painting at home. She had showings around town. She never told us that anything happened.

"She met someone," Jodi says.

"Alex?"

"No, he came after me—that's Hannah's dad. The man I'm talking about is *my* dad. I found out she met him at that fancy art school. Except he didn't want a kid. He didn't offer to help her with any of it. He was a professor, and he was more concerned about losing his job than helping Mom out. Or helping out his daughter. So he forced her to give me away and she listened to him. She left me." A sadness is in her eyes, her mouth quivering.

My sister gave her up. Jodi was abandoned.

But Beth would never. She could never...

"She put me up for adoption," Jodi says. "In Seattle, and she never came back." She wipes the tears from her eyes.

"But why didn't she tell us? She would have told us."

"Nope." Jodi stubs out the cigarette. "Mom went back to Louisville and pretended like everything was okay, that she didn't just have a baby and leave her behind. When I turned eighteen, I looked her up. I found out she married this other guy, and they have a kid together. But she keeps *this* kid. She doesn't give this one away. And then, whoops, Alex takes off and leaves her two years later. He abandoned her the same way she abandoned me." She laughs again, but it's strained. "What goes around, comes around, am I right?"

It's the same words Eli once said to me.

"I'm sorry," I tell her, and I really am. I have no idea if any of this is true, but I need to say something to calm her, sympathize with her for whatever she has been through. Whatever she thinks my sister did, whatever she's gone through since the day she was born, she needs an apology. I think she's been waiting for an apology for an awfully long time.

"It was tough, you know?" Jodi says. "Seeing how my mom and Hannah were so happy. And I kept thinking, why not me? What made Hannah any better? Why was she so special that she got to stay?"

She reaches for another cigarette but stops herself. "Why did Hannah grow up to have a family and I didn't? Why was she so loved while I went from foster home to foster home, one more horrible than the next? I couldn't wait to get out. And that's what I did. I got the hell out of there and moved to Louisville. I checked on Mom for a while."

"I would show up at the art gallery," Jodi continues, "and she never recognized me. Can you believe it? Her *own daughter*. Her firstborn. She never put two and two together, and you can't imagine how much that hurt. She would answer my questions about art and tell me about the techniques she used, and the whole time I was screaming inside, *Please look at me! I'm your daughter. The one you gave up. Don't you know who I am?* But she would say she had to meet with a customer. A real customer. And that was that."

She cries softly. "It's like she forgot I existed, and all that mattered was Hannah. My hair was never as black as hers, not like the rest of you, so I had to keep coloring my hair. I kept showing up at the gallery. She still didn't recognize me. I finally confronted her and told her who I was, the baby she gave up. She denied it at first, but she finally gave in. Threats will do that to a person." And she smiles. "I forced her, and she told me everything: Seattle, my biological dad. I told her that I would tell everyone. They would know what she did by leaving me. I left her notes, checked up on her after work, asked for money. It must have really freaked her out."

I shake my head. "You frightened her?"

"Why do you think she started staying at home? She quit

work. She insisted that Hannah be homeschooled. We tried to talk, and she gave me money. She told me she was sorry and she cried a lot. But, yes, I think I might have scared her a little too much." She grins again. "I might have been a little too intense, and she hid away. I made her feel so guilty. But it wasn't enough. I still wanted to hurt her. Make her pay for what she did." She laughs. "I did eventually."

My eyes bulge. "*You're* the one who set the fire?"

"You bet I did."

My daughter whimpers loudly beside me, but Jodi ignores her.

"It took some time, though, didn't it?" She looks at Patrick. "I needed help. And the more I learned about the family, the more I heard about the drama: the night Grandma and Grandpa died, how you were cut from the will. I learned about the wreck and your involvement with Hank too, the awful way he was killed. And it seemed pretty damn suspicious to me also. So, I reached out to them. I got in touch with Patrick."

She smiles at him. "He was willing to talk. And I thought, here's someone who hates these people as much as I do. Here's someone who wants revenge and might just do anything to get it. And when he told me that you left his dad to die in that car, in that fire, and that my mom might have helped you, well," she pauses, "it was natural for us to team up." She squeezes his hand. "A natural partnership, don't you think, babe?"

He nods, but it's a demented love in his eyes.

Cassie shakes like a leaf. "Mom? What is she talking about?"

"It's going to be okay," I tell her again, but I honestly don't know anymore. There is no guarantee I'll be able to protect my daughter *and* get us away from these people. How will we save the real Hannah?

"There was just so much motivation, you know?" Jodi says. "Patrick and his brother run this company and there's a chance they could land even more money if they could get a hold of your sister's property. The Chandlers' too. Teaming up with them, all that cash, and I'd be set for life also."

"You don't know how angry I was that your sister was holding out on us, either," Patrick says. "Refusing to sell. It's like she was mocking us. I knew we had to get rid of her. Week after week, returning to that area off Route 30, and it made me sick knowing it's near where Dad died. I want that whole place bull-dozed. Get rid of it."

He jerks the gun at my face. "Let's say it brought back a lot of feelings—everything came rushing back to the surface. After all these years of staying quiet, trying to calm my mom down, my brother too, and then I meet Jodi. She tells me her story, what she's been through, and I couldn't believe the lengths your family has gone to so they can cover things up. And I knew I wanted to help. But I never expected we would fall in love, but it happened. So we planned, and we planned, our little plot coming together. And here we are." He smiles, his green eyes flashing at me—Hank's eyes, and I shiver.

I ask, angrily, "So what's your plan? You're going to kill us, and then where will Jodi—Hannah—live? Everyone still thinks she's a minor. She'll be sent to foster care."

"Only for another two years," Jodi says.

"Or we take off." Patrick shrugs. "After we get rid of the two of you, Jodi can pop back up in a few years. She'll have all of Hannah's information. We can claim what is hers."

"You won't get away with it," I tell them. "So much can be uncovered. The death of my sister. The police are already onto you, and it won't take them long before they'll know what you did to us too."

"We'll figure it out," Patrick says. Another smirk. "Don't you worry."

"And no one will question me." Jodi lightens her voice and bats her eyelashes. "What, sweet, innocent me? Like you said, everyone thinks I'm Hannah. We have Hannah's birth certificate, her social security number. She never got a passport or driver's license so we're clear." She laughs. "Even the Chandlers believe that I'm Hannah. I have my black hair." She pulls at the wet, streaky strands. "I mean, hell, you're her own flesh and blood and you bought my story too. You actually thought I was your niece. We've got you all duped."

The tears burn in my throat. *I hugged her*. She hugged me back. I *cared* for this girl.

"Bloodwork," I tell her. "DNA. It will prove everything."

"Who's going to check?" Patrick says. "Someone killed you off, except that Hannah survived this attack. *Again*." He smiles. "She's a great actress as you've already seen. She'll play up the part with even more trauma. No one will question her."

Cassie hunches over in a sob. I grip my hand around hers tightly.

"Please," I plead again. "Please let Cassie go. She won't say anything."

"I promise," Cassie says through her sobs.

"She won't tell anyone," I beg. "Who's going to believe a twelve-year-old?" And then, another idea strikes me. "You can stay with us, Jodi. Live with us. We'll go back home, and we'll carry on like you're still my niece. You don't have to go to school. We can say we hired someone to homeschool you. And that way, you can still be with Patrick. I'll let him visit. You can bide your time..." I'm grasping for straws, but this could work. I can find a way to save my daughter.

There is a shift in Jodi's face, and my hope rises. She might actually be considering this.

"What do you think, Hannah?" I ask, even though it kills me to call her by my niece's name. "You don't have to hurt anyone else, and I can help you. You can still get the money. All of it. You can sell the land to Patrick, whatever you want to do. It's only for two years, like you said."

I plead to him next. "This will be my way of making amends to you. For your dad, your whole family. Everything you've been through. I'm so sorry about what happened, but I didn't want your dad to die, I promise you that." I reach for his arm, but he pulls it away. He points the gun straight at me.

"Nice try, Ms. Jenkins. But no. It's too risky. We'll stick to our plan."

"And Hannah?" I cry. "What about her? Where is she? Are you going to just keep hiding her?"

"Oh, don't worry," he says with a crooked smile. "We're taking care of everything."

# THIRTY-TWO

Patrick pushes his plate away. He's finished eating, and he's the only one who's touched his meal.

"We're leaving tonight," he says. "The four of us. We'll leave the hotel, and you will *not* try anything, do you hear me? You will not scream. You will not break away. I'll take this gun and hold it to Cassie's ribs as we walk out the door. If you try anything, I will shoot her right there on the spot." Cassie gasps, another strangled sob, and the pain tears through me. "Don't think I won't do it. I won't hesitate."

The anger flares hot in my chest, but it's layered with something else—fear.

I must save my child.

The pan Jodi used to cook with is still hot on the stove. It's coated with cooking oil, and the oil shines bright beneath the kitchen lights. I could reach for that pan and bash Jodi's head in. I could smash Patrick's head in too, then grab that knife on the counter, the one she used to slice the potatoes. I'll scream at Cassie to run. I'll tell her to get far away from here.

My daughter, and all that sprinting up and down the soccer field, she would be quick.

But my biggest obstacle is that gun. Patrick won't let go of it, and he keeps it inches from my face. I'm fast—but will I be fast enough?

I don't have time to think. With one hand, I shove Cassie from her chair until she lands on the floor beneath the table. I grab our plates—untouched and covered with food—and throw them at Jodi and Patrick as a distraction. But I don't hit them hard enough, and it does little, except to stun them. But all I need is a second, and it does the trick. It buys me enough time to leap from my chair and reach for the skillet.

I hit Patrick first. With my adrenaline surging, my rage roaring at everything they've done—my sister—what they've done to Hannah—frightening my daughter like this—the rage courses through my veins. Patrick is the one I need to get to first, and I smash him. Nothing can stop me now. They've messed with the wrong person. We won't go down so easy.

The smash of the pan is enough for Patrick to drop the gun, and he howls with the heat of burned oil splashed across his cheeks. It drips to his neck. *I hope it burns your skin off. I hope you burn in hell.*

He staggers against the wall, and I hit him again—hard—until he falls to the floor.

I turn to my daughter. "*Run!*"

She scrambles to her feet and takes off for the door. I wait for her to rush down the hall before I exhale again. I hear her screaming for help. She'll soon be in the elevator. She will be safe.

I turn just in time to see Jodi launching toward me. She has gone from wiping mashed potatoes from her eyes to a full-scale attack. I rear back the skillet and smash her in the face, watching with full pleasure as the blood gushes from her nose. She drops to the floor.

But she's tough, and Jodi tries to crawl back up again. She pushes against the chair and grabs one of the plates and hurls it at my head, but I duck, and the plate shatters on the counter behind me.

I swing the pan and hit her again, telling myself I can beat her to death if that's what it will take. I will do this to protect Cassie. I will do this so she can never hurt Hannah, and we will keep her safe.

Jodi falls again, a loud *oomph* escaping from her mouth. She's bleeding and her face is covered in bits of marinade and oil. I turn my attention to Patrick.

*They should have never come for me*, I rage. *They should have never killed my sister.*

But Patrick remains still on the floor. He's dazed, and the blood streams past his eyelashes into his eyes. He moans, but he doesn't try to stand. Instead, he lifts himself to a sitting position and leans against the wall. His head falls back.

I'm ready to strike—I'll hit him as many times as I hit Jodi— but he holds out his hands as if to call a ceasefire. He knows damn well I will strike him again. He knows that Cassie will soon be asking for help. They'll call the police.

I stare at this man who has stormed back into my life all these years later. Patrick wipes the blood from his face. He coughs, then he peers at me as if he wants to talk. Maybe he wants to apologize.

But I can't stop my hands from shaking, and I keep the frying pan arched over my head, ready to swing.

"Ms. J-Jenkins," he stammers. And in that moment, I see him as that young boy again, the boy who stood in my parents' house, his eyes lowered with so much sadness and fear. I picture him as a child sitting on Dad's knee when he dressed up as Santa, Dad laughing and tilting his head back while Patrick giggled. The weekends when the Robashes would come over to visit. Hank and Gloria would hang out in the living room while Patrick and Eli stayed outside and played on the tire swing.

I once again see the frightened teenager who cowered behind his accusing mother, his outraged big brother. The shock on Patrick's face as they screamed and threatened us.

"I'm sorry," he says.

But I blink and vigorously shake the memories from my brain. That was a long time ago, and Patrick has changed. He's not that timid boy anymore. He planned something awful with a deranged woman who claims to be Beth's child. I clench my teeth. I won't be fooled.

I glance at the gun, but it's on the floor and not that far from his reach. He could still get to it.

I move quickly and kick the gun out of his reach. He doesn't move. He doesn't protest. The fight might actually be leaving him.

"I'm sorry," he repeats. "We've gone too far, me and Jodi. I know that now."

I don't let go of the frying pan, only tighten my grip around the handle. "What did you do to my niece?" I ask. "Where is she?"

"I don't know."

"What do you mean you don't know?"

The blood trickles from his forehead. "Jodi was there. She's the one who set the fire, and I was at the conference. Eli didn't know what we were doing. He still doesn't know. He met with Mr. Chandler, checked on some properties, and then he came back to the conference. Jodi said the house burned, but that Hannah got out. She ran into the fields."

My heart could burst. "Where did she go? Why hasn't anyone heard from her?" I stare at Jodi—we need answers. I kick at her to rouse her. She moans but doesn't get up. Her eyes remain closed.

I stare at Patrick. "Did Jodi chase after her? *What did she do?*"

"The girl ran off, that's all I know. But then..." He looks away. "Jodi said she thinks Hannah ran back into the house. She must have wanted to find her mom and help her." Tears well in his eyes. "She may have gotten trapped inside."

The sickness returns to my gut. The flames, and all that horror. Hannah screaming for her mom and wanting to save her. Hannah's love for her mother is what might have killed her.

"But they didn't find her body," I remind him. "The police would have said if they found my niece."

"I don't know," he pleads. "That's what Jodi told me."

I kick at the woman again. I need her to wake up and tell me what happened, but she releases another moan.

My ears perk for other sounds—the elevator doors opening, the police and their footsteps rushing down the hall. Detective Haygood shouting and telling us that he's here. He'll say that my daughter is safe in a patrol car. But there are no other sounds, and no one is rushing down the hall. Only my strangled breath fills my ears.

Patrick says, "What happened to my dad. What my mom said about the two of you, those text messages she showed us, it's unforgivable. He hurt us, and the two of you should have never done what you did. But we shouldn't have lost him either. He shouldn't have died."

"You shouldn't have killed my sister," I tell him. "Killing Beth was never going to solve anything. Hurting me or Cassie won't do anything either."

He smiles—it's small, but it's there. "But at least we could sleep better knowing your whole family was gone. Knowing that we got back at you and hurt you too." I arch the pan high above my head. "And if we can get access to that land, think of all that money that would come to us. It would be such a bonus."

I raise the pan even higher.

I was wrong—he's not sorry. He will never back down. His apologies and sad eyes are all just an act.

I step forward. I will beat him to death. I will end this right now.

## THIRTY-THREE

I stare at the gun. I could reach for it and tell everyone that I shot him in self-defense. No one could blame me. I could shoot them both, right here, right now, and be done.

But I still need to know what happened to Hannah. We have to find her, and Jodi is the only one who can tell us where she is.

Finally, the stampede of footsteps rushes down the hall. "*Police!*" someone shouts as somebody else yells for a key card. They pound on the door. "Open up!"

Patrick whips his head to the door, then back to me. "Ms. Jenkins..." he pleads.

I hear Detective Haygood. The police are here to save us.

"Open this door right now," the detective says.

"Patrick Robash is wounded, but he has a gun," I shout. I don't tell him it's on the floor. I don't want them to know that I've kicked it out of the way. The police need to come in here fully prepared to take him down.

At my feet, Jodi stirs. She murmurs something as she tries to push herself up.

"A woman named Jodi is in here too," I tell him. "She's been pretending to be Hannah. She's been lying and living with us. She's not my real niece."

Detective Haygood says, "Someone break this damn door down or find me a key card!"

One of the cops suggests they shoot the electronic entry instead. I stand back.

"I'm not going to hurt her!" Patrick shouts.

But I'm not sure if anyone should believe him. No one should believe anything Patrick or Jodi say, not after what they've done to my family. Not after what they wanted to do to me and my daughter if they could have snuck us out of this hotel.

Detective Haygood pounds on the door. "Where is Eli Robash?"

"He's not here," Patrick says. "He has nothing to do with this."

I stare again at the woman on the floor. She is on her knees, and I know I should hit her again. God knows I want to.

"We didn't mean for it to get this far," Patrick cries. "I'm sorry."

"They killed my sister," I shout to the detective. "Jodi is the one who burned my sister's house down. They planned on taking everything away from Hannah. It's all been for the money, the property. It's all been..."

But I don't finish my sentence because I don't want them to know about Beth, not yet, about what Jodi claims my sister did, if she really is her mother.

Because if my sister really did give her up, there were reasons. She was so young, a scared college student, and that man—that shithead of a professor—did nothing to help her. If Beth filed a complaint, would the administration have believed her over one of their own faculty members? He could have come after her if he lost his job, his reputation ruined. She would have been forced to leave art school, and I know how hard she worked to earn that spot.

"We need to find Hannah," I tell them. "She's missing."

On the floor, Jodi opens her eyes. They snap open like one of those monstrous sea creatures that has suddenly come alive.

She wipes at her mouth, a smile stretching across her face as she smears more blood at her forehead. But she winces. I wouldn't be shocked if her nose is broken. One of her eyes is already closing up.

At the door, the click of a key card. The door opens.

I look to see Detective Haygood rushing into the room. He's here—he will save me. But that's when Jodi takes her chance. She pushes me aside and leaps for the gun. She points it at the police officers. I scream as she swings it toward my head. The sharp taste of fear hurtles down my throat.

"You don't want to do that," Detective Haygood warns her. "Drop the gun." He steps forward cautiously.

"Don't come any closer!" she screams.

The sight of Jodi is wild. It's straight out of a horror film. Blood smears her face with globs of it at her forehead, and it drips past her ears. It's mixed with mashed potatoes and cooking oil, her hair still slick with black dye.

Her eyes are wide, her pupils dark, and her teeth cut through the blood in her mouth, a menacing white.

She points the gun at the police officers. She motions to Patrick with one hand. "Come here," she tells him. "Stand with me."

Patrick does what he's told. He's injured and he clutches his head, but he moves beside her.

I lean against the kitchen counter, wanting to get as far away from this potential shoot-out as possible. Because at any moment, someone will fire first, and I'll need to duck. I will hide under that table. I will close my eyes until it's done.

With the gun in her hand, Jodi reaches for Patrick and

slowly walks him backwards. They step past the sofa, the coffee table. They reach the window.

There's nowhere for them to go, and I can't tell what Jodi is thinking. They can't hide anywhere since she locked both doors to the bedrooms. They won't be able to escape. An army of police officers crowd the entrance to the hotel room and another group waits in the hall.

Detective Haygood steps forward. "You need to lower that weapon. Don't do anything that you'll regret."

But Jodi sobs. "She left me! My own mother left me." She cries, and so does Patrick. "We both needed the money, and I have every right to what that family has to offer. That money, that land... I'm *Hannah's sister*. It should be mine!"

The detective's voice hardens. He keeps his hands raised, palms out. "Ma'am, I'm not going to tell you again. You need to drop your weapon."

She ignores him. "Being her daughter. Doesn't that count for anything? But my mom didn't want me. She abandoned me. She helped cover up what happened to Patrick's dad. They lied to everyone and got away with it. We had to come up with a plan. We had no choice. It's what she deserved. You can't blame us. You can't blame us for *any of it*."

Detective Haygood says, "I told you to drop your weapon."

The mood in the room is intense. The detective's eyes twitch as each of the police officers get into position. They grow increasingly antsy, their hands on their holsters. If Jodi makes one wrong move, they will pull their triggers and fire. They won't hesitate. I'm ready to drop to the ground.

"Ma'am, if you don't do what I'm telling you, we will have to take action. And you don't want that. We can talk. We can end this right now."

"End this..." Jodi whispers. In her eyes is a devastated expression.

Patrick meets her look next. Jodi raises the gun, but she raises it at Patrick. Then she points it at her own head.

"*No!*" The word bursts from my lips. All I can think is, *Don't die.* Jodi can't kill herself before she tells us what happened to Hannah.

"Where is she?" I scream. "*Where is my niece?*"

She points the gun back to Patrick's head. He doesn't look scared or outraged. It's like he understands what she's thinking. He's devoted to her. They've run out of options. Jodi nods at him.

My heart slams in my chest. They have to tell me before they do something drastic.

"Tell me where she is!" I scream.

But Jodi turns around and shoots—the gunfire, the sharp blast of it—and I scream again. She fires three more shots, but they're directed at the window. The police surge forward, and it's manic. Shouts fill the room as Detective Haygood lunges forward, his arms stretching toward Jodi, toward Patrick, but he won't reach them in time.

Patrick breaks against the glass with his elbow while Jodi knocks another large piece of glass with the gun. It shatters to the ground five stories below and people in the parking lot are screaming.

Jodi looks once more at Patrick, and he gazes at her. It's so final, that look.

They don't look back, only turn to the sky and the openness in front of them, and they jump.

# THIRTY-FOUR

It takes three more days before Detective Gillespie and the Louisville Police Department find Hannah's body. It's the real Hannah, my niece, and the pain is so unreal, the loss of her, the realization that she is gone and I will never see her again. The teenager who I thought was living in my house, the one whose relationship I hoped to repair, the closeness we were forming as a family, and it was all a sham.

After Jodi and Patrick jumped, the police wanted to find Eli next, but he said he had no idea what the police were talking about. He claims he didn't know what his brother and girlfriend had been planning.

After another search of the family property, the police found Hannah's body in a shallow grave not far from the house. Tucked away from the burned shell of the home, beyond the tire swing and apple orchard where we used to run and play, is where Jodi dragged Hannah's body. With my sister trapped and dead in the upstairs room, Jodi buried Hannah beneath a wood pile.

The belief is that Hannah ran back to the burning house to save her mom. But once inside, she succumbed to the smoke. Jodi must have pulled her out, saw that she was dead, and found the perfect way to become my niece. With her mother and half-sister gone, she fled to the Chandlers' home and took on the role of a sixteen-year-old. She was covered in ash, her hair wild. None of us questioned that she wasn't Hannah.

Detective Haygood assures us that we are safe. Meanwhile, in Kentucky, Detective Gillespie says I have nothing to worry about either. Eli Robash is as stunned as everyone else by what's happened: the death of his brother, his brother's girlfriend, and the tragedy of it all. He said he never intended to hurt us, that Patrick never included him on their plan. He had no idea of the deteriorating mental state of his brother, and the way Jodi cajoled him.

Eli explained why he disappeared. He claims that his car broke down south of Louisville. He was in a rural part of the state, another region to explore for land development, and he planned on coming back. He had every intention of answering the detective's questions, but without a phone signal and with him stranded in the middle of nowhere, he spent the night in his car. He waited for hours before someone finally drove by and picked him up.

It sounds unbelievable, a convenient excuse, and I still don't trust him. He could be making everything up. He might have known exactly what his brother and Jodi were up to. Maybe he's the one who moved Hannah's body while she ran to the Chandlers', then he sent Patrick to Huntsville to meet up with Jodi. Still angry all these years later, he convinced Patrick and Jodi to finish us off.

The fear swirls in my stomach, and it keeps me on edge. I still remember the way Eli responded after his father died. He was so full of hatred and wanted to retaliate. I don't think he got over his anger just because he was busy with work and a family, as Patrick said. I think the fire still burns within him.

That's why I worry that Eli is still plotting and waiting. The task isn't complete since my daughter and I are still alive. Patrick and Jodi failed to get the job done. And now I think Eli is biding his time. He can't strike right now while it's too obvious so he'll wait before he can finish what he and Patrick started. *The strike of a match.* We're still not safe.

The last couple of weeks have rocked me to my core. The loss of my sister, and then Jodi showing up at my doorstep. I let a con-artist into my house, and I didn't know it. It will be a long time before I stop looking over my shoulder.

There is still one Robash family member left.


It's another month before I'm able to pull myself together for a return trip to Louisville. My best friend, Cynthia, says she'll help me, and so will my daughter. They join the long car ride to Louisville, Kentucky. It's the first time I've been home in thirteen years.

Detective Gillespie agrees to follow us to the property. We finally meet face to face and I hug him the moment I see him. I also ask him to follow us closely. I don't want to be caught off guard if Eli Robash comes after us. But Detective Gillespie says he'd be crazy to try anything with all the heat that's on him right now. But I don't want to take any chances.

We have a special reason for returning home though, and it's a heart-wrenching one. Hannah's funeral is the day after tomorrow. It will be a small affair with only ourselves and the attorney present, but it will be a way for us to say goodbye. We'll say goodbye to my sister too.

I also want to show Cassie the farm and where I grew up, where her aunt and cousin lived. I'll describe much happier times before death knocked on our door again and again.

With Cynthia by my side and Cassie in the backseat, Detective Gillespie follows, as promised. We drive down Route 30 and pass the Chandlers' home. I look to see if they're outside, but they're no longer living there. They are not selling the property, thank goodness, but they've relocated to a townhouse where they can be closer to their grandkids. One of their sons is moving to the farm and he plans on fixing up things. His daughter loves to ride horses.

I spot the Chandlers' barn, and it fills my heart to know the stables will once again be full of activity. The property will remain in the Chandler family and the land is protected. For as long as our families can help it, there will be no five-lane interstate or new shopping center cutting through this area.

I sigh at the familiar sound of crunching gravel beneath the tires and proceed slowly down the drive. I find what's left of our family home. My heart breaks at the scorched wood. I've tried to imagine it, I've tried to prepare myself, but it's much more painful in person. Blackened beams and a hollowed-out roof, tumbled bricks and the chimney that has collapsed on one side. The bedroom where my sister hid, the floor buckling until it crashed to the ground.

I can't stop crying even when I pull the car to a stop. Cynthia takes my hand, and Cassie leans forward from the backseat. She hugs my shoulders.

I sob—what they did to our family, killing Beth, killing Hannah. Destroying our family home. What they almost did to me and my daughter.

I cry for my parents too. The grass is scorched, but it's the same spot where I passed out all those years ago. I remember the pain—it's never left me. Our parents died, and in her grief, my sister turned on me.

She was angry. She was confused. And I forgive her. I think I've always forgiven her.

I should have told her I'd forgiven her. We'd both made some tragic mistakes.

My sister had her reasons, her own failed attempts at coping. She's not here to explain them, and I can never know exactly what was going through her mind, especially when she left Jodi behind. But it must have been an act of desperation. She was so young and so lost. After leaving Jodi and going through that heartache, it was one tragedy after another. Beth didn't know how to cope with each one.

With that rage, and after all of those years of anger, it poured out of her body when she set fire to Hank's car. I understand that. It wasn't just about Hank and Alex, and what they did to us. It was about that other man too, the professor from art school. The first man that abandoned her. The guilt of not being able to keep her first child.

I wipe the tears from my cheeks and step out of the car. Nothing about the house is recognizable; only a footprint remains of the front living room and where my sister used to paint. In the back somewhere is the kitchen where Mom taught us to make ice cream. In another corner is the home office where Dad worked.

But behind the house, the apple orchard remains, untouched, including the patio where we held Hannah's party. The flames didn't reach the tire swing either. The rope is frayed, the tire gray and weathered, but it still swings in the breeze.

If I close my eyes, I can hear my sister laughing. I can hear her pushing Hannah in the swing, my niece kicking her feet into the air.

Through the fields is also the creek where we used to fish, the spot where we picnicked. The hay bales we ran past with our kites. It's where Hannah played years later with her dog, her tiny black ponytail on top of her head, the excitement of turning three and having friends come over for her party. The way she used to call me *Auntie Tawa* as I lifted her into my arms.

I've decided to bulldoze the house. While it pains me to see it torn down, we can't leave this burned shell behind either. It can't stand here as a painful reminder of what we've been through. We will erase this blemish from the land and start over.

The reason I can make this decision came as a big surprise. After what Jodi and Patrick did, and Hannah's body was identified, Mr. Fredericks notified me of a clause in my sister's will. She not only left her daughter in my care, but she also included another section. I'm positive Mr. Fredericks encouraged her to do this as a formality. A *just in case.*

If anything were to happen to Hannah, the land would revert to me. If I was still alive and able, I'd be the last family member, which means I would take ownership, my children too. It pains me to know that Cassie and I are the last family members left, that my sister and niece had to die the way they did, but the property is now mine to do with as I wish.

So I will honor them. I will bulldoze the house and build a new one in its place. I'll show Cassie the fields and take her for long walks to explore the creek. We'll pick apples. We'll buy flowers and remember Hannah and my sister.

But something I won't do? I will never sell this land. With the Chandlers' son moving in, we will hold out. We will never sell, no matter how many offers or how much money they shake at us, and that especially goes for Eli Robash. The Chandlers and my family are locked together against their threats, their need for wealth and the unrelenting spread of urban growth. There are other areas they can focus on. For now, this beautiful place will remain ours.

Standing in front of the house, I hold hands with my daughter while Cynthia dabs her eyes. We remain quiet, each of us lost in our thoughts, but I feel their strength beside me. It fortifies me. Their support will make me strong.

. . .

Detective Gillespie waits in his car and gives us our privacy. When it's time, he'll start up his engine and leave. We'll return to the hotel and rest before we say goodbye to Beth and my niece tomorrow.

A breeze blows and I tug my daughter's hand. I nod at her, encouraging her to turn away from the burned remains of the house and watch the setting sun beyond the fields instead. It's the corn fields where we would play, the same fields that we would gaze upon while we sat on the front porch, the four of us: Beth, Mom and Dad, and me.

Mom would hum songs while we rocked in the chairs. Dad would talk about another section of fence that needed repairing. Beth would tease me about sneaking the ice cream spoon for a lick.

Our family has lost so much, and we shouldn't have had to endure all that pain. Beth certainly didn't have to go through her pain alone. She should have told us, and we could have gotten a chance to know Jodi. Maybe things could have been different. Jodi could have spent her childhood with us.

We would have helped take care of that little girl, and Beth could have finished art school somewhere else. There's a chance we could have stopped everything from happening: the hellish life Jodi went through, the additional plotting when she teamed up with Patrick. Beth and Hannah could still be alive right now. Hannah would have grown up knowing Jodi as her big sister.

But I can't rest. I need someone else to be accountable, and I've been spending some time doing a little bit of research. I tracked down Jodi's dad. He's still a professor at the art academy, he reached tenure years ago. My guess is he couldn't risk anyone finding out that he'd gotten one of his students pregnant. He might have even threatened to have my sister expelled if she told.

Beth made her own decision, but I've made up my mind on what I'm going to do. After leaving the farm and getting Cassie and Cynthia settled in at the hotel, I will head to my scheduled meeting with Detective Gillespie. I've asked him to wait for me at a nearby coffee shop, and that's where I plan on telling him about this professor. I will ask for his help. I want to know what this man will admit to. At the very least, I want him to know the damage he's caused. The grief he brought upon my sister, and most of all, the child he forced her to give up. He will know about Jodi. At the very least, he will know her name.

I also want him to feel sorry for what he did. He needs to feel responsible, feel guilty. Because no one's off the hook—least of all him. And it's my mission to make him pay. I will do this for Beth and Hannah. And, yes, I will even do this for Jodi.

# A LETTER FROM GEORGINA

Thank you so much for reading *The Niece*. With the excitement surrounding my other books *The Stepdaughter* and *The Missing Woman*, I wanted to come up with a situation where a family is gripped by fear by those around them. The multiple instances of fire—both hypnotic and disastrous—especially with what has happened to this family in the past, and it was too enticing not to write. I so hope you enjoy this tale. No one knows who to trust until it all comes together with a shocking twist.

If you'd like to keep up to date with all my latest releases, please sign up at the following link. Your email address will never be shared and you can unsubscribe at any time.

*www.bookouture.com/georgina-cross*

And if you enjoy my books, I'd absolutely love if you could leave a review. Getting feedback from readers is amazing and it also helps to persuade other readers to pick up one of my books for the first time.

Thank you so much. And happy suspenseful reading!

Georgina

# KEEP IN TOUCH WITH GEORGINA

www.georgina-cross-author.com

facebook.com/GeorginaCrossAuthor

twitter.com/GCrossAuthor

instagram.com/GeorginaCrossAuthor

goodreads.com/georginacross

bookbub.com/profile/georgina-cross

# ACKNOWLEDGMENTS

Thank you to my agent, Rachel Beck, and the team at Liza Dawson Associates. Rachel, you have been by my side for so many years and you've always had my back. I will forever tell everyone you are the best agent ever. Your #agentsisters love you.

To my editor at Bookouture, Laura Deacon, thank you for giving me the bandwidth to rewrite this book from scratch. The first draft shaped much of this story, but with Maisie Lawrence's keen eye and her original feedback, I was able to make this book that much better. Thank you to everyone at Team Bookouture, including, the publicity team, cover designer, and copy editors.

This book is dedicated to the Decatur Crew, especially to Melinda Jones, the former owner of Second Read Books Store, and now with the Athens-Limestone County Public Library, and also to Mary Ann Hotaling, former Mrs. Veteran America, and her group of amazing friends and teachers who organize book club events and cheer me on. Because of you, this book's setting is Decatur, Alabama. You asked, and I delivered some drama!

Thank you to reader Beth Milner for winning the "Name a Character" contest during one of our author events and silent auctions. Money raised benefited Operation Prom Dress for students at the Decatur Excel Center, Decatur City Schools (organized by Mary Ann Hotaling and Jodi Sue Bair). Students were able to select a prom dress, flowers, and accessories, and I hope they had the best time. For the contest, Beth chose the name Cynthia in honor of her younger sister, Cynthia. This name is featured as Tara's best friend, which seems lovingly appropriate. Thank you for selecting the name, Beth.

To my family—my English aunties, my countless Malaysian aunts, uncles, and cousins, and to my family who put up with me writing every day at the kitchen table—thank you for being my number one support team. You guys are the best for reading my books and telling your friends about them. It's a fun journey and I have so much more I want to create. I'm sorry, kids, but the kitchen table is going to be monopolized with my laptop for a few more years—unless I'm forced to return to the downstairs writing bunker.

To my parents, Kelvin and Cecilia, my sister Davinia, plus her little ones Leo and Elliot, you guys are my heart. We're the original Pilgrims! Thank you for always believing in me. Davinia, I will always laugh at your Mad Cow joke. Thank you to Leo and Elliot for teaching me the worm song.

And most of all, to my husband, David, my sons, Reece and Liam, and my stepsons, Andrew and Matthew, I know that I write a lot and I'm sorry that I don't cook. Ever. Thank you for accepting when I go to bed at 9 p.m. and pretty much spend every day attached to my laptop. I love you guys.

Printed in the USA
CPSIA information can be obtained
at www.ICGtesting.com
LVHW051937250324
775488LV00007B/163